The Radical Novel Reconsidered

A series of paperback reissues of mid-twentieth-century
U.S. left-wing fiction, with new biographical and critical
introductions by contemporary scholars.

Series Editor
Alan Wald, University of Michigan

Books in the Series

Salome of the Tenements

Anzia Yezierska

SALOME
OF THE
TENEMENTS

Introduction by Gay Wilentz

University of Illinois Press
Urbana and Chicago

© 1923, renewed 1951 by Louise Levitas Henriksen
Reprinted by arrangement with the author's estate
Introduction © 1995 by the Board of Trustees of
the University of Illinois
Manufactured in the United States of America
P 5 4 3 2

This book is printed on acid-free paper.

Library of Congress Cataloging-in-Publication Data

Yezierska, Anzia, 1880?–1970.
    Salome of the tenements / Anzia Yezierska ; introduction by Gay
Wilentz.
        p.   cm. — (The radical novel reconsidered)
    ISBN 0-252-06435-6 (pbk.)
    I. Title.   II. Series.
PS3547.E95S35   1995
813'.52—dc20   95-6020
                                                    CIP

Contents

Introduction
Gay Wilentz

In the climatic love scene in Anzia Yezierska's *Salome of the Tenements*, John Manning, the upper-class, native-born Protestant American, rhetorically asks Sonya, his young immigrant Jewish bride: "'Are we not the mingling of the races? The oriental mystery and the Anglo-Saxon clarity that will pioneer a new race of men?'" (108).[1] Yezierska's first novel, published in 1923 and reissued in this series, sets out to answer these questions and to challenge the prevailing theories of education and philanthropy that have affected public policy to the present day. A love story of a working-class Salome and her "high-born" John the Baptist, *Salome of the Tenements* radically critiques the settlement education projects that aimed at Americanization through the melting pot theory (a sociological premise that all immigrants could be molded into Americans along the lines of the dominant culture). Such a move toward inclusion often hid an attempt to efface differences by "Anglo-Saxoning" the immigrant, in this case the Eastern European Jew. *Salome of the Tenements*, still powerfully resonant, addresses as well the problems of interethnic, interclass marriages. Moreover, the novel exposes the hypocrisy of the "good works" of the privileged class, dedicated to helping the poor.

In this introduction I offer a discussion of Yezierska's life and work, the rise of settlement houses at the turn of the century, the famed romance of an immigrant Jewish woman and her millionaire, and how these events are realized in *Salome of the Tenements*. Yezierska's passionate but cynical novel presents a view of an important historical moment through the maneuvers of a larger-than-life female (perhaps even feminist) protagonist who refuses the fairy-tale of America's promised land.

Carol Schoen, author of the first full-length study of Yezierska, writes that in *Salome of the Tenements*, "Yezierska creates an antimyth which rejected the sentimentalized vision of the poor but immigrant girl who . . . marries the kind American millionaire" (qtd. in Henriksen 180). The novel is based on a well-publicized historical event: the romance of Yezierska's friend, the writer and labor activist Rose Pastor, with the millionaire philanthropist Graham (J. G. Phelps) Stokes. However, *Salome of the Tenements* also tells— as does the majority of her fiction—Yezierska's own story, especially that of her short but impassioned relationship with the well-known educator John Dewey.

The Making of the Writer

Anzia Yezierska, author of a semifictional autobiography and semiautobiographical fiction, understood the place of the immigrant, especially that of the immigrant who is also a social minority. She came to America as a young girl (of perhaps eight to ten) from a village in the Pale (the Jewish ghetto that spanned Russia and Poland)[2] during the 1890s, at a time when anti-Semitism was equally rampant in the place she left and the promised land she entered. Living in the teeming ghetto of New York's Lower East Side, Yezierska and her family knew the poverty and oppression faced by Jewish immigrants to the United States. *Bread Givers* (1925), her most acclaimed novel, tells of the coming of age of a young working-class Jewish woman. In her other two novels, (*Arrogant Beggar* [1927] and *All I Could Never Be* [1932]), her short stories, and her semifictional autobiography, *Red Ribbon on a White Horse* (1950), Yezierska portrays the conflicts in a Jewish community struggling for identity in a new land and the tenuous relationship these immigrants had with the native-born, Anglo-Saxon Christian majority. She also details the awful working conditions for the lower-class immigrants as they struggle to make themselves over in order to achieve success within the rigid class-bound structures of America.

For Yezierska, the struggle was personal and political; in her own life she was never able to reconcile her admiration for and repugnance toward the dominant culture, the "higher-ups," as she called them. As part of an underclass, she grew up in a household of women who worked in ghetto factories to support a Hebrew scholar father. Her rise out of poverty and oppression reflected the economic rise of many Jews, but like other authors of the time,[3] she was never able to separate herself from those who were unable to break out of the ghetto. Yezierska's conflicting feelings about this supposed paradise for the poor Jewish immigrant is mirrored in her lament "America and I": "Where is America? Is there an America? What is this wilderness in which I am lost?"(*Open Cage* 26).

Her own move toward success in the wilderness of class- and race-based America came through education. Yezierska worked in a laundry while attending night school and later went to Columbia Teachers College. She married twice during this time; the first marriage was annulled, and the second, to Arnold Levitas in July 1912, ended in divorce. She had one child from her second marriage, Louise, who became her mother's biographer. After finishing college, Yezierska worked at many different jobs, from teacher to settlement house worker. Her job with charity organizations reinforced her feelings about upper-class women who had entered her community when she was a child; however, as a single mother she felt unable to confront the system. She wrote to her friend Rose Pastor Stokes of her feelings about the programs for the poor: "I see how the people are crushed and bled and spat upon in the process of getting charity and I must keep my mouth shut or lose my job" (qtd. in Henriksen 71). Through her work at the settlement house and her role as an educator, Yezierska was first allowed entrance into the world of the higher-ups. This experience increased her political awareness and radical sensibility about the problems of liberal reform, informed by her earlier employment in the sweatshops. It also helped focus her aims in life.

By the time Yezierska was in her thirties, she had decided to become a writer. Pastor Stokes, who was a committed radical and socialist, encouraged her to write stories of the ghetto. With Pastor Stokes as her example, Yezierska formed into thought her feelings about the inequities of American life for the working class, for women, and for Jews. However, despite her similar sensibility to Pastor Stokes's ideals, she was too unconventional and eccentric to join any movement for long. Nevertheless, throughout her life and in her fictional and autobiographical writings, she was always committed to radical change—particularly on a personal level.

Once her writings began to appear, Yezierska quickly captured the public's interest. Like her heroines, she gained phenomenal success—"A Scrub Woman Who Became a Great Novelist" (Henriksen 2–3). She not only began writing for major magazines and newspapers but also had her first collection, Hungry Hearts (1920), published and later made into a movie. She moved to Hollywood in 1921 but soon returned to New York, feeling she could not write away from the Lower East Side that inspired her. Fame and the contradictions inherent in that privilege would prove to be too much for her, however. Productive and popular during the years 1923–32, by 1935, she was a pauper again, working for the Works Progress Administration's Federal Writers Project. America, it seems, had lost interest in the life of the poor immigrant. Yezierska died in California in 1970, writing book reviews and short stories until the end.

One important influence on her life and works was the educator John Dewey. Despite encouragement from Pastor Stokes and others, in 1917 Yezierska was unable to find a publisher for her stories of ghetto life. At first, editors rejected them because they were written in dialect and portrayed a world far from their understanding. Yet, Dewey, having read one of her stories, encouraged her. He felt that her writing, despite its roughness, was genuine. He presented her with her first typewriter and gave her finished stories to his friend Herbert Croly at the New Republic, where her work started to appear.

Yezierska had approached Dewey to gain a better teaching position, but their fateful encounter in 1917 changed both their lives and profoundly influenced her writing. Mary Dearborn notes in Love in the Promised Land: "From their first moment together, [Yezierska] invested John Dewey with all the qualities she felt she lacked, all the avenues that were closed to her, all the possibilities of the promised land. . . . The fairy-tale marriage of her friend Rose Pastor kindled her imagination about such encounters and, as she grew increasingly pragmatic in her struggle to get ahead in America, she saw in whose hands the reins of power lay" (108). Dearborn poses Yezierska's relationship with Dewey as part of her "self promoting" personality (107); however, in examining Yezierska as a radical writer, we can see more than just an aim for self-aggrandizement. For Yezierska, as for her friend Rose, liberal reformers like Dewey and Graham Stokes symbolized the America they had dreamed of—a place where the high-born and the immigrant could work and love together, where they could make a new America that would not break its promise to the poor and powerless. Unfortunately for both of them, reality would turn out quite differently.

Yezierska's short but passionate relationship with the older, married Dewey was based on a mutual desire to expand their limited worldview and create a bridge between apparent oppositions. In *Red Ribbon,* she recalls: "Our need for each other burned away the differences between Gentile and Jew, native and immigrant—the barriers of race, class, and education" (110). For Dewey, his desire rose from his general belief about education—how better to "learn by doing" than to learn about immigrant experience from a young, attractive immigrant woman who idolized him. Dewey, according to Dearborn, "saw in Yezierska a natural counterpart to his own intellectualism, the infusion of emotion he felt immigrants could bring to himself and to America. . . . For Dewey, Yezierska was the archetypal 'other,' the immigrant he sought so desperately to understand" (4–5). Yezierska also realized Dewey's emotional limitations. As much as she wanted to be part of his WASP culture, she found that world unemotional and cold, almost sterile.[4]

During their time together, Yezierska and Dewey both wanted some kind of blending of their heads and hearts; however, Yezierska's heart was a little too much for Dewey. Her uncontrollable otherness (linked to her cultural group) and her refusal to give up the passionate intensity that he saw as hysterical and overdramatized turned him away from her.[5] Dearborn points to the possibility that Dewey's coldness came about because, although professing great love for him, Yezierska did not respond to his overtures and apparently refused to have sex with him (129)—after which Dewey withheld his affection and would not permit her to meet with him. However, as Yezierska recollects in her autobiography, his rejection reinforced her desire to write (117–19).

Returning to the ghetto and seeing the Jewish immigrants attempting to make it in a world that offered only poverty and oppression, she realized she would write their story—to tell the truth about the immigrants that no "cold-headed" sociological study could show.[6] The novel *All I Could Never Be* (1932) is her fictional account of her work with the Polish study and her relationship with Dewey. All of her writings, however, reflect that relationship and what she saw as the failure of the dominant group to accept poor/Jewish/immigrants as equal citizens on their own terms. In *Salome of the Tenements*, John Manning is another version of the Dewey figure, but he is also modeled after Graham Stokes, the millionaire socialist and philanthropist.

Settlement Houses and Millionaire Romances

The romance and marriage of Rose Pastor to the millionaire Graham Stokes and the rise of the settlement programs for new immigrants in the late 1800s and early 1900s provide the historical background for *Salome of the Tenements*. The settlement houses were schools, which would today be called continuing education centers, founded to train new immigrants in the ways of America and to give them the skills they would need to succeed. The settlements were run by liberal reformers who prescribed a method, later taken up by the public school system, to inculcate the poor and ethnically diverse immigrants into the values and traditions of the dominant group. Famous educators like Jane Addams and Dewey himself influenced the movement, at the heart of which was the idea, shaped by Social Darwinism, that the individual could be "scientifically" trained to adhere to society's demands for social order. At the time, immigrants were perceived as a threat to this order and they had to be "Americanized so as to protect the 'American way'" (Karier 88). According to Clarence Karier, Dewey, as a strong advocate of this movement, "viewed ethnic and religious differences as a threat to the survival of society, to be overcome through assimilation" (92). For liberals like Dewey and Stokes, as well as other members of this movement, the relationship to socialism came through a desire for economic growth and progress in a welfare-like state, even if that progress meant the manipulation of the workers. The settlement houses were used as a way to educate immigrants "for [their] own 'good' and that good was defined by the mores of the new liberal" (Karier 89).

According to Rose Pastor Stokes's biographers, the settlement education movement was comprised of "affluent do-gooders and social workers [who] lived in the settlement houses and tried to 'uplift' downtrodden slum dwellers" (Zipser 7). Pastor, herself a first-generation Jewish immigrant, began a series on the settlement houses for her paper, the Jewish daily *Yiddishes Tageblatt*. She interviewed her future husband Graham Stokes for this series at his place of work, the University Settlement. Based on Jane Addams' Hull-House in Chicago, the University Settlement was among the first of the settlement houses to spring up on the Lower East Side of New York. Both Stokes and Pastor were socialists, and their commitment to social justice fueled their fairy-tale romance. If his impending marriage to the "Israelitish maiden" was a problem for the Stokes family, they eventually accepted Rose into their life of privilege (Pastor Stokes 100). In the ghetto, however, this relationship set off the dreams and aspirations of young immigrant women.

For the young women working in Lower East Side sweatshops, daily headlines such as "J. G. Phelps Stokes to Marry Young Jewess" (*New York Times*, 6 Apr. 1905, 1) and "A Ghetto Romance" (*New York Tribune Illustrated Supplement*, 16 Apr. 1905) fired their imaginations. Pastor, working for a time in a cigar factory, was surrounded by her fellow workers calling her the "luckiest girl in America" to marry a millionaire. She comments in her autobiography: "We serve as an ever-renewable fairy-tale-come-true . . . the fairy-tale of 'Democracy'" (101). For both young socialists, the marriage was also a political issue. Graham Stokes "framed the forthcoming marriage so as to imply Labor's stake in it" (Pastor Stokes xxii).

Yezierska saw the Pastor-Stokes union as a bridge over the cultural gulf between Jew and Gentile. To the young "Hattie Mayer" (Yezierska's Ellis Island name, which she later rejected for her given name), Rose Pastor stated that she was about to "make history": "'I am going to be married to the millionaire Stokes,' she revealed. 'Riches and poverty, Jew and Christian will be united. Here is an indication of a new era'" (qtd. in Zipser 43). Yezierska, who saw her friend and confidante as a major influence on her writing (Dearborn 88), was not only thrilled for Pastor but was captured by the story itself. She too hoped to make a physical and emotional break from the ghetto, yet saw her own possible separation as a rejection of culture and traditions.[7]

For the next ten years, the Stokeses worked with the socialists and tried to overcome class and ethnic differences to make their marriage and its democratic aims work. On Thanksgiving Day 1917, however, in the midst of her personal upheaval over Dewey, Yezierska visited with her friend, who was also despairing because her politico-fairy-tale marriage was breaking up. The Stokeses broke with the Socialist party because they supported America's entrance into World War I; however, after the Bolshevik revolution, Rose joined the emerging Communist party, which proved to be a turning point not only for her political career but for her marriage: "She had found [in Communism] an enduring political home, but the commitments inspired by war and revolution led to the dissolution of her marriage. For Graham Stokes the period of involvement with radical activism had come to a definite end" (Pastor Stokes xxxix). What began when Rose poured out her heart to her friend on Thanksgiving Day ended when she left her husband in 1923. She had realized the unsuitability of his liberal ideology for accepting true social change and of his desire to maintain his privileged, elite lifestyle. He, in turn, had become increasingly irritated by his wife's involvement with the Communist party and attempted to limit her activities. For a while, they made meager attempts to work things out. But after her well-publicized trial for espionage[8] and her husband's refusal to allow her "comrades" in *his* house, she decided to divorce him. Despite his total disgust for her personal and political activism, he at once pleaded and demanded that she return, for divorce was unthinkable in his culture. She wrote to him to reject his appeal/ultimatum and to declare that "even the kind of armed truce that existed between us at the house was impossible to maintain, because of the deep-going fundamental difference in our aims, our ideals, our principles and convictions" (qtd. in Zipser 253).

With the breakup of her marriage, Rose Pastor Stokes discovered the depths of the hypocrisy of the liberal reformers who wanted to maintain their privileged status. Yezierska, in her autobiography, alludes to Graham Stokes, on whom she partially based her male protagonist in *Salome of the Tenements*. She gives a thumbnail sketch of an unnamed young millionaire who "dreamed of being a new St. Francis of Assisi," married a factory girl, and lived with the poor on Hester Street. But, she tells us, the poor were too ready to be his "brother" and share his wealth: "This assault of brotherhood was more that the gentle, saintlike millionaire could take. Stunned and bewildered by the tidal wave of beggars, he barricaded himself and his bride behind locked doors and hired two strong-armed men to keep the poor away" (*Red Ribbon* 89). The ironic tone of this passage also pervades *Salome of the Tenements*, a love story and a formidable critique of liberal reformers like Graham Stokes and John Dewey.

By the time she wrote *Salome of the Tenements*, Yezierska had integrated the stories of the two sets of lovers and created a radical and romantic novel. Both Dearborn and Henriksen comment on the similarities between Dewey and Yezierska's relationship and the novel. Henriksen notes: "It was therefore only the externals of [Rose's] life and mannerisms, but mostly Anzia's traits, that went into the vivid personality Anzia created for Sonya" (171). However, I find the interplay and overlay of characters more dialectic than that. Rose Pastor Stokes and Anzia Yezierska were good friends; they were both Jewish immigrants who had worked in sweatshops, had come into their own as writers, and had fallen in love with men not of their race, class, or culture. Both were radical spirits who saw something in the men they loved beyond the typical hypocrisy of the rich do-gooders. In both cases, they were disappointed. Pastor Stokes, who had a lifelong commitment to organized labor and Communist party politics, saw her husband's betrayal of her and the goals he said he believed in within the context of class-based oppression. However, as Yezierska transformed Pastor Stokes's real-life story into her novel, she not only layered her own undeveloped affair with Dewey into the plot but expanded the focus of the young woman's activism from solely class based to include that part of herself denied in the move toward Americanization—her Jewish identity.

Salome of the Tenements

A humorous, poignant, engaging story of a willful young Jewish immigrant named Sonya Vrunsky, who will do anything to get her millionaire John Manning, *Salome of the Tenements* takes place in

New York City and moves from fashionable uptown to the Lower East Side. As in Yezierska's other works, the novel teems with the vibrancy and life in the ghetto; the language is a rich transliteration of Yiddish into English. The novel reflects her aim to tell the real story of this world of immigrants, portraying the pathos and pathology of those in the underclass. Like the biblical Salome (a questionable role model), young Sonya creates an illusion to win over the man who, metaphorically, is a bloodless John the Baptist—all head, no heart. Sonya gets her man, but she finds that the gulf between them is unbridgeable and that the manner in which she must behave to be with him denies her very being. Ostensibly a story about the pitfalls of gaining love by deception, the novel is both an examination of the problems of interethnic, interclass marriages and a harsh critique of the settlement program and the hypocrisy of the liberal reformers who began it.

Typical of the novel's critical reception at the time of publication was the view of Ferris Greenslet, an editor at Houghton Mifflin, which had published *Hungry Hearts and Other Stories* but had rejected the novel. To Greenslet, Sonya was "so unattractive, not to say repellent, that it seems to us likely to handicap the success of the book" (qtd. in Henriksen 174). Louise Maunsell Field called Sonya an "illiterate, hot-blooded little savage" (22), while Scott Nearing of *The Nation* identified her as a "devouring monster," calling *Salome of the Tenements* "an unwholesome book" (676). Even when the reviewers found the book fascinating, they tended to revert to racial stereotype, rarely picking up the critique of the liberal reformers of the day.[9] The critics were alarmed that Sonya triumphs in the end and that the character representing the American ideal—John Manning—is shown to be a sham. The novel appeared morally reprehensible to those who wished to maintain the status quo and who would rather not consider the suffering of the poor or the effects of semiforced assimilation on social minorities and new immigrants. In spite of, or perhaps because of, the infamy associated with the book, it sold well and film rights were bought. Its publication was also timed to coincide with the film version of *Hungry Hearts*.

One reviewer who did identify the progressive themes in the novel was the historian James Harvey Robinson, a colleague of

Dewey's at Columbia. Robinson observed that every sociologist and "miscellaneous moralizer" should read *Salome of the Tenements* so as to expose the "facile, pompous generalizations and academic abstractions . . . of the creatures which he pretends to explain" (14). In looking back on this time period, which affected the whole structure of public education in America, the novel presents for us today a contemporary critique of the contradictions of the melting pot theory and the issue of "good works" for the poor. In "Nationalizing Education," Dewey called for a broad concept of American nationalism, "extracting from each people its special good, so that it shall surrender into a common fund of wisdom and experience what it especially has to contribute" (185). Encoded in this notion is the contradiction underlying Dewey's cultural pluralism: the melting pot ideology covertly demands "that immigrants conform to the Anglo-Saxon model of culture and society" (Feinberg 497). Implicit in his demand is an understanding of the superiority of a certain culture and a certain class that contrasts sharply with Dewey's goal of an expansive American nationalism.[10]

Salome of the Tenements critiques not only the aims of the liberal reform movement but also how these aims were carried out by the social workers and do-gooders who ran the settlement houses. Sonya and the other young women immigrants attend programs at the settlements not for education and assimilation into the dominant culture, but for a chance to escape the ghetto—with luck, through marriage. Sonya, who from the beginning of the novel has rejected the false piety of the settlement house and its "friendly visitors," changes her mind when she, like her model, Rose Pastor Stokes, is sent by *The Ghetto News* to interview a famous philanthropist. After their meeting and initial flirtation, she plots: " 'To think how I once hated settlements. . . . Where else can a poor girl like me meet her millionaire if not in the settlement?' Sonya rationalized her inconsistency. 'How did Rose Pastor catch on to Graham Stokes?' " (82–83). Yezierska uses her friend's name here to both remind us of and separate Sonya from her model. Clearly, in this passage the illusion of love clouds Sonya's clear-sighted understanding of the hypocrisy of the settlement house.

Throughout the novel, references to the "inhuman activities of philanthropy" (138) reinforce Sonya's understanding. Later, when the married Sonya takes up her administrative position in the settlement house, she realizes that her husband's settlement is no different from the charity programs of her youth—designed to keep people poor and grateful for the little they get. In one scene, she watches the social workers, with "the self-conscious look of virtue in their eyes" (135), decide on what the poor deserve. Hearing a "rigid woman in a white starched collar" tell the "friendly visitors" to be on the lookout for the "impostors" (a widow who might add a little chicken to the meager rations given to her by the program) for the sake of the "'worthy poor'" (135), Sonya rages to herself: "'So these are Manning's social experts! So this is their plane of reason—"reason" forced down the throats of the people!... All of them lying to him! But they can't lie to the people" (138).

Sonya, at this point, believes that she can tell Manning what is going on and that together they will change the settlement programs for the better; however, in trying to talk to him, she faces his untested idealism, based on his life of privilege. He rejects her questions about class divisions with soothing phrases right out of Dewey's works: "'[We will] show the world that all social chasms can be bridged with human love and democratic understanding'" (119–20). Sonya retorts: "'Tell me in plain words how can there be democratic understanding between those who are free to walk into steerage and the steerage people who are not allowed to give one step up to the upper deck?'" (120). Manning's response that she always "'emphasize[s] differences'" reflects his inability to see the hypocrisy behind his liberal reforms.

The novel details the contradictions of Dewey's philosophy for a national culture on the most intimate level. In the primary love relationship in *Salome of the Tenements,* Yezierska sets up a binary opposition that resists displacement: Anglo-Saxon upper-class man/Jewish immigrant woman. Most of the comic moments of the novel ensue from this opposition; however, underlying the humor is harsh social criticism of ethnic prejudice and class privilege. In the first third of the novel Sonya schemes to catch her millionaire. She is embarrassed to meet Manning in her shabby clothes and to show him her tenement room, so she manipulates and cajoles the ghetto to present something beautiful for him. She convinces the famous designer Jacques Hollins (né Jaky Solomon) to make her a dress for free, but her worst deed is to bind herself to the pawnbroker "Honest Abe" by saying she'll pay back the $100 she borrows *after* she's married. Following along with Sonya's daring maneuvers, we hear with incredulity Manning's remarks on entering her room. Demonstrating the irony of noblesse oblige, Manning walks into her newly painted, decorated room and is impressed: "'Why, it's the glory of poverty that it enforces simplicity!... The thing that appeals to me so much about the East Side ... is their directness, their unscheming naturalness'" (73). Manning has been hoodwinked into believing his own fantasy about the nobility of poverty, but as we see later, Sonya also is fooled by the belief that Manning will be her savior, and the ghetto's as well.

Of course, with so much at stake, the marriage cannot work. Its breakdown is guaranteed when Sonya, a willing victim of Honest Abe, must expose her own deceit, and her savior reacts with anti-Semitic slurs. However, as the authorial narrator tells us, the marriage was deceitful on both sides: "Sonya and Manning, tricked into matrimony, were the oriental and the Anglo-Saxon trying to find a common language. The over-emotional Ghetto struggling for its breath in the thin air of puritan restraint" (132). Yezierska moves artfully from cultural group identity to stereotype, although some readers may find the reliance on stereotype—from the Shylock pawnshop owner Abe to the composite of sterile, unfeeling WASPs—somewhat disconcerting. One reviewer at the time focused on this use of representation and called Manning "a frosty prig that some readers may consider unreal, but that satisfied me as being true to type" (Roberts 26).

As in most comic novels, stereotypes are often used to make social points, and in this novel, Yezierska exposes the foibles of her community and the dominant culture to sharpen her social criticism. One of the best examples of this in the novel is the wedding reception scene; not only does it predate Woody Allen, but it politicizes that vision as well. Type and stereotype clash as the ghetto dwellers meet the uptown snobs; the Lower East Siders are the unlikely guests at a sometimes cruel comedy of manners. The examination of a stereotype's relation to issues of cultural unity is of concern in this historical moment of ethnic revival; moreover, the opposition of Sonya and Manning reflects other considerations of the present day: the intersection of race, class, and gender. Throughout the novel, Sonya is the emotional, oriental other to the " 'cold in the heart and clear in the head' " Manning (66). Through them Yezierska examines the historically based image of the ethnic woman as perceived sexual other to the Anglo-Saxon male. In the fallout from this intimate relationship, and within the context of the time period, she questions whether there can ever be a coming together of these groups as equals.

The one character who appears to be able to mediate these oppositions is the ghetto success Jaky Solomon (Jacques Hollins). His stamina and vision take him from a downtown tailor to a famous designer of clothes. For some readers today, the fact that he has had to change his name to become renowned may diminish that success, but it is not critiqued in the novel. And it is Hollins who first identifies the hypocrisy behind Manning's social reform: " 'I suppose . . . playing with poverty is more exciting than knocking golf balls' " (30). Hollins's cynical retort to Sonya's adoration of Manning sticks with her and resonates throughout. By the end of the novel, she has triumphed, but on her own; her accomplishment comes from what she makes with her hands. In a return to culture and "her people," Sonya designs beautiful clothes for the poor and working class, helping Hollins to reconnect as well. However, in the novel's denouement, even Manning becomes human, for Sonya realizes that " 'at bottom we're all alike, Anglo-Saxons or Jews, gentleman or plain immigrant. . . .—even a gentleman when starved long enough can become a savage East Sider' " (183). Her universalist vision at the end of the novel is somewhat mitigated by her final critique of her once savior, now an exposed failure of social reform: "She had thought of him going through the years making speeches in educated language, using handed down words in high sounding phrases that were as empty, as meaningless as the scientific goodness of his settlement work" (183).

With the reissue of this engaging, radical novel, *Salome of the Tenements* has outlived its critics. Today's readers can enjoy it as much as its first readers did. A novel that questions the basis of liberal reform and the roots of philanthropy, *Salome of the Tenements* anticipates many of the themes in later works such as Richard

Wright's *Native Son*. Indeed, the radical vision presented may reso-
nate more for today's readers, as we reassess the welfare system,
reassert the right of people from a variety of ethnic backgrounds to
succeed without accommodation to the dominant culture, and
reexamine the roots of liberal education. Furthermore, although
perhaps not a feminist by today's standards, Sonya has a strong
feminist impulse, and the critique of liberalism and its limited
vision is part of the move to redefine "American" culture. Finally,
Salome of the Tenements is a wonderful read, full of the rich language
and humor that made up the immigrant Jewish Lower East Side in
the early years of this century. To be sure, today's readers will not
condemn Sonya as a "devouring monster" but will perceive her as
a young woman with three strikes against her, trying to make her
way in America, that wilderness in which she is lost.

NOTES

I would like to thank Louise Levitas Henriksen for her careful reading
of this introduction and her clarification of certain historical facts. All
page numbers for quotations from *Salome of the Tenements* are from
this reissue.

1. The labeling of the Jewish people as a "race" is a historic treat-
ment now in disuse, at least in the United States. However, during the
time period of the novel, Jews were so identified, and Yezierska also
used the term; hence, I have used "race" to include the cultural,
religious, and ancestral aspects of Judaism.

2. Yezierska emigrated from the village of Plotsk/Plinsk on the
Russian-Polish border around 1890, with her parents, three brothers,
and three sisters. She was unsure of her date of birth, but her daughter
states that she was between eight and ten years old when she emigrated
(Henriksen 13–14). For the Jews in the shtetl, living in the Pale, there
was no particular national identity with either Russia or Poland, due
in part to frequent border disputes. This may be one reason why
Yezierska—and the heroines based on her—identified herself sometimes as a Russian Jew and sometimes as a Polish Jew. In addition,
because Yezierska tended to fictionalize her life, it is difficult to pin
down with complete accuracy certain dates, times, and places.

3. See, for example, Cahan.

4. Not only does the majority of her writing reflect what Yezierska
felt to be the inability of the Anglo-Saxon to respond emotionally, but

even "Prophets of Education," her review (written after their breakup) of Dewey's book *Democracy and Education,* attacks him in a most personal way. She called the writing of the book both inhuman and undemocratic, adding: "Can it be that Professor Dewey, for all his large social vision, has so choked the feelings in his own heart that he has killed in himself the power to reach the masses of people who think with the heart rather than the head?" (497)

5. In Yezierska's short story "Wings," collected in *Hungry Hearts,* the Deweyesque character identifies hysteria, overdramatization, and servile aggressiveness as characteristics associated with immigrant Jews. Repulsed by the young woman (who only wants him to help her with her English) and her "outburst of demonstrativeness," he thinks: "The whole gamut of the Russian Jew—the pendulum swinging from abject servility to boldest aggressiveness" (10).

6. Yezierska's objections to the project behind the *Conditions among the Poles in the United States: Confidential Report* reflect her concerns that the experts did not listen to the people. For more on this study, as well as the anti-Semitic behavior of the project director, Albert Barnes, see Dearborn (122–25) and Feinberg.

7. For a fuller discussion of the problems of mediating traditional Jewish culture and individual freedom in Yezierska's work, see Wilentz.

8. Rose Pastor Stokes was arrested under the Espionage Act in March 1918 for speaking out against the war. She was convicted and sentenced to ten years in prison, but the verdict was eventually overturned (Zipser 176–98).

9. See, for example, "Hungry Souls," W. Adolphe Roberts's review of *Salome of the Tenements.*

10. For further discussion on this educational policy, see Karier, Spring, and Violas.

BIBLIOGRAPHY

Works by Anzia Yezierska

All I Could Never Be. New York: Brewer, Warren and Putnum, 1932.
Arrogant Beggar. New York: Doubleday, 1927.
Bread Givers. 1925. New York: Persea, 1975.
How I Found America: Collected Stories of Anzia Yezierska (Rpt. of *Children of Loneliness.* 1923). New York: Persea, 1991.
Hungry Hearts and Other Stories. 1920. New York: Persea, 1985.
"The Immigrant Speaks," *Good Housekeeping* 70 (June 1920): 20–21.

The Open Cage: An Anzia Yezierska Collection. Ed. Alice Kessler-Harris. New York: Persea, 1979.

"Prophets of Education." *Bookman* 52 (Feb. 1921): 497–99.

Red Ribbon on a White Horse. 1950. New York: Persea, 1981.

Salome of the Tenements. New York: Boni & Liveright, 1923.

Reviews of *Salome of the Tenements*

Atherton, Gertrude. "Fighting Up from the Ghetto." *New York Herald,* 7 Jan. 1923.

Field, Louise Maunsell. Review of *Salome of the Tenements* by Anzia Yezierska. *New York Times,* 24 Dec. 1922: 22.

Goodman, Henry. "What Anzia Yezierska Doesn't Know about East Side Fills Two Books." *Forward,* 25 Nov. 1923: English page.

Nearing, Scott. "A Depraved Spirit." *Nation,* 6 June 1923: 675–76.

Roberts, W. Adolphe. "Hungry Souls." *New York Tribune,* 17 Dec. 1922: 26.

Robinson, James Harvey. Review of *Salome of the Tenements* by Anzia Yezierska. *Literary Digest International Book Review,* Feb. 1923: 14.

Smertenko, J. J. Review of *Salome of the Tenements* by Anzia Yezierska. *Literature Review,* 20 Jan. 1923: 395.

Z.F.P. "Those Who Welcomed 'Hungry Hearts.'" *American Hebrew,* 2 Feb. 1923.

Other Sources

Cahan, Abraham. *The Rise of David Levinsky.* 1917. New York: Penguin, 1993.

Dearborn, Mary V. *Love in the Promised Land: The Story of Anzia Yezierska and John Dewey.* New York: Free Press, 1988.

Dewey, John. *Conditions among the Poles in the United States: Confidential Report.* Prepared for the Military Intelligence Bureau. N.p., 1918.

———. *Democracy and Education.* New York: Macmillan, 1916.

———. "Nationalizing Education." *National Education Association Addresses and Proceedings* 54 (1916): 183–89.

———. *The Poems of John Dewey.* Ed. Jo Ann Boydston. Carbondale: Southern Illinois University Press, 1977.

Feinberg, Walter. "Progressive Education and Social Planning." *Teachers College Record* 73 (1972): 485–505.

Henriksen, Louise Levitas. *Anzia Yezierska: A Writer's Life.* New Brunswick: Rutgers University Press, 1988.

Herzog, Kristin. *Women, Ethnics, and Exotics: Images of Power in Mid-Nineteenth-Century Fiction.* Knoxville: University of Tennessee Press, 1983.

Hymen, Paula E. "Culture and Gender: Women in the Immigrant Jewish Community." In *The Legacy of Jewish Migration: 1881 and Its Impact.* Ed. David Berger. New York: Brooklyn College Press, 1983. 157–68.

Kamel, Rose. " 'Anzia Yezierska, Get Out of Your Way': Selfhood and Otherness in the Autobiographical Fiction of Anzia Yezierska." *Studies in American Jewish Literature* 3 (1983): 40–50.

Karier, Clarence J. "Liberal Ideology and the Quest for Orderly Change." In Karier et al. 84–107.

Karier, Clarence J., Joel Spring, and Paul C. Violas, eds. *Roots of Crisis: American Education in the Twentieth Century.* Chicago: University of Chicago Press, 1973.

Neidle, Cecyle S. *American Immigrant Women.* Boston: Twayne, 1975.

Pastor Stokes, Rose. *I Belong to the Working Class: The Unfinished Autobiography of Rose Pastor Stokes.* Ed. Herbert Shapiro and David L. Sterling. Athens: University of Georgia Press, 1992.

Sachs, Susan Hersh. "Anzia Yezierska: Her Words Dance with a Thousand Colors." *Studies in American Jewish Literature* 3 (1983): 62–67.

Satlof, Claire R. "History, Fiction and Tradition: Creating a Jewish Feminist Poetic." In *On Being a Jewish Feminist.* Ed. Susannah Heschel. New York: Schocken, 1983. 133–62.

Schoen, Carol B. *Anzia Yezierska.* Boston: Twayne, 1983.

Sullivan, Radna. "Anzia Yezierska, an American Writer." Ph.D. dissertation, University of California, Berkeley, 1975.

Wilentz, Gay. "Cultural Mediation and the Immigrant's Daughter: Anzia Yezierska's *Bread Givers.*" *MELUS* 17.3 (Fall 1991–92): 33–41.

Zipser, Arthur, and Pearl Zipser. *Fire and Grace: The Life of Rose Pastor Stokes.* Athens: University of Georgia Press, 1989.

Salome of the Tenements

To Horace Liveright

1

Salome Meets Her Saint

"My dear Miss Vrunsky," said John Manning, bowing courteously. "You need not thank me. If you are pleased to get this interview for your paper, it has been a pleasure for me to give it."

His low voice of cultured restraint thrilled through the girl like music. Even his formal manner—his unconscious air of superiority—roused in her the fire of worship.

"It's not just an interview you've given me," she flashed breathlessly. "It's high thoughts fit for poetry—the most beautiful language that ever went into print in our *Ghetto News.*"

Her ardent words embarrassed him. "I trust," he replied, bowing with high-bred aloofness, "that this opportunity to reach the public through your press will materially aid the progress of the work."

She lifted her shining face to him. "Your words—they'll burn into the hearts of the people like the fire of a new religion. Never before did a born American talk out to them so prophetically—what means it America!"

A network of little lines crinkled above the high cheekbones. Her smile broadened, warmed in the radiance of that ardent appreciation. But in spite of the emotional stimulus she gave him, his frosty blue eyes failed to kindle.

"You are the poet. It's your live imagination that could make my poor words flame—" And he checked himself at "flame," his Anglo-Saxon austerity shocked at having been trapped into using so colorful a word.

"What do you mean?" cried Sonya impetuously. "You, a great philanthropist, to say that to me—a nobody? There are millions like me—"

"Are there?" And for the first time during their talk, his eyes twinkled venturesomely, as he searched her face.

"Of course there are." The color of her cheeks seemed to catch the reflection from her glowing eyes. The whole face was alight. "There are millions of us here."

"You are one of them—yes—but you are distinctly yourself." The strangeness of his own words caught in his throat. His brows puckered. He suddenly became aware that he was self-conscious. For the life of him he could not prevent his fingers plucking nervously at the lapels of his coat.

"You mean it? Something you see in me different?" blurted Sonya. She clasped her hands gratefully. "Thank God! Other people—they think I'm only crazy."

"My child," he said, trying to withdraw into the shell of safe abstractions. "With your ardor you can become the voice of your people."

"But how? What do you want me to do?" She had to restrain herself from leaping toward him in her eagerness. "Only tell me!"

He drew back a trifle, studying her. "That's not so easy to answer, but perhaps I can find a way to help you. I'm willing to try if you'll let me."

"Help me? For myself alone, I don't need no help, because I got nothing to do but my column on the paper, and I'm tired of that. But only let me work for *you* and you'll save my soul."

Oblivious of the squalid humans that swarmed about them, indifferent for the moment to the myriad needs that drove the crowds here and there from pushcarts to shops, from tenements to factories, restaurants and coffee stands, unaware of the raucous orchestra of voices, the metallic bedlam of elevated trains, the pounding of horses and humans scuttling through the middle of the street—this man and this woman stood wholly absorbed in one another.

Head swung back, Sonya looked up in admiration at Manning, her heart pierced by the cultured elegance of his attire. Not a detail of his well-dressed figure escaped her. His finished grooming stood out all the more vividly in this background of horrid poverty. A master tailor had cut his loose Scotch tweeds. His pale brown pongee shirt was lighter and finer than a woman's waist. The rich hidden quietness of his silk tie; even his shoes had a hand-made quality to them! she thought.

Less definitely, but with equal interest, the man's glance took in the girl. Of severe blue serge, shiny from wear, there was about her dress the nun-like austerity of the intellectual East Side. But personality, femininity, flamed through this unrevealing uniform.

"You have a greater work to do than I" went on Manning. "You have the burning fire of the Russian Jew in you, while I am motivated by a sickly conscience, trying to heal itself by the application of cold logic and cold cash. The real liberation of your people must come from within—from such as you."

A smile born of the spirit lit his face as he bowed his bared head in regretful dismissal, "A week from to-day then, lunch at the Russian Inn."

Sonya Vrunsky had no words as she took the hand he gave. She felt the kindness of his spirit brush against her very heart-strings. She longed to throw herself at his feet and weep. "Ach! America— God from the world! Ach!"

As if by magic, the force of her will had materialized her desire into flesh and blood. Here, in the teeming Ghetto, among haggling pushcart peddlers, in the dirt and din of screaming hucksters, stood John Manning, millionaire, philanthropist—the man of her dreams, talking to her, inviting her to lunch with him.

Through a tear-dimmed mist she saw his tall slenderness, the shoulders slightly stooped as though by a head too heavy for his frail strength. The premature greyness of his hair was to her a nimbus—a cloud of white light, adding the final touch of divinity to the luminous features.

"And you mean it?" she faltered. "I—I didn't waste your time?"

She was at once filled with an embarrassment so painful that for a moment she stood facing him without a word. "From all your business to stop to talk to only me—"

"You shame my business," he reassured her. "To get my work done, I fear that my time is usually only too well protected. How much I would have missed if you hadn't come!"

"I can't yet get over it, my luck. I, a wild stranger, stop you in the middle of the street and you answer me so naturally like you knew me from always."

"You were no stranger, the moment you spoke."

Sonya's eyes were pools of light as she looked up to him.

"I didn't think it possible that a born higher-up, no matter how much he wanted to come down from his educated manners, could be so plain from the heart like you. Why, you make me feel so natural, I could go on talking to you forever like you were nobody."

This response from one of the people filled him with a new faith, a new hope for his work.

"My child, you have been a revelation to me," he said, once again extending his hand in final parting. "The next time you must tell me more about yourself." And John Manning was gone.

Sonya stood looking after him. She seemed unable to tear her body away from the burning bush where a moment before he had stood. The rough pushing and jostling of women with their market baskets failed to violate her ecstasy. Her lips were parted, her hand lightly clenched, her whole body posed as if for flight in ardent pursuit of him.

"My child! You have been a revelation to me!" she repeated. She—Sonya Vrunsky—a revelation! Every nerve within her quivered with joy—a joy so sharp, so poignant, that it hurt to draw breath.

She tried to free herself from the bewitching spell of him. "Six months—no—a lifetime—ten full lifetimes, have I waited for him!"

His presence, so ethereal, yet so vivid, still breathed over her—reached forth tenuous feelers toward her. The very air was pungent with his spirit—the light of his smile still enveloped her.

Through a blur of dazzling brightness she found her way back to Suffolk Street. The slattern *yentehs* lounging on the stoops, their dirty babies at their breasts, were transfigured into Madonnas of love through the light of his face. The noises of the street, the shrill screams of hucksters, cries of children merged into the echo of his voice.

As Sonya entered the dingy tenement where she lived, she lifted a transfigured face to the sputtering gas jet. It was mean and dingy no longer. The blaze of it was like the blaze that whirled at the top of her brain.

The very ground under her feet seemed to expand and glow. It was not solid. Nothing she touched was solid. Even the crooked stairs that led to her hall-room changed into a Jacob's ladder that led skyward where dreams opened upon dreams.

Sonya darted to her mirror as soon as she reached her den. Then poised in front of the glass she gave herself a passionately critical scrutiny. With hands pressed against her cheeks she studied the reflection of herself. Luminous black eyes flashed back at her—keen-edged swords of desire. "He—he is for me as the sun is for the earth—light—life. He is the breath of all that is beautiful. Ach! How I could love him! I'd wrap my soul around him like a living flame."

"My child! You have been a revelation to me!"

The music of that sentence rang in her ears all night. The day had been too much for her. She could not sleep. Her thoughts were on fire. Toward morning at last she dozed, to dream of him and the new life of friendship with him.

Then she awoke and before her eyes was the light of his eyes and in her heart the breath of his voice.

Still under the spell of him, she went to the window, looking out on a fire-escape where she kept her can of milk and groceries for her breakfast. The roaring tumult of the noises from the street below woke her from her dreams. Wedged in, jumbled shops and dwellings, pawnshops and herring-stalls, strained together begging for elbow room. Across the alley a second-hand store protruded its rubbish. Broken stoves, beds, three-legged chairs sprawled upon the sidewalk. The unspeakable cheapness of a dry goods shop flared in her face—limp calico dresses of scarlet and purple, gaudy blankets of pink and green checks. From the crowded windows hung dirty mattresses and bedding—flaunting banners of poverty.

She slammed the window with a crash. "God from the world! How did I stand all this till now?"

The grimy walls of her little room pressed in upon her—suffocated her.

"An end to darkness and dirt! I've found my deliverer! Already I'm released from the blackness of this poverty. Air, space, the mountain-tops of life are already mine!"

She wanted to shout her triumph to the world. "What will they all say at the office—Lipkin—Gittel Stein?"

An hour later she burst like a whirlwind into the office of the *Ghetto News.*

"Wild woman, what is the matter with you?" From her desk in the corner, Gittel Stein peered over her thick-lensed glasses. "You're so on fire! Your eyes are jumping out of your head."

Sonya Vrunsky threw her hands up in the air. "It's come—it's here—my life is made!"

"Who? What? You crazy?"

"I met the greatest man in America! John Manning, the millionaire! It was I who told Lipkin to let me interview him and ask why he gave up his limousines to come among pushcarts; why he left his swell place on Fifth Avenue for a bare room in a settlement."

"*Nu*, I remember—but that was weeks ago."

"It's easier to see the President of the United States. Board meetings, conferences at Washington, labor arbitration committees—his secretary kept giving me excuses—"

"Ye-yes." Gittel's brow knitted into a frown, duly resentful of the younger girl's exuberance.

"So I decided to go for him direct. You know the old saying, 'Everything comes to him who goes to fetch it.' So I waited in front of his settlement house till he came back from lunch. Then I stopped him! I felt like Joshua who stopped the sun!"

Gittel Stein took in Sonya with deliberate, envious eyes. For the hundredth time she tried to analyze the secret of her charm. The shirtwaist Sonya wore came from the same shop in Hester Street. It cost no more than her own. Sonya's hat, her shoes, were of a cheaper grade, yet from the crown of her head to her slender feet the girl sparkled with the magic of youth—the flame that drew all men.

"Think only," went on Sonya, "that millionaire invited me to lunch. But why shouldn't he?" Sonya drew herself up proudly. "I ain't a cheap nobody!"

"You're crazy for power, Sonya Vrunsky," Gittel hated her own pettiness but she could not resist the jibe. "You don't want to do big things. You only want to shine for a big person. You'd sell your soul for a million dollars."

"Dollars?" Sonya Vrunsky tossed her head in arrogant denial. "It draws me only to his culture, his fineness—the beauty that grows amid beauty. The struggle for a living makes men coarse-grained and greedy—"

"It's not only men that the struggle for bread makes coarse-grained and greedy—" and Gittel paused significantly.

"You've said it. It's just to get away from the sordidness of this penny-pinched existence that I got to catch on to a man like Manning." Her heart tightened with fear as she noticed for the first time the pinched face of her companion—the grooved lines of wear and want that had eaten into the softness of the neck.

"Your American millionaire can't hold a candle to our own editor, Lipkin—a poet whose words are wine to the soul."

"*Ut!* Lipkin! For all his fine poetry, he has a poverty-stricken dent in his chest. A poet is not a poet if he has a pitiful *nebich* look even though he is starving and in rags. A real poet should be able to clothe himself with the heavens and feed himself with the stars."

Sonya was again caught up by the beckoning vision. A transforming fire sprang into her cheeks and her hands moved feverishly. "The spirit—the spark of inspiration—the flash from the eyes that lifts me to the heights—these are the things that I seek in a man."

"You are only a creature consumed by the madness to rise."

"A woman should be youth and fire and madness—the desire that reaches for the stars. A man should be wisdom, maturity, poise. John Manning has everything I need to save my soul. He can give me the high things of heaven and the beauty and abundance of the earth."

Gittel glanced at Sonya with amused pity. "You poor *yok!* He, a rich, cultured American—a born blueblood—and you, a crazy from Hester Street, a nobody from nowhere—you want to catch on to him!"

Sonya's eyes flashed disdainfully. "Why, Manning and I are more alike than born equals. He is trying to get rid of his riches and I'm trying to get rid of my poverty. Both of us we want to get away from the things of the earth that hold us down from the freedom of the stars."

"You faker—you bluff! Sometimes I wonder if there is anything real in you."

But at the words there flashed before her another Sonya—on her knees before the rusty grate coaxing the kettle to boil, while Gittel lay helpless with an aching chest—a Sonya whose vibrant voice and glowing face were the only sunlight in her room during the lonely days of her illness.

"I take back what I said." Gittel reached for the girl's hand. "There is a real spark in you somewhere."

"The only thing real is that I'm to have lunch with Manning in a week from to-day." She blew a kiss to the shaft of sunshine that slanted across the desk. "And I'll rob, steal or murder if I got to—for clothes to make myself beautiful for him. Come to look for a new hat with me?"

"Where would you get the money? Only yesterday you borrowed a fiver from Lipkin."

"Come, I say! Any brainless fool can go buying with money. If I could get an invitation from Manning, everything else got to come to me," she challenged with the devouring egotism of youth. "I feel the gods are holding out their hands to me. 'Sonya Vrunsky,' they whisper to me, 'dare to want what you want and you'll have it. Let loose your soul on the wishing-wings of your dreams and we'll give you the fulness of your heart's desire.' "

Fascinated, the older girl watched her. Sonya was a being from another world—one bound by invisible laws of her own making. Memories of Gittel's own youth—a youth still-born—struck at her heart. Never had she felt so poignantly the loss of that which she had never known. Never had the unlived, untasted years been driven back upon her with such crushing force as now.

Appraisingly, Gittel's eyes surveyed this visionary March hare. "Sonya, it's Don Quixote you make me think of. Only, he tilted at windmills, but you, you got the sense to land the solid things."

"The first solid things I got to land are some decent clothes," laughed Sonya, plucking at her threadbare jacket. "These stuffy things are begging themselves to be taken off! See only through the window! Even the street-cleaners have on their white wings. Even the shriveled trees in Seward Park are putting on little new leaves. I could tear a new spring hat from out the blazing sun."

"You'd draw the very dead from their graves when you begin to burn for a thing." The envy in her tone was ill-concealed. "Poor people have no right to let themselves want—"

"You call me poor because my pockets are empty?" Sonya turned her pockets inside out. "I can catch on to the golden hills on the sky when it wills itself in me."

"*Nu*, my American Cinderella! Try to catch on to new clothes without money—"

"*Ut!* Always hammering money! What's money anyway but

dead metal? The only thing that counts is the living breath of desire. Let me only give a look on something worth while and money or no money I get it. Come only—you'll see."

"I can't waste my precious time watching you stand on your head and turn the world upside down. I got my job—"

"No, stick to your job. The life in me cries out for life. I got to have what wills itself in me—"

The door swung open and there entered a drooping figure with dreamy eyes.

"I got him—Manning—the interview."

"Is there anything our Sonya cannot get?" Lipkin's pallor deepened at the nearness of her.

With a vision of the fastidiously groomed Manning before her eyes, Lipkin's slovenly neglect—his broken shoes and torn coat-sleeve—filled her with a pity that was almost contempt.

"Sonya, you'll be famous yet," beamed Lipkin, gratified to have got the interview with the much-talked-of John Manning. "Have you enough material for a Sunday special?"

"Look only!" Excitedly Sonya opened the pages of her note-book. "I didn't try to write a word while he talked to me, but the minute I got home, it leaped like lightning from my pen. Listen only to this: '*I came to teach and I am learning. I came to give and find myself receiving from those who I thought had nothing. Right here in these crowded tenements is the spirit that is beauty and power!*' "

Exultantly, Sonya handed the note-book to Lipkin. "The rest is yet all in the rough but you can patch it together. The inspiration is there. The grinding it into shape is not for me."

"It is for you only to feel and to fly. Let lesser ones do the grind." Gaunt and dragged down from overwork—yet the task that Sonya thrust so lightly into his hands was like a boon of life to him. The thought of having a part in anything that she touched put new light in his tired eyes, a new glow into his pale cheeks.

Gittel Stein turned away to hide the hurt she felt at the joy that shone in Lipkin's face, as his eyes rested on Sonya.

Sonya glanced from the pale Lipkin to the worn and faded Gittel. "What a selfish, unfeeling person I am!" she thought. "I, who have the whole of life ahead of me, who am going to have the luxuries of love, beauty, plenty, the companionship of Manning."

She could almost have wept with pity for these two. The perpetual shadow of sadness in Lipkin's face and the hungry wistfulness that cried out of Gittel's lusterless eyes smote her with a sense of her own undeserved good luck.

How she would help them—once she had the power! Lipkin would be free to devote himself to his poetry without the worry for bread. And Gittel—she would introduce Gittel to some of Manning's millionaire friends and get them to take her out to the theater and concerts and wake her up from the deadness of her joyless existence.

Having settled the golden future for them all, Sonya flew back to immediate desire. "To-morrow you will see me a bird with new feathers," and she was gone in search of her new hat.

Through the window, Lipkin watched the threadbare little jacket as it turned the corner and disappeared. "How it dances from her the joy! The very earth she steps on wakes with new life! The childlike innocence of her!"

"Pfui! The blindness of men! That girl innocent!" thought Gittel. And unable to control her rancor any longer she exploded. "It wills itself in her to marry John Manning. Already she got him to invite her to lunch."

"The little witch!" chuckled Lipkin as he turned into his inner office. "And she hid that under her sleeve. But why shouldn't Manning invite her?" he defended her with a wry smile. "She's the very spirit of springtime. She's sunlight and moonlight and song!" apostrophized the poet dreamily.

Somehow Gittel could not resume the thread of her work. The girl's disturbing youth still lingered about the place and stabbed her into a realization of her own futility, the unlived, wasted years going on endlessly.

"Good God! What a jealous hag—what a green-eyed snake I am!" mused Gittel, as her eyes fell on the gay pot of geraniums on Sonya's desk. That bold bit of color brightened the dinginess of the office like a symbol and banner of beauty among the paste pots and chaos of paper smudged with printer's ink. "How eager she is for a little beauty! Even in this clutter of dust and dirt her flower pot shines like a light from a happier world."

Her rancor gradually gave way to a sane mood of reason.

"In a way I like the girl for the very wildness that I hate. She with her bluff, her four-flushing, her bedeviling of men, can move mountains. After all, why should I hate her simply because she stretches out her hands to life as I'd like to do, if I only had it in me! Why can't I be glad for her little gladness? How long will it last, her bubble of joy? What is her whole happiness but a rainbow of glamour and illusion bound to melt like mist with the first breath of reality? Then why do I eat out my heart envying her?"

With such platitudes, the lonely spinster tried to console herself. But the very next moment the joy-starved face went greyer with envy.

"Ach! Be it glamour and illusion, but while she lives, she is *alive*. I am dead. I never yet lived. I never was young. Never in my whole childhood or youth did I ever know the rainbow light of illusion. I don't envy her. I don't want to tear away from her her little star of joy, but why have I been cheated out of the chance to grow, to live—to love?"

In a rush of self-pity, her whole past flashed before her like pages of an open book. They were grey, pictureless pages filled with reason and philosophy on how to suffer and endure—pages unlit by one live experience, by one act of divine madness, by one flare of assertive youth. Never since she was born had she ever looked into the eyes of love.

Longingly her glance strayed to where Lipkin sat in his office smiling over Sonya's papers, utterly unmindful of his drab assistant's devotion.

"How I could love that poet!" She clasped her hands over her shrunken breast, swept along into a confession for the first time. "How I could be father and mother and lover and friend to him! How I could feed him and bring the best poetry out of him! And to that crazy, heartless one, he pours out the finest, the deepest, from his soul!"

Her words, though unspoken, seemed to her curiously shameless. Rigidly she suppressed the emotions that had brought them to the surface and assumed a knowing air—a challenge of self-justification—a fatuous sense of superiority over the younger girl's power.

"Women like Sonya are a race apart," she philosophized. "They can no more help vamping men than roses can help giving out their perfume."

2

Shopping for Simplicity

Jostling throngs, haggling women, peddlers and pushcarts. The smell of fishstalls, of herring stands. Sonya Vrunsky headed for Essex Street unmindful of them all.

Earth and air and sky blazed with vision crowding upon vision: John Manning's life-giving look—his thrilling words, "You have been a revelation to me!"—John Manning kissing her lips, clasping her in his arms, pressing her to his heart, his being flowing into her being till she swooned in blinding bliss.

She looked up and smiled to herself in rapture at the dazzling mirage that danced before her. Every tenement roof became a gilded spire throbbing heavenward with the great Miracle in her heart.

"It's my worship for him that lifts me out of myself! What's beating in my heart is back of everything—suns and planets and systems."

She said it passionately, prayerfully, with lifted face as one facing her Creator for the first time.

"So that's why Keats and Shelley had such deathless music in their songs—because it was love and the life-giving glow that love gives that sang itself in them!"

In one leap she had ceased to be a self-centered, self-seeking thing, wasting her soul in the sordid struggle for food and clothes. No more would she lose precious hours night after night in such sordid trivialities as washing collars, ironing waists, darning patches in her threadbare suit. As Mrs. Manning, maids would do all this sordid work for her. She was star-high above the drag of material things. She lived now for the world. Her interests were as large as humanity and its problems.

Already Sonya felt she had joined hands with those large humanitarian forces for which Manning was famed: model tenements, play-grounds for children, old-age pensions, the abolishment of poverty and want in every form.

Anticipation leaped thirstily to pleasures ahead.

She saw herself the center of all eyes. People drew back in wonder as she passed. Envious fingers pointed her out. Hushed voices whispered her name—"There she goes, Mrs. John Manning, who gives away millions to the poor!"

Through her luck the whole Ghetto is saved. The hungry and the homeless lift their hands in blessing everywhere she turns. The ragged children scamper from hovels and tenements and cling to her in childlike affection as she scatters handfuls of money among them.

To the rhythm of her light footsteps and the lilt of her singing heart, a hand-organ catching the contagion of her happiness started up the latest popular air. Snatching hungrily at the joys of the street, a group of ragged waifs began to dance with the abandon of the children of the poor.

Edging her way into the little circle, "Sing it, sing it," Sonya cried. "Don't stop at dancing." She picked up the ends of a short brown braid tied together with a shoe-lace and hummed the words of the chorus, "Just a little love, a little kiss, I will give you all my life for this."

An aching pity for these helpless little ones smote her—their future swallowed up in sweatshops. If only America had a few more John Mannings to give to the poor! And in the surge of her great compassion she slipped a copper into the brown braid's grimy, little fist.

"Step right in! Selling-out sales! Bargains!" Sonya's arm was seized by a puller-in who dragged her down from romance to Essex Street.

"Who wants your bargains? Have you no eyes? Have you no ears?" Shaking herself free from the obnoxious hand, she picked up the littlest of them all and waltzed him around the lamp-post.

"Holiday hats! Shine yourself out for the Passover! Everything marked down cheap!" Another importunate puller-in reached out for her coat-sleeve.

"Worms should eat you and your cheapness," she hurled at the offender. The sordidness of haggling and bargaining—all she had ever known till now—broke in upon her high mood. Suddenly remembering that she had gone out to buy her hat, she waved a hurried farewell to her little friends and made her way to Abramson's—the only one-price store on Essex Street.

"What can I show you, dearie?" fawned a full-bosomed woman from behind the counter.

"The best you got," Sonya ordered, looking about the display of spring millinery.

"The stuck-up thing! How she blows from herself!" the saleswoman whispered to the girl with coral earrings across the aisle.

One after another, Sonya picked up and flung down the hats.

"I thought I could get one decent hat in Abramson's! I hate cheap feathers. I hate cheap stuff!"

"Did you ever wear anything but a shawl over your head in the old country?" was the quick retort. And at an approving nod from Sadie—in Trimmings, "The minute they come to America nothing is good enough for them. The dirt under the feet they were at home, and in America they blow from themselves like born millionaires."

Sonya gave the woman one contemptuous glance and turned to go.

Fearing to lose her customer, the woman encircled Sonya's waist in an affectionate embrace. "I should live so, dearie! These hats are the latest thing in style!"

"A fire should burn out all your styles," Sonya exploded. "God from the world! Haven't you got something simple?"

At which the woman jerked from the bottom drawer a stiff sailor, hurling it on the table-top. "Here's one simple enough, Gawd knows."

"*Gottuniu!* What hardness—what ugliness!" Sonya turned up a scornful, young nose. "Something simple, I want—yes, but soft and formed on the lines of the head."

"Something soft and formed on the lines of the head." The mimicry was for the benefit of the clerk with the diamond necklace at the near-by tricolette rack.

"Ach! It drives me wild to have to wade through so much junk to get something simple." Up went Sonya's arms with the abandon of a tragedy queen. "I ask only, how can a person like me stand the cheapness of these ready-mades?"

"What you want ain't in existence at all." The woman's patience was exhausted. "It's a wonder you ain't having your 'simple' hats made special for you. Why not go up to these millionaire stores on Fifth Avenue? There you might maybe find your 'simple' Vanderbilt styles."

Fifth Avenue! The very name was magic. The dancing lights came back into Sonya's eyes as she beamed on this fountain of wisdom. "What a *yok* I was to waste my time on Essex Street!"

"Maybe a plain store on Fifth Avenue wouldn't have anything 'simple' enough for the likes of *you*." The woman winked derisively to her friend across the aisle. "Why not better go to Jacques Hollins direct? He got those 'simple' nothings in hats and dresses that costs fortunes."

"Tell me only—where is he?" cried Sonya.

"Where is Jacques Hollins?" Sadie of the Trimmings joined in the laughter. "I guess you ain't been long in America!"

At last she had found something to impress this stuck-up prig. She'd give her an earful. "He don't remember no more none of his old friends what knew him when he was Jaky Solomon, but just the same I worked before he began rubbing sleeves with the higher-ups, when he was only tailoring on Division Street. It was me he talked to when he was on fire to go to Paris to learn designing," she tapped her bosom boastfully. "But when he landed back as Jacques Hollins on Fifth Avenue—hm-m! His nose was in the air like he was born and raised by Vanderbilt."

Sonya was a-tremble with excitement. "How can you get to him?"

"Nobodies from Essex Street would faint away from the shine of the brass buttons on his footman. His models—do you know how much they get for showing off his designs on their shapes? Fifty dollars a week. Only the Four Hundred are rich enough to pass through his door."

"How does he get it so good?" Sonya questioned breathlessly.

"Rich women with no worries on their heads but how to catch on to men, they don't care what price they lay down for a dress so long it'll make them shine out different. They're begging themselves by him he should only take their money. And Jaky Solomon, with his head for the dollar, he knows how to let himself be paid good for his time. So he studies their faces and their shapes and color of their hair and the shade of their skin. Ain't that what wills itself in you?" she taunted.

"Ach!" breathed Sonya. "I always knew there must be clothes artists that could make me look like myself."

"*Nu!* so go to Hollins then," scoffed the woman. "He's the only designer that could suit you."

Unconscious of the sneering voice, Sonya cried, "To him then I'll fly. Quickly only. How can I the soonest get to him?"

"Hire yourself a taxi," jibed the scandalized woman, "and then his footman will give you a kick out!"

To the sound of the mocking laughter Sonya darted from the store to the nearest telephone directory. With her single remaining nickel she took the uptown surface car.

"Bug house! Crazy!" jeered the woman. She tapped her forehead significantly with the index finger as the tittering chorus surrounded her.

"The nerve of a landlord! The bold thing!"

"The stuck-up'dness of a newly married bride!"

"You'd think Rockefeller's son is falling on his knees begging to pay for her hats."

"I'll bet not a penny in her pocket—heels turned down—gloves full of holes."

"Penny-pinchedness from her feet to the head."

"Yet it wills itself in her clothes from Fifth Avenue!"

"Maybe Jacques Hollins yet!"

Another peal of laughter—"Jacques Hollins yet!"

3

Jaky Solomon and Jacques Hollins

Every now and then the Ghetto gives birth to an embryonic virtuoso. Out of the crucible of privation and want, from hovels, basements, and black tenement holes, the unconquerable soul of the Jewish race rises in defiance of its environment.

As Zangwill emerged from the abyss of London's East Side, as Heifetz strove for self-expression on the violin, and Pinsky wrestled in his Bowery printing shop with the ghosts of his future dramas, so Jaky Solomon struggled blindly in a sweatshop as a designer in the dress trade to create clothes that would voice his love for color and line.

The finely moulded, sensitive lips of the boy curled daily into more restless discontent. He had gone from factory to factory in search of an employer who would see the value of his creative ideas. But always he had encountered opposition and dense stupidity. Even now, though he had come to the best house on East Broadway, he still had to bend to the will of an ignorant boss.

Mr. Epstein, the president of the Star Dress Concern, swung around on the swivel chair and contemptuously faced his designer.

"So this last swatch of goods don't suit you neither?" he exploded.

"You can't drape the models I designed from this shoddy stuff." And Jaky Solomon's sensitive fingers ran across the bale of silk that grated his flesh like a file. "This ain't got body, nor color."

"Body—color! Who heard from such words! We're in business for the dollar and the cheaper silk means thousands saved for the house."

"Without art it chokes me. I can't breathe." His long fingers worked spasmodically. "*Gottuniu!* Can't you see there's too much red in that brown? It cries to be softened in shade!"

"I put up with your high airs long enough." Mr. Epstein shifted the stub of his cigar to the other corner of his mouth. "Why don't you hire yourself a flying ship to Paris and design out styles for the queens?"

Jaky Solomon glanced deprecatingly at his underfed, puny body. Why couldn't he realize that he was only a common tailor? Why this futile search for color and fabrics that were only for the rich?

Paris!

Suddenly he saw himself in Paris.

Why was he hoarding his money—going without proper food, living in a dark hovel, if not for Paris—Paris!

Back in his rat-trap of a room he lifted the mouldy mattress from the floor and groped with trembling hands for the hoarded wad, the lever that would lift him into the world of freedom and opportunity. Feverishly, he counted the thumbed, evil-smelling money. Each bill as he held it in front of the smoky gas-jet was a magic wand. It dissolved walls, burned down barriers, released the talents in the free air of limitless expansion.

He was on his knees before the future queen of England, draping the shimmering chiffon and velvet of her coronation robe. Great stars of the Parisian stage tapped impatient dainty feet in his mauve-hung reception room. The famous courtesans of kings and princes bowed before him in recognition of his genius.

The gas-jet flickered, sputtered. And with it his dreams were extinguished.

Darkness.

He fumbled in his pocket for another quarter for the meter. Five minutes later he rewrapped the grimy bills. "Only sixty dollars," he groaned. "How far is yet my dream from Paris?"

*   *   *

Jaky Solomon had been with the house of Sussman Bros. on 42nd Street but a few months when he was made head designer. More and more was he in demand by the difficult, rich customers whose friends had worn gowns of his exquisite workmanship.

Mrs. Isenblatt, the banker's wife, turned a cold, fishy eye upon the proprietor. "But only Solomon I want to fit me," she flashed her diamond-covered fingers in arrogant finality. "That last velvet suit of yours is laying in my closet yet. I look like a barrel in it. Only Solomon knows how to push away my fat."

Sussman threw up his hands in despair. The stupid flattery of these fool women was ruining his head designer, encouraging him to demand an ever increasing wage.

"We got other designers just as good and better," he urged. But with an impatient gesture, Mrs. Isenblatt repeated her request. And Mr. Sussman was too shrewd a business man to risk the loss of his richest customer. He summoned Solomon.

"Nobody can hide away my hips the way you can, Solomon." Mrs. Isenblatt was all dimpled creases, as she watched him drape the cloth around her. "And honest I look like a perfect thirty-six instead of forty-eight around the bust," she simpered at her reflection in the cheval mirror.

"There ain't nothing a tailor can't do if he takes his time to study the shape," he smiled with a mouthful of pins. "I could make you look thin and a thin woman fat."

"Ach! Solomon! Could you fatten out a skinny girl by your fit? My Sadie is nothing but skin and bones. She's a girl in years and eats out her heart that she ain't got the luck for the right man."

"Any woman without a positive hump I can make beautiful. It's for a tailor to fit a shape into a woman. Otherwise he ain't got the right to call himself a tailor."

"Money ain't no money if you could only put a little stylishness into her fit. The way the tailors make her look, she's like straight sticks."

From the corner of his eyes Solomon appraised Sussman's richest customer. In one swift glance he took in the glittering stones on her fat fingers, the pearl and the platinum lavallière that was lost to sight in the three folds that had once been her chin.

"I'm going to take her to the swellest hotel in Long Branch where come the richest of the rich American Jews, the Jarmulowskys and the Perlmutters and Goldbergs," Mrs. Isenblatt continued. "There ain't no money I wouldn't spend to give my Sadie a chance to marry herself good."

Solomon looked up from his stool and there entered a square-boned young woman whose duvetine suit seemed to have lost the quality of its softness on the gawky frame.

"Oh Sadie! Solomon is going to make for us our clothes for the summer." Impulsively she turned to him. "How much ask you to come for a month to do nothing but design for me and my Sadie?"

"I can't leave my job. I got to make a living."

"Only do this for me," she wheedled, "and I'll pay you so much as you get in six months here."

The Jew in him measured her. The rapacious greed of his race for money, power, leaped up in his dark eyes. Paris—ach, Paris!

"I can make you clothes that will shine you out over all the Fifth Avenue dresses of the swellest hotel."

At last his opportunity. At last after years of struggle! The order would mean enough money to take him to Paris where he would develop the talent he knew was in him. He would be the greatest designer in the world.

"A thousand dollars for a month will you pay me?" he challenged recklessly.

"I promise you five hundred dollars more if my Sadie gets herself engaged through your clothes."

Two years later Solomon returned from Paris with a personal wardrobe which any man of the fashionable world might have envied.

When his Paris employer had offered him fifty thousand francs a year, he knew that his education was complete, that he was ready for New York.

And he saw himself the new Oracle of Fifth Avenue fashion— Jacques Hollins.

4

The Inner Temple of Fashion

Still in her high mood, Sonya mounted buoyantly the brownstone steps of a remodeled mansion. An attendant in green broadcloth and gold braid opened the door.

"I want to see Mr. Hollins."

The immobile flunkey stared at her from under lowered lids. His long experience had trained him to discern at a glance between customers and the rest of the world.

"The other entrance if you want a job," he directed in lifeless tones.

"I've come to order the best from this house," Sonya announced, pulling herself to her full five feet two.

"Mr. Hollins sees no one without an appointment."

"I must see Mr. Hollins *now—and at once*," she commanded.

The flunkey was moved by her arrogant manner though his reason told him that he should bar her out. "Maybe Miss Bernice, his assistant—"

"I don't wish to see any assistant," she said imperiously. "I wish to see Mr. Hollins."

Sonya pushed by the flunkey and entered.

"What is it?" Miss Bernice cast a swift appraising glance at the intruder. Sonya stared through the well-gowned creature as though she hadn't heard. Haughtily she brushed by the woman as though she were a piece of furniture. Sonya now felt quite superior to such menials as Miss Bernice with her Paris gown. She headed straight for the office marked "Private."

"What is it you wish, please?" Miss Bernice's voice and manner grew respectful. And now that the hireling knew her place Sonya deigned to notice her.

"Tell Mr. Hollins an old friend of Jaky Solomon is here."

In the dimly lit arch window of the drawing room, a slender man dressed with meticulous care paused in the midst of a confer-

ence with Mrs. Van Orden. Summoning an attendant, he bade
him show the lady to his private suite.

Before Sonya had time to take in the exquisite furnishings of the
mauve-hung reception room into which she was ushered, Hollins
entered with quick, silent tread. He thought he had buried his
Division Street pedigree under five years of Fifth Avenue success
and was puzzled as to who this "old friend" might be.

"I have never seen you before." Between eyes half shut he tried
to place this young person in the shabby suit.

Sonya looked at the artist's narrow face, with the hair growing
low over the forehead, brushed back fastidiously; the full-lipped
sensuous mouth, the nose with quivering nostrils. A thrill of aesthetic delight stabbed through her from head to foot, as her eyes
were held in admiring awe. This was the god of clothes! In every
fiber of her being she felt a kinship with him—a divine understanding of beauty!

"You know me—don't you feel you know me?" she cried impetuously. "Anyway—I feel I know you."

"Know me?"

"I heard how you worked yourself up from a Division Street
tailor to a Paris designer. Your story was wine in my head," she said
in her breathless, eager way. "I felt that you, a Russian Jew, would
understand this great, consuming passion for beauty that drove me
to you."

He stared bewildered at this blazing comet from out of a clear
sky.

"Jaky Solomon!" She hypnotized him with the impassioned
earnestness of her voice. "You—you alone know what it is to be
driven by day and by night—not to eat—not to sleep—not to
rest—to feel only one longing—to know only one urge—to dream
only one dream—*Beauty*—and the dazzling, shimmering shine
beyond reach. And—" she flung out her arms with tragic abandon,
pointing sorrowfully to her shabby coat. "I who feel so burningly
the quiver of every line, the breath of every shade of color, I must
wear this hideous ready-make stuff."

Hollins was struck dumb—entranced by the guileless face, the
erect live figure poised bird-like with desire. Fascinated, he watched

every gesture of the eloquent hands, every change of expression of the mobile face.

"Jaky Solomon!" The cry burst from the depths of her. "There are people who will sympathize with a girl starving for bread, but only an artist like you can sympathize with a girl starving for beautiful clothes. And only you can know that the hunger for bread is not half as maddening as the hunger for beautiful clothes. Why, day after day, for years and years, I used to go from store to store, looking for a hat, a dress that will express me—myself. But something that is me—myself, is not to be found in the whole East Side. Sometimes I'm so infuriated by the ugliness that I have to wear that I want to walk the streets naked—let my hair fly in the air—out of sheer protest. My soul is in rebellion. I refuse to put clothes over my body that strangle me by their ready-madeness."

Not since Jacques Hollins had left the dark tenement in Division Street had he seen such naked, passionate youth. Here was inspiration, stimulus—an ardor for beauty that he had not believed anyone but himself possessed. How starved he had been these years of Fifth Avenue success, starved for something more than the appreciation of his art in terms of money!

"You from the East Side, you know how the greatest doctors come to the clinics to heal the poor free of charge. I too am sick—dying from the blood poison of ugliness!"

Charmed by the changing colors of her flaming speech, he listened. One minute she talked like an East Side *yenteh*—the next minute the rhythm of the Bible flowed from her lips.

"You doctor of beauty! Why shouldn't you save a poor girl's life with your life-giving power to make beautiful? But if money you got to have, then just add the cost to your rich customers' bills. There's enough money in America to give me the clothes that are me—myself."

A pleading thing of youth and flame reached up to him. Her hands fluttered up and down his arm like antennae of rapacious famine. It brought back to him the thrill of his own emotion when he first touched fine silk. It was irresistible. She pierced to the core of him. Everything he had was hers. Hollins had an impulse to rush over to the rack of original designs and thrust some gorgeous costume into her pleading hands.

The knob of the door was turned. A pompous silk-clad figure entered unannounced. Mrs. Van Orden's voice shocked him back to reality.

"Mr. Hollins, you must give me your attention immediately, my chauffeur is waiting and I have a bridge luncheon."

Hollins had been working mechanically that morning on the problem of Mrs. Van Orden's irrepressible fat that would take all his genius to veil, but now he looked with sharp distaste at the beefy shoulders and bulging bust across which the satin of her gown was stretched as she bent forward in aggressive self-importance. The body of this bourgeois was dead wood—not worth working over—he thought contemptuously! Slowly his eyes moved to Sonya. His face was expressionless, but he noted with aesthetic delight her slender figure. Sonya's neck was like the stalk of a flower, and through the coarse serge of her shabby suit he sensed the bud-like breasts.

His decision was made.

Turning with suave politeness to Mrs. Van Orden he said, "Work on your orders, madame, must go over until our appointment to-morrow, I regret to say." And he bowed her out of the room.

Then he turned back to Sonya. With long tapering fingers he shaded his eyes as though to veil from his sight the radiance that filled the room.

"You are so beautiful!" he breathed in a voice that he scarcely recognized as his own. "Dreams, romance, prophecies, are in your eyes—you—you Ghetto Princess!"

"Ach! A princess in rags! Who wants a beggar princess? I want men to grow blind with the shine of my beauty when I pass."

Good God! This girl was an electric radiance divinely formed of flesh and blood. "Every line, every fine thought in the creation of my gowns would breathe on her," thought Hollins. "She has the figure of a born dancer, of a Bernhardt in her youth. But how does she walk? How does she carry clothes?" he wondered, with professional sensitiveness.

He called Miss Bernice:

"Bring me that new Challais model and take this miss to the fitting room to try it on."

A transformed Sonya re-entered the room, "with a queen's tread," thought Hollins. So beautiful, so vibrant, was her carriage that the composure of the artist was shaken by a sharp personal thrill that came straight from the racial oneness of the two of them. He saw in this countrywoman of his a living expression of his ideas and ideals. How much better could she, with her fine feeling for beauty, show off his creations than the thick-skinned, rich women who used his art as tinsel for their vanity!

"I can promise you you shall have your first costume a week from to-day. And I myself will design it."

In gratitude her arms went out to him. "Oh savior of my soul! God of the beautiful! Are you real? Or am I only dreaming a dream?"

Afraid of the threatening tears she rushed to the door. All at once she remembered she had no car fare and shamefacedly she hurried back.

"Oi—I forgot," she colored apologetically. "I came to you with my last nickel."

He proffered her a bill.

"Oh no—just a nickel," she protested, forcing the bill back. The mischievous twinkle in her eyes gave way to the condescending manner of the visionary Mrs. John Manning. "Keep the bill for a deposit on my clothes." And helping herself to a five-cent piece from his handful of change, she darted from the room, passed the now obsequious doorman—down the brownstone steps.

5

The Democracy of Beauty

"As I told you, Sonya Vrunsky," Jacques Hollins stood away with his head thrown back to get a better perspective of the full length costume. "With your color and verve there must be nothing but simple lines. That's why I wanted this nun-like grey with a touch of sheer batiste against the whiteness of your throat."

He put his hand on her shoulder and smoothed the fabric with the thrill of the creator who has taken formless clay and breathed into it the flame of life, the eternal glamor of beauty.

"When you came to me that first time in your plain blue suit, you were a picture of Russian youth as only Rembrandt could paint. And now," he breathed in reverence at the vision his genius had created. "Now, I see before me a new Esther, dazzling the King of the Persians."

Impetuously, she grasped his arm. "You made me look like Fifth Avenue-born. Only—I don't want to have the tied-up manners of a lady."

The surging life of her step, the supple swing of her lithe body, fascinated Hollins as she moved around, admiring herself candidly in the revolving mirrors.

"You don't have to be a second-hand pattern of a person—when you can be your own free, individual self," he said.

"I feel I can conquer kingdoms in this dress. Could any man alive refuse me any wish if I came to him in this beautifulness?"

"You'll certainly make my art shine to the heights of your wishes," gloated Hollins. Her frank sense of power—her open egoism delighted the artist because it was the same quality that had made him, Hollins, the unconquerable.

With the grace of a born princess, she sank on the divan. "Jaky Solomon!" she cried. "Immortality is in every line of this dream-dress you have made." Her sensitive finger-tips fluttered here and there, touching the cloth where it was draped most delicately over her body. "The feel of it must pass on forever."

Swept into her poetic mood, he felt himself transported to a land of illusive beauty, dressing a fairy princess. For the first time he had the experience of designing a gown for the sheer joy of it.

"You've given me back my lost soul. You, Sonya, are my first real work of art."

He gazed fascinated at the transformed Sonya. For she was transformed completely.

"It's not only from the outside, but from within out, to feel myself so fine," she murmured.

A surge of gratitude rushed through her as she realized with what consummate tact Hollins had given her the intimate personal necessities of dress. And in so impersonal a manner! She remembered her dilemma when she came for her first fitting. As she removed her suit in the gorgeous dressing room the horror of being seen in her coarse cotton undergarments "made it black for her eyes." Suddenly, she saw undergarments and every little detail of the toilette laid out on the dresser—obviously for her—even shoes and silk stockings. The understanding, the delicacy of this big-hearted giving marked Hollins as a being above the oppressive charity she had known as a child.

"Talk about democracy," laughed Sonya in a way that told him subtly that she felt his fineness, his unbounded generosity. "All I want is to be able to wear silk stockings and Paris hats the same as Mrs. Astorbilt, and then it wouldn't bother me if we have Bolshevism or Capitalism, or if the democrats or the republicans win. Give me only the democracy of beauty and I'll leave the fight for government democracy to politicians and educated old maids."

A smile of amused delight lit Hollins' features as he listened to Sonya. With one brain section he carried on the conversation, while with the other he tried to analyze the secret of her charm. Now he told himself it was the vibrant quality of her voice. Now it was the shimmering bits of original speech that dropped from her lips like colored flame. Now it was the virgin bloom upon her flesh that triumphed above the squalor of the tenements from which she had sprung. "So even dirt can nourish beauty," he mused.

"It must be all real—you—me—me dressed up in my dreams."

She looked at Hollins with her piercing black eyes, suddenly dazed by the overwhelming reality. "But somehow it ain't from this earth. I always knew that I was up in the air. It was knocked into me from childhood on that I was crazy. But you—you too must be out of your head. Why should you put yourself out to so much trouble and expense for a penniless nobody like me?"

"You—a nobody?" And the reflected beauty of what he read in her, illumined and softened the thin hawk-like features. "The least of us have the blood of poets and prophets in our veins. Ach! If I could only tell you how with all my success and French-American name, it draws me to our own with a force that is stronger than me."

"Then why did you cut yourself off from the name of your own people?"

"I'm a Jew—yes—but I'm more than a Jew. I'm an artist. An artist transcends his race. When I returned from Paris, I saw that my living must come from the millionaires. And a Jaky Solomon, though he were a wizard of style, could not command the prices of a Hollins. Heine, the poet, let himself be sprinkled with Christian convert drops and went through the hocus-pocus of changing his religion, not because he was ashamed of his race, but because it left him free to give his art to the world unhindered by racial prejudice."

"But an artist shouldn't work for money, only for love," she flared at him capriciously. In her new outfit she had a triumphant sense of spiritual superiority. He was indeed the great genius of color and line, but like Lipkin there was something sordid about him somewhere. "How could you have sold yourself to the Fifth Avenue millionaires?" she challenged. "It's as if Keats and Shelley should be singing their immortal poems for a luncheon of bankers at the Waldorf Astoria."

Sonya's accusation brought him up standing. Was it true? Had he indeed sold himself? His unhappy, discontented mouth tightened as he strove to conceal his suffering. "Does Zanwill work for love? Does even Gorky, who is the voice of the poor? Money is the least that the world can offer the artist for the long years of privation. . . .

"How little you understand—you Ghetto child! You, who dropped down to me from the open sky, you have given me the first chance of my life to work for love."

He paced the floor with a tread that carried him back to the bleak years of his youth and early manhood, oblivious for the moment of Sonya's presence.

"Other artists who forged up from nothing like me, had patrons to free them from the worry for bread during the years of learning and preparation. I had to work at both ends—my art and the selling of my art to pursue my art. Always there had to be two sides of my brain at work—the love of color and line, and the need to earn money so as to work out my dreams of color and line."

A silence as the even pacing continued.

"I always dreamed of designing clothes that would express and reveal the human soul, but it was only bodies that came to me for gowns. Sometimes fat bodies to be disguised, sometimes beautiful bodies to be suggested." He smiled reminiscently. "But this is the first time that I clothed the living frame of a soul. You are the most radiant being—"

"I feel like a radiant being." Sonya peeled off a grey glove, touched the grey suède pumps, put a timid finger on the sheer silk stockings and felt in each movement of her supple body her skin vibrate with the luxuriant feel of her silken undergarments. The snug-fitting turban of dove's breasts seemed poised for flight on her shapely head.

"I've taken so much from you and yet I don't feel as if I've taken anything," she said simply. "What you've given me is like air in the lungs, light for my eyes, wings for my soul!"

"Ach! Ghetto princess! You have proven to me your thorough-bred soul because you are not grateful. You have given me something more profound than gratitude—more than the humble thanks of servile souls."

"Jaky Solomon!" she bantered mischievously. "Even if you'd be as rich as Jacob Schiff, you'd never know how to be a philanthropist. You couldn't be like those kind rich ladies who felt they saved my soul when they handed me down an old pair of shoes or cast-off corsets—and expected me to gush my gratitude to the end of my days." She paused and looked up to him frankly. "No, I don't thank you." And at these words she felt her eyelids stinging. In spite of her efforts at self-control a mist blurred her eyes. Smiling as she tried to blink back her tears, she reached out for the handkerchief he wore in his sleeve.

"To think that I might have died in ugliness if I hadn't the crazy push to walk over your doorman and over your stuck-up Miss Bernice and get to you!"

"Tell me, Sonya," he asked, with sudden intuition. "What started the hunger in you—so you had to come to me?"

She drew up and looked at him as though he had suddenly pounced on her secret. For a moment she was all on guard. But their relationship of mutuality, he as the artist and she the subject—he, the giver; she, the receiver—made her feel how absurd subterfuge would be.

"What makes any woman want clothes more than life?" she flung the question at him by way of answer. "Poets when they're in love they can write poems to win their beloved. But a dumb thing like me—I got no language—only the aching drive to make myself beautiful."

He wondered why that inevitable reason for her coming had not suggested itself to him before.

"Who is he—what is he?" he asked eagerly.

"He is one of those American-born higher-ups—all class and coldness. I could no more look into his eyes than into the burning sun. The minute I only see him, even miles away, I'm so on fire I don't know where I am any more."

"What does he do for a living—this *yold* on whom you spend so much fire?" he asked with a tinge of contempt. But Sonya was too absorbed in her eagerness to tell of Manning to notice his tone.

"He never touched the dirty work of making a living. He's one of those born millionaires who came down to the East Side to preach democracy. He only loves to rub sleeves with beggars and nobodies."

"You mean," scoffed Hollins, "he is one of those philanthropists who come with a gilded cane to tap ash-cans and garbage heaps? I suppose," he added cynically, "playing with poverty is more exciting than knocking golf balls."

"But he don't just play with poverty," defended Sonya. "He spends his days worrying how to get rid from his riches."

"The stupid fraud! The self-deceiver! It's his wealth that has made him spiritual enough to want to get rid of his wealth."

"But he ain't like you or me. He's a born saint—a follower of Tolstoy—"

"Follower of Tolstoy—that faker?"

"Is Tolstoy a faker?" Sonya was shocked at the sacrilege.

"Wasn't he a faker pretending to make himself for a coarse peasant when he had back of him culture—education—art, and all that money can buy? Wasn't he faking when he preached the gospel of celibacy after having nine children of his own?"

"Manning is a follower of Tolstoy but he's no faker. Yet even if he was the biggest crook and the greatest liar I'd be just as crazy for him."

Sonya was in that divine state of amorous illusion that no touch of reason could reach. And Hollins did not even wish to argue.

"Be happy with him, Sonya, if you can. But that holy saint don't deserve you."

He cast a final glance of approval at her dress. But already his mind was leaping ahead to other costumes and other combinations of color in which she would shine.

"I'm almost not jealous of your trying-to-get-poor millionaire who don't want the things of the earth, because he wouldn't know how to make you beautiful as I know."

He sank his chin in his palm, two slender fingers lying across his cheek. "How can I go back to business now?" he protested in whimsical pathos. "Dressing you has been art."

6

Manning Touches the Pulse
of the People

Even as a boy the tragic history of the Russian Jews had stirred John Manning with heroic longings. The desire to reach out to them, to help lighten the burdens of the race of sorrows intensified with the years.

Sick from the restraints, the deadly conventions of his class, he had finally broken away and had gone to live among the Ghetto people.

He had made every advance of which his native reserve was capable, only to find that his culture proved a barrier that held him out, apart—labeled him "philanthropist," "uplifter." He had come to resent his wealth. It was the handicap which kept him from being accepted, defrauded him of the warm, personal contact he sought.

Then had come this girl with the naked soul of her race shining in her eyes. Among the colorless greys of his years's futile gropings, Sonya Vrunsky stood out as the single vivid flame he had encountered. Through her he would yet touch the pulse of the people. His eyes filmed with the vision of her vibrant self—as he had taken leave of her a week ago. She was the pulse! Within her lay the power to make articulate his life's purpose.

The corners of his lips twitched in a semblance of a smile as phrases of her "Sunday Special" recurred to him: "The face of a Lincoln, the soul of a St. Francis, an American Tolstoy." Again the twitching of the mobile lips. Impatiently he looked from his watch to the door.

John Manning was not entirely comfortable in this restaurant that was a transplanted corner of Russia. It seemed a trifle theatrical to him, the walls with their futuristic designs of grotesque birds and prehistoric vegetation. About the tables short-haired women and heavily bearded men waved long cigarettes and chattered incomprehensible Russian. He thought he had never seen so much tea drunk; tall glasses of it stood at every elbow. Waitresses in stagy peasant costumes flitted from table to table and sputtered and purred a language he did not understand. He was glad to recall that Miss Vrunsky was not so bizarre and sophisticated as these women about him.

A wave of magnetism! John Manning looked up. A vision in grey, a glowing face rising above morning mists came toward him. If Sonya had planned to arrest and astonish Manning she certainly succeeded, for he stared at her—she could have sworn it—without at first recognizing who she was.

"Ach! So you remembered our appointment!" Sonya Vrunsky grasped his outstretched hand in both her own.

"Did you think there was a risk of my forgetting?"

"But you have so many world worries on your head." She was guilelessness itself as she drank in the tribute of his glance.

For the first time Sonya knew the intoxication of being well dressed—release from the itching shoddiness of ready-mades—the blotting out of her personality in garments cut by the gross. Never before had her clothes been an expression of herself—she an expression of her clothes. It was like being free from the flesh of her body, released from the fetters of earth. Her eyes opened dreamily into his.

She felt that it was the first time in her life that the woman in her had looked into the eyes of a man with the full force of her personality and awareness of her charm. "How glorious—just to breathe—just to be alive!"

"You are so different!" He restrained himself from touching her to make sure she was real. "I hardly knew you!"

"Is a bird on the wing ever twice the same?" She was so filled with life, with youth, she could have sung aloud with the bursting joy in her. "I'm as changeable as a rainbow in the air. A million worlds leap up in me at the breath of a real person like yourself."

Where was the girl he had come to meet—the girl with the quick, shy look, the bird-like movements—the pleading tone?

Her abandon, her nakedness staggered him, and John Manning, the product of generations of Puritans, retreated into his shell.

"Even a bird on the wing must have food sometimes," was the impassive comment as he handed her the menu card.

"Ach! You man of earth! How can you think of food! Can't you feel it is Spring in the air?" Audaciously, she flung the bill of fare back at him, "But if eat you must—you'll do the ordering!"

She knew that food was put before her—that she ate. But it was a relief when the waitress cleared the plates and they faced each other across the little round table. At last they were free from the interruptions of service.

"My life is one endless running away from the things that drag me down," was her answer to his request that she tell him about herself. "From afar off I see the free air of where I'd like to be, but no sooner I get there than unseen walls rise up to shut me in. Even as a little girl, holding on to my aunt's skirts, on the ship to America, the sea, the sky called to me 'Fly, fly, free, like the sea-gulls!' But I was roped off, herded, like cattle, in the steerage, choked with bundles and rags and sea-sick humanity. Then later, in the factory, tied to a machine, windows barred and iron doors—and yet my heart was still on wings. I saw myself a stenographer in a beautiful office with space and light and time to think and to dream between work. But when I came, it was nothing but hammering, hammering at a typewriter till I thought I'd go *meshugah* from the very sight of it. Then the newspaper office! That would be the chance of America for me, I thought. But it's only another kind of drudgery dragging me down."

Eyes tense, brilliant, held his own as he nodded in sympathy.

"What I never had till now is comprehension. Anyone less than you would have thought me crazy the way I'm talking myself out to you. But you—you know that if I'm mad it's because I'm choked with great desires that I had no chance to live out."

John Manning had the sensation of being swept out of himself upon strange sunlit shores. The bleak land of merely intellectual perception lay behind him. Her intensity, her earnestness swung him toward her high peaks of emotion—robbed him of the power of speech.

"But I hate to talk about myself all the time. It's not fair for you to ask me about my life unless you tell me about yours."

"I've never done anything to speak of," he murmured dumbly.

"Who are you—what are you? Haven't you got the words to tell me what you've been on Fifth Avenue, before you came to us?"

For the life of him he could not find the words to tell her of himself. He kept plucking at the lapels of his coat with his nervous fingers. "You don't know what a handicap it is to be born into the easy life of wealth. I couldn't get hold of anything till I came here where the struggle is elemental."

The girl wondered how she could get this tongue-tied man to talk. "What do you think of my write-up in the paper? Did I understand enough to put down your high thoughts?"

"I wish I were all you saw in me," he answered, pained by what must seem to her absence of feeling, lack of appreciation, when his dead ancestors, his rigid training, prevented him from being warm and spontaneous as he wanted to be.

"What I said was nothing to what I feel. I feel I know you better than your own people. I knew you on the first look more than you can ever know yourself in ages."

John Manning looked at this primitive woman, masking instinctively the fear that she understood him too well. Was it true that she knew him better than he could ever know himself? He felt an irresistible attraction in her clairvoyance and her strength.

"I'm ashamed of my isolation from life," he said.

"You want me tell you why you're so far away from the people? You live too much inside your head. Too much ashes from book-learning is choking up your natural feelings."

Again he wondered if that was true. "That was why I had to see more of you," he said with the nearest approach to recklessness that had ever been permitted in the well-ordered life of his emotions.

Manning struck a match to his cigarette and over the flame let his eyes rest on her, not appraisingly, but as if studying the woman he did not know.

Sonya's face, her figure vibrated with something more powerful than strength, more poignant than beauty, more potent than character. That something which through the ages has swayed kingdoms, toppled empires—the resistless magnetism—feminine mystery.

She looked down swiftly, then up. In her eyes was a far-off look of longing for things beyond reach.

"You and I, coming from the opposite ends of society. You, a somebody, and I, a nobody. But here, in America we come together and eat by the same table like born equals."

A pause fell between them. She frankly studied the sensitive lips, the brow expansive and noble that denoted a high order of intelligence. And yet she saw that this man was bound in with centuries of inhibitions that would take a cataclysmic love to break down.

"Why is it that I in my ignorance can see through him and all his high education?" thought Sonya, "and why can't he, with his high education see through the workings of my plain mind?"

"You're scared of me just because I'm myself. Because I can't help being real," she said aloud, unaware of her ruthlessness. "But only the real things interest me. Tell me only, of what use is all your learning in the head if it shuts you out from people who come to you? What's the use of education and polite manners if it makes people fear themselves and each other?"

For once John Manning was swept out of his poise. He could not let this challenge pass. Afraid of her? It was absurd. And he told her so. But as she had seen fit to remind him, he came from another world, a different class where there were social rules and regulations to be observed. He had never known a human being like her. "And it is because of that, that you have so much to teach me," he ended humbly.

"Right this minute, I can teach you the most important thing you got to know. You're born with the same feelings like us—like plain people, but you hold your feelings in. Just coming down to live in the settlement ain't yet enough.

"If you're hungry for the real life, then stretch out your hand for it—eat it and drink it wherever you can find it. If it's beauty that you want then snatch it from the air. That's what I got to do all the time," ended Sonya passionately, remembering how she had got the very dress that at this moment made her more worth while to Manning.

"I believe you're like that," he said wonderingly. "You're different, more vital than our American women."

"Your American women! I couldn't be like them if I stood on my head!" The little dove's breasts on Sonya's toque fairly trembled with her scorn. "In their company, I feel like a wild savage in a dressed-up parlor of make-believes. Every gesture I make, every word I say is a shock to their lady-like nerves."

A thoughtful frown puckered her brow. "They can hold in their feelings like they hold their little dogs on chains. They can do tricks with themselves all day long. Their heads are like ice over their hearts. Always calm and cold and correct. God from the world! I only wish I could be like them. But with me, my heart is over my head. No chains of training can hold me in. My feelings let loose in me like the suppressed avalanche of centuries."

Here was life rushing toward him, flooding him with an emotion he had not dreamed was in him. His boyhood wish to idealize the poor, to find the spiritual response that his own people failed to give him, took substance and form in this creature of air and fire. And without shame, without reserve, without self-apology he listened. He knew now, and he knew well why he had left the anaemic conventions of his own people and come to the East Side among hers.

Manning was fired by an intense curiosity. He must fathom the mystery of this new personality. From whence had this immigrant girl come by her force? What manner of antecedents had passed down to her such resistless power that transcended her lack of schooling? Her very ignorance seemed to burn like a torch in her breast. "Child! Who are you? What are you?"

The gift of a thousand tongues possessed her. Her pulses leaped. An unwonted fluency surged from her lips as she leaned toward him—this man from the other world, in whose presence the *Weltschmerz* of her race found voice.

"I am a Russian Jewess, a flame—a longing. A soul consumed with hunger for heights beyond reach. I am the ache of unvoiced dreams, the clamor of suppressed desires. I am the unlived lives of generations stifled in Siberian prisons. I am the urge of ages for the free, the beautiful that never yet was on land or sea."

"And I," he breathed, impelled by her sublime candor to apologize for himself. "I am a puritan whose fathers were afraid to trust experience. We are bound by our possessions of property, knowledge and tradition."

He paused—and she, watching the rapt expression of his face, felt her awe increase.

"Traditions have been the heaviest millstones about our necks. In Russia, it's youth, inexperienced youth that leads the elders. With us, dried-out professors are the priests. Our colleges are temples of Moloch into which youth is poured to come out, stamped and moulded in the old forms—cheated of its ardor for the sake of sanity, prudence and material success."

"God from the world!" she cried, tears welling up in her eyes. "You can be real when you let go from yourself. So much you can teach me and so much I can teach you!"

Her voice fell upon a deeper note. Her whole face was alight with her impassioned earnestness. "You got a head. I got only feelings. I never know where I am. I'm bewildered by the dazzle of visions that melt at my touch. You understand so much. You got to save me. Who else shall save me if not you?" she finished by pressing sensitive hands against hot eyes.

"Hungry sheep look up and are not fed." The words from Chaucer rang in his ears as the potency of her plea gripped him. Was it possible that this divine spark of hungry humanity who had come to him to be saved, had in reality come to save him? Even the mother who had borne him had not given him more richly than this waif—this immigrant from the Ghetto streets.

Till now, he had been sterile—impotent. This woman of the people was the divine finger of God toward the realization of dreams of service as vast as humanity and its problems. A vision of all the world's wrongs flashed before his eyes: the diseases and crimes of poverty; landlordism; the greed of capital, under the guise of patriotism propagating wars and race hatred; people relying on leaders who use the people for their own ends. . . .

This woman would be a divine force for righting all social wrongs. Their combined personalities would prove a titanic power that would show the world how the problems of races and classes, the rich and the poor, educated and uneducated, could be solved.

With uncanny clairvoyance she pointed the way. He might almost have spoken aloud his thoughts.

"One way, and one way only, through which you can save my soul and help me save the world. You must let me work with you."

The nails of her slender fingers dented the soft flesh of her upturned palms. "I'll not let you say no to me. I'll make a place for myself even if you got no place."

"Good God! What miracles we could accomplish together!" thought Manning. And the flame that consumed her leaped from the eyes of the man back into hers, scorching her with its intensity.

Blindly, he groped across the white cloth toward the little clenched hands.

"You must come and find your place in the settlement," he said, enthusiastically. "But we must meet to talk things over where there are no distractions. Can I visit you at your home?"

"Oh—I—you don't know in what a terrible tenement I live."

"If it's only a place where we can talk undisturbed, that's all I care about."

Sonya checked the impulse to tell him to come at once, that very evening. She had to have time to think how to make the place presentable for him.

Woman's instinct prompted her to put off his calling on her. How could she possibly receive him in her room the way it looked? She veiled with playful hesitancy the exasperation she felt at the necessity of delaying his coming.

"Let me see," she fumbled evasively. "So much is on my head to attend to—but how about in two weeks?"

Taking out his memorandum book, he made a note of the appointment. Sonya craned her neck to look at his memorandum.

"My! A visit to me, you yet have to make a note of it?"

This naïve remark that Manning smiled down discreetly was wafted clear across to a lone figure at a near-by table. Unobserved by Sonya and Manning, a slender, meticulously-dressed man had come in soon after Sonya had taken her seat opposite Manning. He had drifted warily to a table partly concealed by an elbow of the wall. With the delicate fingers of his artist's hand, he shaded his eyes, as his gaze rested on the flaming East Side girl and her Anglo-Saxon saint.

Hollins did not have a very clear idea as to why he had come. Sonya had inadvertently dropped the remark that she was to lunch at the Russian Inn with Manning, and that whole day Hollins had found resentment smouldering within him that Sonya's vivid youth should be gowned by his artistry to meet a pale-blooded puritan. He had paced his workroom up and down. His next creation could take no form. He smiled satirically at his confused emotions. Then he had shrugged his shoulders, dropping the matter until the morning of the luncheon. A creature of impulse in all things not directly connected with his art, he had decided suddenly to go to the Russian Inn—left Mrs. Van Orden in the midst of a fitting. To see how Sonya looked in a public place? Or to appraise Manning? He could not analyze his motives. He only felt he must see her.

As he gazed at the pair, each enamored gesture that Sonya made, each burning word, was a subtle stab to Hollins. His narrow, faun-like forehead puckered and his mouth twitched. "So much ardor!" he mused wistfully. "And she pours herself out on his fake philanthropies. Never will he understand her. Only I understand her."

When Sonya and Manning rose to go, Hollins lowered his head, covering his face with both hands as if he were plunged in thought. They walked by him without noticing him, but he heard Sonya's words as they passed out:

"How happy I am to work for you!"

She to work for him! He could not bear to think of this live creature in the colorless atmosphere of philanthropy. He could see her only giving life to color and line, putting soul into velvet and fine silk.

7

Sonya Stoops to Conquer

Sonya walked home from the luncheon drunk with triumph. Manning's anticipated visit was like a mirage that had suddenly turned into a dazzling reality. "The sky is falling to the earth! Manning invited himself to visit me!" she breathed exultantly. "If I could only keep my head!"

But as she entered the hallway of the tenement where she lived, the depressing squalor fell like ashes over her high hopes. Never had the grimy walls seemed so grimy. The flaked plaster of the crumbling ceiling rained its foul dust on the floor. Rotten boards shook at each step of her climb up the rickety stairs.

She looked about her room. Her cheap, pitiful attempts at beauty mocked her. The flimsy curtains from the ten-cent store, whose color had once concealed the cracked panes, now flaunted their dusty cheapness. The faded pictures that covered the stained walls shouted their pretense at parade.

"Manning's tolerance of poverty and dirt is all very nice in talk," she mused. "But if he sees this dump where I live, he'll think I'm only one of the Ghetto millions—an object for charity and education, fit only to be uplifted."

She would brook no compromise. No patchwork in the staging of her personality when the prince of princes came. She had to have her room plastered and painted and decorated with an artistry as fine as Hollins had shown in the creation of her costume.

But how? Mrs. Peltz with whom she roomed stood in such awe of the tyrannical landlord that it is useless to ask her to appeal to him. If she wanted it done, she must see to it herself.

And why not? she reasoned. Everything comes to him who goes to fetch it. A girl who dined with John Manning, a girl who could get the Fifth Avenue Hollins to design her clothes for her, such a girl ought to be able to manage any landlord, even an Essex Street tyrant.

*   *   *

Mr. Rosenblat was pacing his office in a stamping rage. He had had a lawsuit that morning with one of his tenants and the judge had forbidden the raise of the rent.

"What's America coming to?" he cried waving his fist. "A greenhorn, a beggar, got more right by the court as me, a landlord. Is it worth to pay so much taxes—to be an American citizen, if a dirty immigrant of a tenant can win over my head?

"Pfui!" he raged. "Even the judges are a bunch of Bolsheviks! And all the Liberty bonds I bought to keep going the war!"

His vituperative railing was halted by Sonya's voice, "Are you Mr. Rosenblat, the landlord?"

"Yes, I'm the landlord," he shouted, too enraged to look at the intruder. "But I'd be better off for a janitor."

"I live in one of your houses," began Sonya. "Would it be possible for you to fix—"

"Fix what?" he growled. "Another sink stopped with your grease? Another pipe bust to give you a shower bath? Or did maybe the ceiling fall down again and kill a dozen babies?"

Sonya mustered all her conscious power trying to get the man to look at her, but he was blind with wrath.

"*Nu?* what is it, quick? My minutes is money."

"I came to ask you to paint—"

"Paint yet," he sputtered, his coarse face suffused with blood. "The freshness from those beggars! Paint them up one day and it'll be dirtier the next. Why don't you better stop throwing garbage from the windows so I shouldn't have the expense to clean up the air-shaft every year?"

"But Mr. Rosenblat," she pleaded. "The falling plaster got to be fixed."

"So fix it yourself," he retorted, turning to his inner office.

Sonya followed him with one last appeal, "I heard you got a daughter who is getting herself engaged."

"What's that your business?"

"I too want to marry myself sometimes and I could sit till my braids grow grey before any man would call on me in that dirt. You know it's the duty from every good Jew to help an orphan get herself a husband, and all I ask you is to fix up my room."

"You Bolshevik!" he choked. "Because my daughter got it good, so you got to have it too? Maybe you'd want me to divide with you her dowry and cut up her piano for you in two? The world is going crazy from those Bolsheviks."

He slammed the door in her face. "Go—go to your socialists and anarchists and divide up the world with them. You beggarin!"

"Cossack! Pogromshchik! Dirt-eating muzhik!" Sonya's thoughts raged wildly as she rushed out of the landlord's office.

"Manning! Ach! Manning!"

This minute she would go to Manning and tell him of the landlord's tyranny. Let Manning know how hopeless it is for the poor to be clean—to be decent—when their housing is in the hands of such savage beasts—Russian czars who squeeze the poor of their last penny to choke them in stink-holes of darkness and dirt.

Like a beacon of light in a tunnel of darkness, like a song of freedom to one choked with oppression the vision of Manning came over Sonya. Ach! It was more than the landlord's insult that cried out of her to him. If she could only tell him of the wrongs and injustices she had suffered since she was a child! The dark days when the friendly visitor of the charity office called. The gifts of cast-off clothes from kind rich ladies. The free dispensaries, the working-girls' homes. All the institutions erected to help the poor. She had gone through them. She had known the bitter, biting, galling shame of them.

Tears zigzagged down her cheeks as she heard herself telling it all. But at the sight of the settlement, self-pity was swept away in a blinding tumult of emotion. Her heart beat till it hurt. Her brain swirled in the vague, chaotic struggle for the mastery of things as she entered the outer office.

A lady with a social worker's smile and a white starched dress with a high collar, rose in professional welcome. "What can I do for you, dear?"

The mechanical kindness was like a lash on the raw spot of the wrongs she had planned to confide to Manning.

"You can do nothing for me," came from Sonya. "I must see Mr. John Manning himself."

The woman stiffened. The mask of the social worker's kindness dropped from her face. She glared at Sonya with the resentment of a teacher who hates the children she teaches, the charity agent who nurses her enmity against the thankless poor.

"I make appointments for those who wish to see the director," said the woman curtly.

"You—you—work for Mr. John Manning?" Sonya stared the woman out of countenance. She clutched both hands at her heart and kept staring in unconscious amazement.

"To think that even he—even he's got charity workers of the same brand as in other settlements," thought Sonya. But aloud, she said imperiously, "Where's Manning? Immediately I got to see him."

"He's at his town house for the rest of the day," said the woman, hypnotized into obedience by Sonya's commanding personality. The next moment she seemed to regret her submissiveness and opened her mouth as if to warn that bold-faced hussy against intruding on her master's privacy. But already Sonya was gone.

With quick decision Sonya took the car to Manning's Madison Avenue residence. "All my luck," she reasoned hopefully. "I want to see him alone—without interruptions. And in the settlement there are always secretaries and office clerks nosing about. Pfui! That old maid! I couldn't open my heart to him in that poisoned air of make-believe kindness. If that white-livered, starched-up thing smiles to me again, 'What can I do for you, dear?' I'll thrown an inkwell into her face."

Soon, however, Sonya's natural buoyancy returned. Her eyes shone like pools of light at the vision of herself seated opposite Manning in his private study. Above his stooped shoulders, his saintly head leaned toward her in thrilling responsiveness. She saw the network of little lines crinkling above the high cheekbones, his blue eyes shining with the look of radiant comprehension. The poignancy of his words that inflamed her at their luncheon came over her with a rush of sweetness and pain. He would say to her more transcendent things to-day.

Suddenly it came over her that such fusing one-ness of sympathy rested upon feeling, not upon words. "Ach! What fools we'd be to stop to talk when it's all between us in our eyes!"

She brushed away from her mind all the speeches she prepared on the way. Speech between her and Manning was as superfluous as it was inadequate. "Only silence has depth enough to voice our togetherness," she told herself. "I came with so much to say and I can't say anything. I only want to close my eyes and be alone with you."

She could have wept with compassion for all those people sitting opposite her and around her in the car. How sorry she was for them who had nothing but the sordid, lonely struggle to get on—to push up—to wear out body and brain in sordid, selfish ambition! Out of all these people that sat in the car, she alone was free from the need to push and climb. She was there. She had arrived at the heights the moment she met Manning. Ach! If she could only share with them all the divine revelation of life that had transfigured the earth for her!

Browning's lines from "Pippa Passes" occurred to her.

"How soon a smile of God can change the world!"

"How we are made for happiness!"

"How work grows play, adversity a winning fight!"

So happy she was, she could afford to be generous and forgiving to that brute of a landlord. As long as Manning understood her so thoroughly she wouldn't have to fix up her room for him. He must come to the place she lived in in all its dinginess. She was glad she happened to be wearing her shabby serge. Manning would see the beauty of her soul without Hollins' art. Their togetherness was a light—a spirit that burned through all surfaces into the flaming core of reality where nothing existed but beauty and love.

A drizzling rain had begun to fall as she got off the car. But Sonya was not aware of the rain. She seemed treading on feathery substance like clouds. Her pulses sang with the joy of life.

And then!

Sonya's eyes opened wide as she reached Manning's residence. A half dozen sleek limousines were standing in front of the house. Persian carpets lined the sidewalk and the brownstone steps over which a rich awning was suspended. A pug-nosed butler in broadcloth and livery stood in front helping guests out of their cars.

At sight of the rich gowns sweeping up the carpeted steps Sonya's joy smouldered out like a flame on which water had been thrown.

It grew black before her eyes. She suddenly felt as though a knife had turned itself somewhere in her body. Such grinding pain was tearing her to the earth that she could not move. She became aware that the rain was beating down her face and she was shut out—shelterless. Like a gathering dark her loneliness rose over her. The Persian carpet, the awning, the butler and the limousines stood like iron bars between her and Manning. Every window of that gorgeous mansion became a letter of fire that cried out to her, "You nobody from nowhere! How dare you push yourself in here?"

A young girl in a low-necked, silver gown and silver slippers stepped out of the car followed by an older woman and a man evidently the girl's father and mother. A pang of hate shot through Sonya's breast as she realized how easy it was for that girl to approach Manning on a plane of equality merely because she was rich, merely because her father and mother belonged to his social set.

"Crazy lunatic that your are!" Sonya laughed in bitter scorn of herself. "A nice figure you'd cut if you went in to him now. Your old serge beside their millionaire evening gowns!

"What would he—what would they think when you'd come in? A beggarin? A charity applicant!"

Her heart hurt as if it had been crushed between brutal hands.

"How could he—how could any of them understand how the landlord insulted me merely because I wanted to have my room made decent enough to live in.

"What does he and all his rich friends know about life? They who have Persian carpets spread out for them at every step? And fat footmen in kid gloves to fling open doors for them!

"But how can I tear him out from my heart—only because he's a millionaire? Can his eyes stop burning me up even if he is the biggest Rockefeller fraud?"

A wave of hate swept over her against the world from which Manning came. All that wealth was like an armor that she could not pierce to reach the *real man*. But was he a *real man*? Were rich people ever real?

Hollins' words defining Manning flashed before her. "The stupid fraud! The self-deceiver! Making believe he wants to be poor! I suppose playing with poverty is more exciting than knocking golf balls."

In a mood of bitter dejection she struck her breasts with the ferocious desire to destroy herself.

"*Meshugeneh yenteh!* How you fly away with your dreams!"

A swift flash of lightning came into the black of her eyes. Her hands grew tight at her side and bright spots burned in either cheek.

"I can't help it. I want him. Him alone from the whole world!"

Her hate was transferred with a rush to the people who surrounded Manning—the soulless rich who kept her idol a prisoner among them.

"Who are they—these stupid, stuck-up swells who stand themselves between Manning and me?

"But what chance have you beside that doll-faced heiress with her father and mother to help her catch on to him? She don't have to dry out the marrow from her head worrying for every little thing she wears. She don't have to eat out her heart fighting with a landlord to have a fit place to receive him. The world is made to order for her. Life and love and beauty awaits her everywhere she turns."

Self-pity drowned Sonya in blacker depths than any she had known. "I have no one. No father, no mother, no money, no friends. For every little thing I got to fight, fight till I'm nearly dead."

She threw her arm in front of her eyes and leaned her forehead on it sobbing till she was exhausted.

"Fool! Stop pitying yourself!" She forced up her shoulders and lifted her head in revolt against her momentary weakness. "You got more than all those hothouse débutantes with their silks and diamonds. You have a head. You have brains. You got a will that will burn through everything and everybody to get the thing you will."

She shook her fist at the mansion and its guests.

"Life is to them that have life. Love is to them that have love. Life and love shall be mine even if all the New York millionaires got to pay for it."

Her rebellion leaped higher and higher like a conflagration. There was nothing too desperate for her to think or say, until she was spent with her emotion.

Leaning back to collect her thoughts she realized one salient thing. She could never approach Manning in his setting.

"He has to come to me. Never I to him. If I go to him I'm only a nobody from nowhere, begging for pity and help. When he comes to me, I'm me—myself. A somebody of my own making. . . . And not in my working-dress shall he see me. And not in my dingy room as it is."

Resolutely facing her immediate problem she turned and went back undefeated to the room she was determined to make beautiful for Manning. That night when the rest of the world was asleep, Sonya's mind weighed the prospects of conquering Rosenblat. Yes, he had insulted her, but she would not admit defeat. She would have to think out a different angle of approach. She realized she had been too direct in her request. And without really looking at her the landlord had classed her as one of his many slovenly tenants. How could she make him understand that she was not one of them? "After all," she mused, "man is only man." The hardest of them must have some sensitive spot that she must touch in the conquest of her desire.

The next morning as Sonya raised herself upon her elbow in bed, she saw her shabby serge suit lying on the chair. "No wonder Rosenblat was so hard with me. Even such a Scrooge of a piker must have an eye for beauty. I was too stingy with my Hollins dress trying to keep it only for Manning."

She realized that she had a weapon in her hand. Leaping out of bed she slipped into her outfit of conquering beauty designed by the divine Hollins. She moved her wall mirror up and down to see every angle of herself. From her silk stockings to her winged toque the reflection met with her own approval. The sleek, sumptuous feeling of her finely fitting silk underwear flowed into her being like wine. It was her hour of battle. And she felt she could win.

"But nine o'clock in the morning is not the time to touch a man's heart with Fifth Avenue clothes," she thought. Impatiently, she waited till afternoon.

*   *   *

"Mr. Rosenblat is not yet back from lunch," replied the stenographer in answer to Sonya's inquiry. "Don't you want to wait, lady?" ventured the girl obsequiously, dazzled by the air of uptown that breathed from Sonya's dress. "He'll be back in a few minutes. He's only over by Weingarten's on the next block."

"I'll telephone him later," Sonya said haughtily, sweeping out of the office. But to herself she admitted, "If I could only get hold of the man right after lunch, it will be easy to get from him anything I want."

Her eyes alert for the landlord, Sonya started down the street, but she reached the restaurant without seeing him. Evidently he was still at lunch. For a moment she hesitated and then walked boldly in.

The landlord sat before a dinner containing all the foods of his heart's desire—*wiener shnitzel*, cabbage soup with raisins and a *lokshen kugel* swimming in chicken fat. Luxuriating in his gluttony, Rosenblat raised a forkful of *kugel* to his watering mouth. Then his eyes were caught by a vision of loveliness hesitating at the door.

"Hah! Such a little queen!" The forkful dropped back to the plate as the girl started down the aisle in his direction.

He glance quickly around at the other tables, wondering how near to him this enchanting creature might find place.

Before he had realized it, she stopped at his own table. "Is this seat taken?" she asked sweetly, as she laid her hand on the back of a chair opposite him.

"No," he flushed. "That chair is like waiting for you."

"Thank you," she said formally, but letting her eyes rest on him with coquettish innocence.

"Waiter," shouted Rosenblat importantly, seizing the passing white apron. "Can't you see a somebody is here?"

As the waiter started to hand Sonya a greasy, ketchup-stained bill of fare, Rosenblat snatched it from him and threw it on the floor. "Get a clean one," he blustered. "Don't you know a lady when you see one?"

"You are too kind," breathed Sonya letting her eyes rest on him for a longer moment.

"Those immigrant waiters," the landlord apologized, "they got no respect for class. With me it's different, I know what is a lady on the first look."

Sonya dropped her eyes artfully. Then, as she slowly lifted her lashes, she smiled at the man with a non-committal air of distinction. The Essex Street plutocrat felt keenly that a superior being from another world had dropped down from the sky. And he flushed like an awkward schoolboy not sure of his manners.

Involuntarily, he fumbled at his tie. "Thank God!" he thought. "I got at least a starched collar on."

From the clean bill of fare Sonya now gave her order: light omelette and toast.

Rosenblat looked up solicitously. "You look like a little bird and you eat like a little bird. Ain't you afraid you'll starve?"

She laughed playfully. "One must starve a little to keep one's figure in style."

"Some men got no taste," he confided. "They see no beautifulness in a woman unless her shape is busting out from her clothes. With me it's different. I got an eye for what is art."

It jarred Sonya's sensibilities that she should stoop to conquer such a rough-neck. But she determined to be remorseless to get her end.

With Hollins it had been so different. A flash of the eyes between them and he knew her, knew everything she needed and everything she wanted, but Rosenblat had to be knocked on the head with a club before he became alive to her wishes.

"I'm glad to know you're a man of good taste," she murmured, cautiously watching and measuring his advances.

Emboldened by what he thought was a complete mark of approval, he asked daringly, "Do you live near here?"

"Not so far away," she parried as she bit daintily into a piece of toast.

Rosenblat ordered another glass of tea and lit a cigar. Through the curling smoke Sonya was aware of his pleased scrutiny. She had finished her omelette and was sipping her tea, racking her brains how to make this thick brute knuckle under her without sacrificing her pride. If she could only show him her room while he was in this softened mood she felt sure she could wring concessions out of him. But she could not bring herself to ask him outright to go there. Instead, she said lamely, "Do you eat here, often?"

"Why do you ask?" he mouthed huskily.

"I was just wondering," she evaded, "if I'll see you again."

His eyes sparkled gloatingly. "You want to see me again, little bird? Anywhere I'll come to your nest."

Sonya blushed crimson.

"Oh! I couldn't—oh!" She shrank back horrified at the implication.

He leaned across the table, his thick hairy paw edging toward her hand. "Why couldn't you, little queen? You got me going. . . ."

"Well—but," she stammered, "I got no parlor." Her heart pounded as she realized the questionable depths to which her guileful flirtation was leading her.

"Parlor? I'll come to you anywhere."

"Are you sure it's all right?" she baited, desperately wondering if the end justified her means.

"Sure it's all right," he urged, his eyes bloodshot and rolling as he pursued his desire. "Trust yourself only on me. Don't I tell you you're a lady?"

"How could that thick-neck turn so quickly into a house on fire!" she marvelled. "And what'll he do when he finds I'm only after the painting of my room?"

"I hardly know," Sonya stalled. "I'll think about it."

"Don't think, little heart," he begged throatily. "Tell me only when I can come."

"This evening," she plunged recklessly.

"Where, my little dove?"

"If I tell you where I live, maybe you'll not come, maybe you'll think I'm not so swell a lady."

"You honey sweetness! Anywhere under the sun I'll come to you."

"Very well, then." Sonya took out a little card from her purse and with hands hidden beneath the table wrote the address. Then she put the card beside her plate, face down. Still resting her hand on the card she asked, "Will you promise anything?"

"Anything, little witch."

"Don't look at this card before I leave the restaurant. If you do, I'll not be there when you come. Promise?" she said enigmatically.

"My word is like a bank check," he boasted.

Sonya rose, walked quickly to the counter and paid her check. From the corner of her eyes she saw him sit up stiffly, staring at her. She passed out of the door and turned down the sidewalk. The last glance through the plate glass window revealed his bear-like paw reaching greedily for the card.

Rosenblat bit back his eagerness waiting till the girl was out of sight. Then ravenous for a morsel of romance, he scanned the card. Purple blood rushed to his face as he realized that it was the address of one of his own tenements.

"The nerve from those chorus girls!" he hissed self-righteously. "Ain't there enough rooms for them, uptown on Broadway? To move themselves in by my own respectable house!

"The sly, little devil! And she knew that it was I, the landlord. Otherwise why did she hide from me the address till she got away?"

He smoked furiously for a time. This enticing creature was indeed a high-flying chorus girl, to be shunned and despised by respectable citizens, but the wily witch had got him so stirred up his head was swimming away from him. He must see her again. But he must not let any shadow of disrepute cloud the moral integrity of his good name.

"I got it," he muttered, slapping his thighs. "I'll go to her—only to put her out—if I can only make myself cold enough to do it."

All afternoon Rosenblat's passion was at war with his business ethics. "Ach! Such a peach! Such a milk-white doll! But *Gottuniu!* I got to keep my houses respectable."

He raged savagely against the injustices of fate. "What bad luck I got! Why couldn't she be Applebaum's or Rosalsky's tenant?" Then his mouth sagged. The veins of his temples stood out like cords. "*Oi weh!* Such a catching beautifulness! I got to have her!"

Again, the landlord in him fought his amazing wildness. "Such a business in my own tenements? No—no! I got to keep my houses respectable!"

By the time he reached the block where his temptress lived, he was not at all certain that he would put out the most beautiful tenant he had ever had. His heart began to beat till it hurt. Never since he was a barefoot boy in Russia—never since he was young and free to pursue his desire had he experienced such reckless emotion. His hard eyes grew moist and tender as there flashed before him a vision of Sonya's sinuous youth crushed in his arms.

About to enter the house he stumbled into Itzek, the fish-peddler. The innocent "Good evening" of his old tenant seemed to accuse his guilty conscience. The gossiping group of slatterns in the hallway who scattered at his approach, the slamming of a window, the opening of a door terrified him with a sense of his guilt. Condemnation was in every face he met, in every whispering voice he heard. Everyone seemed to know and shriek aloud why he had come. Even the children, playing unconsciously on the stoop, seemed to point accusing fingers at him.

In a moment he grew tight and hard with wrathful self-righteousness.

"The little witch! I'll put her out," he hissed, as he knocked at Sonya's door.

"Oh, I'm glad to see you," cried the girl.

The landlord ignored her greeting and remained standing stiffly at the door.

"I came all right, but only to tell you you got to get out from my house."

"Why?"

"Because my tenants is all respectable. . . . And you ain't."

Sonya's eyes flamed. "How dare you? Are you respectable?"

Her shy approach in the restaurant had been alluring, but now in her anger she was so ravishing that all his "taxpayer's" virtue broke down.

"Little heart! I'm crazy for you," he growled huskily. "I'll get you a swell little place on Second Avenue. There I can come any time and not be afraid they'll see me."

"I thought your tenants were so much dirt to you. But you're scared of them after all. The minute you think they'll see you, you turn so damned respectable that you threaten to put me out. Don't you?"

"It ain't that," he stuttered. "But this place ain't fit for a classy little queen like you. You don't have to live in a dirty tenement good enough for kikes and immigrants. I'll get you the swellest little flat—"

"So!" hurled Sonya. "If I were one of those you could buy with money then this place would not be fit for me, but if I'm a decent, respectable girl—"

"You respectable? Then where did you get them swell clothes?"

"None of your business!"

"Why did you meet me like—like a restaurant pick-up and invite me to—to—"

"Come to my room, of course. I wanted you to see with your own eyes in what hell-holes of filth your respectable tenants have to live."

The tone of her voice suddenly recalled to him the girl of yesterday. In a flash he recognized her. "Fooled by a skirt and a pair of silk stockings," he muttered. "So you're the same beggarin who wanted my daughter to divide herself up with you? Paint your house yet?"

Sonya braced herself for the fight that had now precipitated.

"Yes, you'll paint this house—not because you want to, but because I have the power to make you do it."

"No tenant yet bluffed me," he blustered.

"In my hand I hold your whole lying respectability," she menaced with her little fist tight-clenched. "I came to you yesterday and appealed to you in the name of human rights. I can tell how you threw me out with your insulting language. And then I can tell how when I met you in the restaurant, you were grovelling before my fine clothes to—to—"

"Whom will you tell?" he scoffed, terrified at heart.

"I'll tell all your respectable tenants. I'll tell them at the synagogue where you are president. I'll tell them at the charity places where you're chairman. I'll write it all up in the *Ghetto News*. But above all, I'll tell John Manning, who has put more than one landlord in prison for bad housing."

Rosenblat cowered before the multiplicity of these threats. The day before he would have brushed her aside—a mere complaining tenant. But a spit-fire who could wear such Fifth Avenue clothes was a different proposition. She seemed mysteriously dangerous if antagonized.

"John Manning?" he gasped, uncomfortably aware that a landlord had indeed been heavily fined the week before on the millionaire's complaint for unsanitary housing.

"Yes—John Manning is coming to see me. I shall marry myself to him," she announced with low-voiced superiority that carried conviction.

"You marry yourself to him—the millionaire? Who are you? What are you? A witch or a detective?" he blurted, feeling like a thing trapped.

"Never mind who I am," her voice was hard and metallic as steel. "Never mind who I am," she repeated, her eyes like sharp arrows, piercing him, and her finger pointing directly at him. "But know this—as soon as I marry myself to him, I shall use all my power as well as his millions to prosecute you for daring to keep human beings in such stinking dirt as your tenements are."

So imperious was her indignation, so crushing her scorn that he cowered before her as though condemned. A new meekness, a meekness born of fear possessed him. He turned to her with whining apology. "Nu, what is it you want done, lady? If it's that millionaire that's coming to see you speak out for anything you wish. I ain't going to shame myself in Manning's eyes when he comes."

"I want first of all this ugly paper torn, down," she commanded. "My walls are to be painted a light soft grey to match this dress I'm wearing. I want white woodwork and a new hard-wood floor. Not only do I want to have my own room done. But the entrance hall and the stairway to be plastered and painted and cleaned."

When she was through with her orders, so submissive had Rosenblat become to her superior will that he turned to her and lifted his hat in grovelling surrender.

"Thank you, little witch, for not asking for more," he mumbled, with a touch of humor in his defeat.

8

The Lily Out of an Ash-Can

The painting of her room completed, Sonya surveyed it triumphantly. Not only her room, but the hall and stairs, the whole house had been transformed by her desire. She looked at the walls approvingly. How cleverly those delicate shades set off her costume! What a splendid background for the sheen of her brilliant black hair!

"Where do I get all that smartness for beauty?" she asked of the glowing face in the mirror. What is it that drives me to make them do the impossible? Hollins, the unconquerable Hollins, with his own fingers designed my costume. I loosened even the tight fist of that tight-fisted Scrooge of a landlord. Benjamin Rosenblat who needed a policeman's club on him to force him to fix the roofs when the melted snow was leaking into the tenants' beds—Benjamin Rosenblat let the most expensive paint flow free like water when it willed itself in me to have my room beautiful."

"Come, Mr. Soskovich! Come, everybody!" she heard the shrill voice of Mrs. Peltz, her landlady. "Come and see my golden roomer!"

In another moment, her door was flung open and Soskovich, the butcher, and two other neighbors crowded in behind Mrs. Peltz.

"That miser, Rosenblat, to take his hand away from his heart like a millionaire!" said Soskovich.

"And really a millionaire is coming to see her, ain't it?" chuckled Mrs. Peltz knowingly, digging Sonya with her elbow. "My *roomerkeh* is born to rub sleeves with higher-ups."

"*Nu*, she don't need no matchmaker to help her with a man!" cried Soskovich.

Sonya beamed with tolerant pleasure at her friendly neighbors. She glowed with the admiration they had bestowed on her, even after they had gone.

Preening into the mirror, gloating over her success, she did not hear a new insistent knocking at the door.

"I didn't recognize the house," cried Gittel, bursting in. "The whole block is talking their heads off. Everybody is coming to look on the wonder. So much Fifth Avenue paint on an Essex Street tenement!"

Gittel's eyes narrowed and her lips tightened with ill-concealed envy. "How did you vamp him—that stingy piker?"

"I'll tell you the truth," laughed Sonya. "Men ain't such hard stuff as they think they are. They melt like wax in my fire for beauty. I need now only about a hundred dollars more to furnish my room fit to set off my Hollins costume and my stage setting will be complete—"

"A hundred dollars to furnish one little room? Why, Iky Applebaum from Third Avenue can do it for a dollar down and fifty cents a week."

Sonya drew herself up in arrogant pride. "What do you think I am? Installment furniture for my room?"

"You big bluff," laughed Gittel. "You were born on an installment bed."

Ignoring the insult, Sonya went on: "These installment thieves— they got only the ready-made shoddiness fit for waps and kikes. They got only red plush over wood shavings, faked mahogany varnished with glue. I got to have *real art*—delicate colors—soft hangings to set off me—myself."

"Then why don't you break into a Fifth Avenue decorator, like you did to Hollins?"

"Those swell sports wouldn't bring their art to Essex Street even if I had the money to pay for it."

"*Nu,* if you're the kind that can get the world for nothing, then why don't you move yourself over to Riverside Drive. There they'd bring their Persian rugs and French settees and sit themselves on them."

Again ignoring the innuendo, Sonya replied, "I wouldn't move myself to an uptown apartment if they weighed me in gold for it. I got to make beauty shine from an Essex Street tenement. For Manning I got to be a lily blooming out of an ash-can."

"Shah! You should be a Christ-child in a manger and then maybe your wise man will come to you with his presents of perfumed riches—"

"You green-eyed knocker! He'll come in spite of your mudslinging."

"Then tell how you'll bring down the moon to get your hundred dollars furniture money."

"Don't worry yourself. I'll get it all right! And just because you're such a doubting Thomas, I'll give you an earful. I'll get my money from Honest Abe."

"Honest Abe?" Gittel leaned back, shrieking with laughter. "That miser? He'd steal the whites out of your eyes. He'd suck the blood from a baby's fingers. Which of your things do you want to pawn by him, your steam yacht, Rolls Royce car or—"

A hard, venomous gleam shot through Gittel's eyes. "I'll give you advice. Pawn your Hollins dress and stand yourself before your millionaire only in your diamond necklace. Maybe then, you'll get him."

"You shameless old maid! It's virtuous ones like you who got nakedness on their brain."

"But what else but your Hollins dress could you pawn?" demanded Gittel, scornfully.

"What else? Only my pound of flesh—only my hopes for the future."

"You'll find that Honest Abe is not that kind of a Shylock. He's got no blood in his veins. Only gold flows in his body."

"I got to get that hundred dollars and I can't see any way to get it quick enough but through Honest Abe."

"We'll see if you can squeeze blood out of a stone."

"I'll show you," cried Sonya tremulous with consuming desire. "Blood from a stone—gold from a miser—generosity from a Shylock. I can melt ice into burning fire—so I'm driven to make myself beautiful—for my saint."

"Nu meshugeneh Salome! We'll see where your wild love-madness will land you—whether with all your crazy dances you'll get the head of your John the Baptist." And the older girl slammed the door behind her in disgust.

9

"Honest Abe"

Honest Abe was known in Delancey Street as the shrewdest bargain driver that ever shrugged his shoulders and rubbed his hands beneath the three gilded balls.

He had no family, no friends. No cat nor dog ever came near him. The grey pallor in his face added an icy coldness to the granite hardness of his features. But more terrifying than his forbidding features was the hissing hoarseness of his cracked voice.

His one passion was his cash-box. And the world existed only to fill it. People had long ago disowned him, had long ago ceased to approach him for any charity. Poverty and want, sickness and woe of those about him were the assets upon which his profits piled.

And to this heartless, gold-greedy barterer, Sonya dared to come for her loan of money, without security, without pawn.

Erect, unconquerable, Sonya swept into the pawnshop. "I must have a hundred dollars." She hurled the words at Honest Abe with the assurance of a Rockefeller offering his check to his tailor.

The pawnbroker was so startled by the commanding confidence of the voice that he hurried forward from behind the counter—forgetting even to close his cash-box.

In his twenty years of business, Honest Abe had never been commanded. People who came to him were either broken wrecks or fleeing thieves. If they were of his poor victims they whined for pity. If they were of the better dressed they slunk from shame. By the tremble of their voices, by the cowering fear in their eyes, he measured his power over them. And now, for the first time, he found himself abashed—disconcerted by the dominating presence of a mere girl.

"A hundred dollars?" he croaked hoarsely, his steely eyes peering from under their bushy brows. "A hundred dollars?" he repeated. "On what?"

"On my hopes for the future." Sonya stood there looking down at him with the assurance of an heiress whose credit had never been questioned.

"Solid dollars on future hopes?" Galvanized by the audacious challenge, he stared at her for a full minute. Instinctively he moved closer and felt a fold of Sonya's dress. "Fifth Avenue goods, all right," he mused. Then growing bolder, "Where do you live?" he asked.

As Sonya told him the address quick comprehension dawned on him. He had heard of the Essex Street witch who had bedevilled the hardest landlord to paint new a whole house to please her. But Honest Abe was too shrewd a man to admit that he knew of her, so he merely muttered derisively, "Solid dollars on airy hopes?"

"My hopes are more solid than dollars." The words shot through him like anvil beats.

Ripples in the dark pool of memory began to break through the hard surface of his being. "Hopes more solid than dollars?" he kept repeating. Dim voices, vague shapes, echoes long forgotten began to stir within him. Ach! Ages and ages ago, there had been a time long buried in his youth when hopes and dreams were more solid than dollars.

Hands clutching at his heart, he stared at Sonya as though in a trance. Who was this girl? What was this girl? Her eyes, big, fearless, unwavering, were not just eyes. They were the magic mirror of his whole past.

He saw himself back in his native village, the cantor of a synagogue on the Day of Atonement. His voice of prayer prostrated his hearers in penance and humility. Another chord! Another swelling of violins from his miraculous throat! And they were lifted to heaven in exaltation of hope. So transcendent was his power over the people that they looked up to him as half divine. For he could move them to ecstasy or break them with woe by the magic of his art.

Ach! Then life had purpose and meaning. Then was he the soul and spirit of his people. Their reverence for his genius was the breath that sustained him. It drew out of him the color, the spiralling range of his voice, stimulated his unceasing capacity for giving and giving.

Suddenly! A cloud of disaster descended upon him. He could

scarcely credit the tragedy when that golden voice grew hoarse and began to fail. His swollen tonsils almost choked him. The terrible fear of losing his precious gift drove him to Warsaw where he hoped to get the help of the great throat specialist.

He came there. The physician examined him. Yes, he needed an operation immediately. Only the greatest skill could save his voice. The professor was confident he could do it. It would cost a thousand rubles.

In vain were all his pleadings. Without money, he had to go to the charity hospital.

And he went to the hospital—to the free ward.

The operation was performed—by inexperienced students, who cut up the poor for nothing to learn how to operate on the rich. They removed his tonsils—and also his voice.

The one spark of divinity died in him. He ceased to have a soul. His thwarted power of song festered in him and became a galling goad for vengeance. But what vengeance can a penniless man take upon humanity? Abe saw that he must have money—plenty of it—enough to have a strangle-hold on entire villages, as Rothschild, the banker.

In Russia, even if he had the burrowing nose for money of the born usurer, it would take him half a lifetime to accumulate enough to wreak his vengeance. Then a light flashed over his brooding darkness—America! To America he would go to get the shekels.

Abe was too cunningly concentrated on his obsession for gold, to begin with pushcart peddling or second-hand clothes as his immigrant country-men did. Straight into a pawnshop he leaped.

His first job was only to sweep and tie up parcels. But his keen head for figures soon made him the book-keeper. Each pawn-ticket he handled was like a human throat he could squeeze between his bloodless fingers.

Masterfully, inevitably, he rose to the ownership of this store and many others. By that time, there was no more need for him to go back to his native village. Many of those who had refused him the money to save his voice were now in New York, herded in the Ghetto where he was czar—his cash-box, his throne and scepter. They had pledged all their dearest possessions over his counter, from their Sabbath candlesticks, their brass pots for *gefülte* fish, down to their last feather-beds.

Idealism and sentiment had long been stamped out of his scheme of existence. But now, confronted by the unconquerable illusion of the girl before him, the long-buried soul in him quivered anew with a spark of life.

"And what are your hopes that are more solid than dollars?" he demanded. The wrinkles made by the phantom of a smile were like cracks in the stony hardness of his face. His grey, corpse-like pallor was lit up suddenly by a flush of life—a dawning interest. "Hopes more solid than dollars?" he repeated, his gimlet eyes piercing the girl with almost human curiosity.

"My hopes of love are more solid than dollars," her eyes flamed valiantly into his. "I'm going to marry myself to a millionaire."

The word millionaire jerked him back to his habitual dollar sense. With practiced eye, he scrutinized her as if she herself were an object offered for pawn. One by one he checked off her assets in his mind. She had youth, beauty. She had fine clothes. She had all that and more. He felt in her a driving force, a resistless passion that could not be thwarted until it reached its goal. The all-conquering power that flamed within her and radiated from her broke through the petrified crust with which the gold-greedy years had encased him. He sidled from behind the counter and offensively began to finger the quality of her dress.

"Who gave you this Fifth Avenue goods? Where did you get this Vanderbilt style?"

"That's my own affair." She turned from him with a supercilious curl of her lips. "I came to you for a hundred dollars, not to tell you my private business."

To his own surprise, Honest Abe found himself apologizing. "I didn't mean nothing. But I got to know where I risk my good dollars."

"People got to believe me, my word," came with a coolness that staggered him. "Wherever I go, my wish is law. The highest places fling open their doors to me. The stingiest pikers take their hands away from their hearts the minute I ask for anything. And you—for a little hundred dollars, you want to know the whole history of my life, as though I were asking you for charity, when I only came to do business with you."

A gleam of wolfish amusement flitted across Honest Abe's face.

"I know now, who you are," he cried with diabolic delight. "You're the *mazik* who bewitched Rosenblat, the sucker, to shine up his rat-hole rooms into a Fifth Avenue palace for you."

Sonya waved her hand and turned up a scornful young nose. "*Ut!* Rosenblat is only the least of them."

"And John Manning is your millionaire?" he probed craftily.

The beloved name on those sordid lips sent a pang of revulsion through her, but she could not contradict him.

With swift appraisal, Honest Abe weighed the risk of his hundred dollars against the girl before whose unquestioning power men abdicated their reason—a temptress who bedevilled Rosenblat to turn into a crazy spendthrift. Even he felt himself staggering before this siren, shaken in his business conservatism like a brainless drunkard.

"Maybe you're smart enough to get him—the millionaire," said Abe, impelled by a superior force. "Yet just the same, I don't know you from before and I don't know how many skirts are trying to catch on to your Rockefeller prince. But I look on you now, and I take my chance on the look—ten to one. I want a thousand dollars you should pay me on the day you marry yourself."

"For only a hundred you want a thousand?" remonstrated Sonya indignantly.

"What's a thousand to a millionaire?" he smiled foxily, as he shrugged his shoulders and rubbed his hands. "He got a thousand thousands. Why shouldn't I get one bone to lick when I help you hook such a pot of fat?"

Sonya frowned disdainfully.

"I'm above sordid bargaining, but I'll meet you halfway. Five hundred dollars for your hundred. Take it or leave it."

Once more his eyes measured her calculatingly. Then, he reached under his counter for a blank note. Sonya drew back in horror as he pushed the tell-tale paper toward her.

"Take it or leave it," he repeated her words gleefully, excited by the novelty of the unusual transaction.

With quick resolution, she picked up the pen and wrote the

words he dictated: "For value received, I promise to pay Five Hundred Dollars, to Abraham Levy, within one month of my marriage to John Manning. In case the marriage is delayed beyond two months from date this note must be renewed."

"Now sign," he commanded. And Sonya signed, as he pushed across the counter two crisp fifty-dollar bills.

"*Gottuniu!* Honest Abe lends a whole hundred dollars on airy hopes," he mumbled, wagging his head cryptically, thinking of the days forever lost when he, too, had been a dreamer and an artist.

10

Passion and Roses

Sonya's eyes surveyed every corner of her room. She had achieved the vivid simplicity for which she had longed all her life. Her personality breathed through the fabrics and colors with which she had surrounded herself. The white dimity curtains that looked so inconspicuously attractive cost ten times as much as the former gaudy prints. The simple couch-cover looked like cheap burlap but for its delicate color and soft weave she had paid more than a week's salary. "Seven dollars a yard only for the plainness of it! Only for its sensuous quietness," she mused.

She recalled how many days and nights of planning and experimenting it took to make that casual-looking corner possible. With what zeal she had studied the color of every single cushion cover of her couch to give the appearance of spontaneous harmony!

Turning to the mirror she indulged in a long, passionate look of self-discovery. "Has all this struggle for simplicity and perfection been only for him?" she asked herself. "Why am I so driven? Is it only to get him? Is there nothing beyond the getting of him?

"Yes," she defied herself. "He is the end, the purpose of life. To get him I'd pluck the moonbeams out of the moon. I'd draw the sun-rays out of the sun. I'd dry oceans and level mountains—only to get him!"

In the tidal wave of her tumultuous confession her self-consciousness was blotted out. She was a planet on fire rushing toward a darker star with which she must merge to complete their double destiny.

A flame of unrest stormed through her on the evening before Manning's visit. Her room seemed too small to hold her. Her erratic mood drove her from corner to corner. She threw herself into a chair to leap up almost instantly and stare vaguely out of the window. Then she resumed the tortured pacing without gaining relief.

Actresses after a long rehearsal know the torment of uncertainty just before their first appearance. Generals after a long siege of preparation for war know that the most racking agony is the night before battle. Sonya on her own small stage was a star, a leader of armies, a priestess of the religion of beauty all rolled into one. More than that. In her intensity of emotion, she was the Russian Jewess rapacious in her famine to absorb the austere perfections of the Anglo-Saxon race.

She could not think. She was a burning desire. But back of her consuming passion her brain struggled feebly. "What chance have you with him when you're going to pieces before he comes? You got to get hold of yourself or he'll see you're dying for him the minute he comes."

Wearily, Sonya sagged into a chair.

"I have prepared my room with all that's in me. My dress is Hollins' most beautiful dream, but I myself am unprepared. With all my brains I haven't the sense to get cold in the heart and clear in the head like the American-born women of ice."

She pressed hot palms to her head as if she would crush in her temples to blot out thought.

"I'm burning up trying to catch on to life—and I wish I were dead."

A shudder of hope and fear shook her at the thought of death.

"Ach! So there will come a time when I'll cease to feel and to suffer!" She tried to console herself, half knowing it was sophistry. "There will be a time when I'll be free from the driving madness of my desire. . . .

"But even dead in my grave my bones wouldn't rest. I'd keep on wanting him even after I'm dead."

Spent with the futile struggle, she crept into bed and lay flat on her back, her eyes moving slowly from one dim object to another. She had no hope of sleep but her tingling nerves made her body feel like tightly drawn wires that threatened to break at any moment unless she relaxed.

"How will I look for him to-morrow if I don't sleep?" she tortured herself by asking over and over again. "My eyes will be shadows of tiredness."

She thought if she could only concentrate on his face until it became visible in the darkness it would quiet her nerves. Instantly the features of Manning, more vivid than life, rose up from the contour of a vase on the shelf. Her heart leaped in her throat at the clarity of her vision. It almost terrified her as she closed her eyes. Now every sound in the stillness seemed like his voice. The opening of a lock—footsteps in the hall, the clatter of a passing wagon, all were Manning hurrying toward her repeating the phrases that had sunk into the soil of her consciousness.

"My child, you have been a revelation to me. . . . That's why I had to seek you out. . . . I am a puritan whose fathers were afraid to trust experience."

It was exquisite agony to hear his voice beating so violently in her brain. But she knew this was madness if it was to take the place of sleep. She jumped out of bed and lit the gas in an effort to dispel the haunting phantoms that thrilled and lacerated her spirit. She lay down again, but to control the forces she had unloosed was byond her power.

The morning found her still sleepless but keyed up to a pitch of self-intoxication that banished fatigue until the crisis should be over. Work that day was out of the question. So she telephoned to the office of the *Ghetto News*.

"Is this you? Lipkin? Yes, you recognized the voice. It's me, Sonya. I'm not exactly well enough to come to work. I haven't slept a wink all night. Oh, nothing the matter, only I'm like in a fever, or something! Oh, all right, come if you want to!"

Indifferently she accepted the prospect of having someone to talk to to while away her restlessness. The half hour it took Lipkin to get to her, she spent brooding over her love, phrasing tender things to say to Manning. The sight of the shabby poet leaning forward eagerly as he came through the door was distasteful to her. She was blind to the pathos of his narrow, stooped shoulders, and black eyes that burned with thwarted desire from deep sockets. Sonya had sometimes noted impersonally the high-bridged aquiline nose, the full red lips that were the only sensuous note in that ascetic face. But to-day she saw nothing in him but a face that bored her.

"What you done with yourself that you ain't well?" he asked solicitously.

"The way I burn up with so much excitement will be the death of me," confided Sonya. And as Lipkin looked at her sympathetically, she added: "Ain't there some way I can learn to get myself cold in the heart and clear in the head like sensible people?"

"Like the Americans, you mean," said Lipkin with an indulgent smile.

Sonya looked at her countryman poet earnestly.

"I used to turn up my nose at the American gospel of sweet and reasonable sanity, but maybe it was only my jealousy. There must be something superior to a people that have themselves under their feet all the time."

"Then middle age is superior to youth," said Lipkin sadly.

"Put it that way if you want to. But all the same the Anglo-Saxons are a superior race to the crazy Russians. The higher life is built inch by inch on self-control. And they have it. They're ages ahead of us. Compared to them we're naked savages."

He scanned her face with sharp inquiry.

"Why, that's the opposite of what you've always said. I guess," he added shrewdly, "you changed a lot since that interview with Manning."

"Always I'm ready to change when I meet higher people."

Lipkins seemed to shrink into himself. His stooped shoulders stooped still lower as if to receive a blow.

"How you hurt, Sonya!" The words came from twitching lips without his volition.

Sonya opened her black eyes very wide.

"What mean you? In what way do I hurt you?"

"If you don't even understand, it would be better for me the less said," he evaded, coloring with confusion.

Sonya shrugged impatient young shoulders.

"Bitter and sweet it is to love the moon," he quoted wryly.

"You get me tired always making poetry out of everything you feel."

Lipkin felt as though he were under Sonya's feet and she were trampling on him. But even at that moment of anguish he grasped at the futile hope of touching her by offering some new tribute of his own creation. Diffidently, he drew from his pocket a crumpled page. "All last night," he stammered, "this wrote itself to you."

Sonya scanned through the poem and then bluntly handed it

back to him. "That's why I never could love a Jew or a Russian, because they let loose their feelings too much."

"Don't you like it?" he asked, incredibly hurt.

"As verse it's all right. But why write it to me?"

Lipkin drew in his breath and stiffened against the wall. "*Oi weh!*" he moaned. "How you hurt me!"

Sonya met his eyes for a moment and then looked indifferently out of the window. Try as she would to be sympathetic, he only exasperated her.

"We either hurt or are being hurt all the time," she said. "If I hurt you, somebody hurts me, and you hurt Gittel."

"I—hurt—anyone? I hurt Gittel Stein?" he asked, startled.

"She's in love with you—that woman who worked with you for years. And you don't even see it—you who hurt no one."

"Oh, I'm sorry," he said wonderingly. But he forgot his compunction as he read the rejected poem in his hand. "You don't even want this heart's blood," he sighed, folding up the manuscript and putting it in his pocket.

"Ah, Lipkin!" Sonya turned to him in sympathy for the first time. "Don't you see yourself how little you care how you hurt others, you only feel it when others hurt you? Here I was telling you how Gittel is eating out her heart for you and you forget it in a minute thinking only of your own hurt."

The poet and lover gave way to the philosopher in Lipkin. "I guess we're all like the fishes in the sea," he admitted, mournfully. "The big eat up the little, till the circle is completed."

"That's why I'm willing to die—willing to spend the last breath in me for only a look from Manning," she said with deliberate intention to let him see how the matter stood.

For many minutes the poet stood as though paralyzed by the import of her words. His eyes wandered in bewildered confusion from object to object. It was only after he had vaguely noted every detail that the significance of this transformed room spelled out its meaning to him.

"Ah, I see! You're waiting for Manning. You made your room beautiful as a jewel-box for him."

"Yes," replied Sonya, ruthlessly. "He's coming here, this evening."

Blindly, Lipkin turned and walked out of the house.

Try as she would to be sorry for Lipkin, Sonya only felt a calming sense of power in the declaration of his love. Lipkin himself had reasoned her out of any possible pity or sympathy when he said: "We're all like the fishes in the sea. The big eat up the little, till the circle is completed."

"To love—to love someone beyond reach, that alone is the highest ecstasy of being," she thought. "I ask for nothing more than to spend myself in worship of Manning."

"But ain't you turning over the whole earth trying to get him?" The challenge was flung by the room she had wrested from the landlord—by the gown her flaming personality had won from the artist Hollins.

"Yes, I can't help it using all that is in me—every thought of my brain—every feeling in my heart—every beauty of my body to win him. But even if he kicked me aside—trampled on me, I'd thank the stars to have been the dirt under his feet," she finished triumphantly.

An inward smile irradiated her features. Like a sunflower burning for the dawn, like a prisoner counting the seconds of his last night in jail, Sonya strained to shorten the interminable hours before Manning's arrival.

She wondered whether her ceaseless thoughts of him day and night had penetrated to him. She saw before her the austere, saintlike face—calm—aloof from the desires of earth. She saw his frosty blue eyes—impersonal, miles away from her, and speech by speech she heard herself drawing him out of his remoteness— thawing him out of the winter of his intellectuality till those eyes twinkled with human responsiveness—with a vibrating nearness to her ardor.

"Will he guess how much I've prepared for him?" she wondered. "Will he see this room? Can I quicken his understanding that I and all that's around me is only for him?"

Her eyes wandered about the room searchingly. "That empty vase cries aloud for flowers!" she exclaimed, impulsively. "Roses—red roses, with tall, strong stems—as high as my head! Red roses such as only the rich can buy. I got to have 'em! I got to have 'em for him!"

Such imperial flowers could be found only uptown. But the

prospect of using part of the long day in an errand for him filled her with delight.

Passing Hollins' shop she saw in the window some imported chiffon veiling suitable for scarfs. One radiant length, an opalescent shimmer of blue and green, held her fascinated. The more she looked, the more she felt she must get it. "What a lovely hide-and-seek of color it'll make over my grey dress!"

She plunged into the store, and was not deterred by the extravagant price of twenty dollars. As she waited to have the veil wrapped, Hollins passed through the department and stopped, pleased and startled to see her.

"Why, Miss Vrunsky—buying things in my shop! You shouldn't do that. You should have come straight to me."

"Oh, take up your time for only a scarf!" she said vaguely, possessed by her own inner turmoil.

He took the scarf from the saleswoman's hand and laid it along Sonya's shoulder. "Yes," he said, masking his personal thrill, "it will go beautifully with your grey dress."

"You think so, you think so!" she repeated rapturously. She took her parcel and moved toward the door, with a light nod and a far-off lover's look in her eyes.

Hollins winced at the certitude that everything she did and thought and felt was for a man he believed incapable of appreciating her as fully as he did. Through the shop window his eyes followed her buoyant step. "There goes an egoist with driving force that will carry her anywhere," he murmured to himself.

Holding tightly her precious scarf, she entered the most select of the Fifth Avenue flower shops and asked for the very best red roses in their stock. She did not stop to ask for the price but thrust the man her last twenty-dollar bill, not stopping to count the change.

Sonya decided to walk back from Fifth Avenue. She tore off the paper wrapping and threw away the cover of the box. And as she walked through the spring air, she stopped and pressed her cheek against the crimson satin of the roses, drugging herself in the richness of their perfume.

In the Fifth Avenue shopping district the people were too busy, too absorbed with their own errands to give more than a casual glance at Sonya. On Madison Avenue fat butlers stared out of bay windows with the blank superiority of pug dogs. But as she reached the Ghetto streets eager faces lighted up with her coming. Children stopped their play and scampered out of alleys and gutters reaching out importunate hands.

"Lady, give me a flower!"

"Only a smell!"

"Only a touch!"

Sonya's first impulse was to hold the roses tightly to her and save them from the clutching hands.

"You greedy kids," she protested whimsically. "You'd only tear them to pieces and I got to have 'em for my room!"

But as she spoke her eyes were held by the dumb, ardent look of an adolescent girl. Lanky, self-conscious, she stood farthest away of the crowd but her eyes devoured the red roses. The need for beauty, the famine for bright color cried to Sonya out of that girl's eyes. With quick recognition of a kindred spirit, she drew out a rose and handed it to her. "You look to me like you know yourself on beauty."

The girl was too overwhelmed to answer. Her eyes filled with tears as she pressed the flower rapturously to her heart. Instantly a dozen little hands snatched and tore at the vivid petals, unmindful of the pricking thorns that drew blood from them.

The ruthless piracy of the children was too much for the girl and she burst into tears.

"They're all crazy for roses!" Sonya laughed joyously. Then she foraged in her box and threw all the flowers except one to the victorious children. While the little savages fought for the petals, Sonya put her arm about the shoulder of the adolescent girl and hurried her down the block. At the corner she handed her the last rose.

"Get away from the kids with it alive. And may you have the luckiest first love!"

Sonya walked on without waiting for an answer. "I don't need the pull of red roses for Manning," she told herself. "If there ain't enough redness in me to draw him out of his ice, then all the flowers of the world can't help me."

11

Manning Himself

Manning had prepared to meet Sonya in a tenement hall-room. She herself had apologized to him for her bare quarters. But he found the very house unusually clean and distinctive. And when he entered her room, he paused in amazement. It was the setting of a woman of culture and refinement and not of a girl of the tenements. Every corner breathed harmony and beauty. The very furnishings seemed animate like a garden watered by a living presence.

"How nice! How simple!" exclaimed Manning in pleased surprise.

"Poor people are forced to be simple," smiled Sonya, glancing shyly at the innocent saint.

"Why, it's the glory of poverty that it enforces simplicity!" responded Manning earnestly. And so eager was Sonya to please the man she loved, to mould herself into the form he desired, so all-consuming was the urge to act the part he approved, that for the moment Sonya actually believed she was simple because she was poor.

"The thing that appeals to me so much about the East Side," went on Manning, "is their directness, their unscheming naturalness." As he spoke, he settled himself luxuriously into the cozy corner which had taken the girl so many days and nights of ceaseless planning, the painstaking persistence of the most studied artifice.

"So you like my simple den?" Sonya's eyes lifted toward him unconscious of any subterfuge. "There's so little here."

"Of course," assented the philanthropist. "That is the whole point. Little is needed to create beauty. All that is needed is a selective taste."

"But suppose one's tastes are expensive," she ventured in spite of herself, remembering how she had signed away her future to Honest Abe to buy the tasteful comfort he enjoyed so lightly.

"I maintain that beauty is *not* expensive," argued the rich man, naïvely. "Pardon me for being so personal, but your charm lies in that you instinctively know how to choose the simple. Your dress for instance. . . . I'm sure you have no time to waste on thoughts of clothes, but how absolutely successful it is! Again a matter of taste."

Under Sonya's lowered lashes a devilish twinkle sparkled. She had indeed been successful, because the effect of spontaneous beauty and simplicity was exactly the impression she desired to create. It would have ruined her chance with him if he guessed for a moment the effort, the struggle it had been to meet him on this plane of harmonious beauty.

"One reason why I came to the East Side," expanded Manning, "is because I must have simplicity. I had to get away from people who waste themselves on unessentials. Our women are the worst in the energy they waste on clothes, on the care of their bodies that leaves so little time for the spirit."

"You like the working-girl in her working dress," Sonya wheedled. "You like her with the natural sweat and toil on her face—no make-up—no artifice to veil the grim lines of poverty?"

"Exactly!" he beamed enthusiastically, unconscious of any shadow of hypocrisy. "Poverty and toil are beautiful crowns of the spirit and need no setting off."

His eyes lit as he glanced at the girl approvingly.

"You are the personification of what I mean. All cannot be as beautiful," he admitted. "You represent poverty—toil, and it is beautiful, because unveiled by any artifice." He paused, seeking for the right word. "I've come to propose something to you." And he paused again, gazing at her in embarrassment as he struggled for the next word.

The blood pounded in Sonya's throat. Her eyes dropped with terror at the crisis that seemed imminent.

"I don't mean anything personal," he blurted in an effort to break through his self-consciousness. "I come to propose that we join forces in the work to which I've given my life. Will you consider being my secretary?"

Sonya shivered as though an icy wind had struck her heart. But as her eyes slowly lifted to his, she knew that any association between them must inevitably be closer, more vital than secretary and employer.

Manning plucked with both hands at the lapels of his coat and thrust his head out with the tense earnestness of a reformer about to preach to an audience. Sonya was all the stimulation he needed. By the flattering absorption she showed in his every move, every glance, she constituted herself a perfect audience.

"The service I feel myself called upon to render the East Side is to teach the gospel of the Simple Life," he launched forth. "I try to make my settlement house an exhibit of what I mean. I have studied out the furnishings with the most competent artists. Only the inexpensive materials are used. Cheap woods, muslins and cheesecloth, cotton and scrim, but combined in a way to bring about beauty."

"But an artist who knows how to make beauty of cheap woods and cheesecloths must be pretty expensive."

The philanthropist looked up in gentle surprise.

"But the man is employed by me specifically to show them how to achieve inexpensive beauty. I trust them to carry out the idea once they are shown. Why, you have achieved this beauty I speak of without expense in your own room—in the clothes you wear."

"You really think so?" murmured Sonya. And she recalled what Miss Bernice had told her in confidence: an outfit such as Hollins had designed for her would have cost a customer a thousand to fifteen hundred dollars, depending on the income of her husband.

"Indeed yes," responded Manning, waxing warm. "That is the very department you are splendidly equipped to organize for me. The department of dress. I believe the working-girl could be vastly helped by instructing her to avoid the gaudy, vulgar styles and showing her how beautiful it is to be simple."

"But they buy those gaudy styles because they're cheap and ready-made."

"Ready-made?" he repeated, vaguely. "We want to get them away from that. We want to teach them how to make their own clothes. I venture to say that you make your own."

"Yes, I know what I want in clothes," she evaded artfully. "I'd be most unhappy in ready-made, stylish things."

"I'm depending on you to imbue them with your taste."

A glance that was a silent caress lingered on her.

"If you think my ideas of dress would be good for the East Side," she parried, "I'm willing to try."

"You can do wonders," he insisted. "For I repeat that beauty costs nothing. All that is necessary is education—to show them how. Why, I have seen alleys transformed by the use of flower-boxes which my assistant has introduced. Whole families have been regenerated by the work of the friendly visitors and their follow-up talks on hygiene and nutrition."

At the words "friendly visitor," Sonya saw a stiff starched dress with a high collar. She heard the mechanical greeting "What can I do for you, dear?" She saw again the irritating smile of professional kindness that guarded the approaches of Manning's office. A host of earlier memories flashed through Sonya's mind. She lived again her childhood days when the entrance of the "friendly visitor" brought fear and hate into their home as she lectured the family how to do without meat, without milk and without eggs. Sonya recalled Hollins' denunciation of the philanthropist. "The stupid fraud! The self-deceiver!" All of Hollins' angered words flashed through her mind only to be rejected in a gush of unreasoning admiration.

"Benefactor of humanity! Savior of the world!" Her face lifted toward Manning in hero-worship. "You will really let me work with you?"

She held back from throwing herself into his arms. But her heaving bosom with her hand pressed on it, her fingers curling inward were far more disturbing to the man who had been taught to distrust emotion.

"I needed an understanding woman in my work. And I have found her!"

Manning gazed at Sonya with an unwavering glance that gave emphasis to his words and established almost a personal, intimate chord between them for the first time.

"Whatever I'll do, whatever I'll be, you've inspired it," sobbed the girl. "The minute I gave a look on you, I knew you'd be my savior."

She was terrified at the answer her declaration invited. A need for air, for space possessed her. She wished that he might have asked her to go out to the park, to the river front, anywhere, because the atmosphere in the little room had grown too tense with the tumult they had created for one another. But as he sat staring at her without any words, she suggested nervously that they finish the evening on the roof.

For a long time they sat in absolute silence looking down from the height of the tenement on the tightly packed buildings of narrow streets.

"*Our* East Side which we are going to save!" she ventured, at last.

"To save—together—*our* East Side," he repeated after her with the fervor of religious conviction.

12

Lipkin the Dreamer

After Manning had said good night to Sonya, he walked away, his head in the air, feeling that now at last he was justified in his faith that he had a great work to do on the East Side. With that girl as his secretary, his settlement would become a vital force in the community, a neighborhood house that would be a beacon-light of human brotherhood, a center where his dream of democracy would find a growing realization.

Absorbed in these weighty thoughts, he was unaware of a figure on the opposite pavement that had begun to walk in his direction as soon as he emerged from the tenement.

It was the heart-broken Lipkin, slouching forward as if he were yielding to a shameful weakness. His humped back and sunken chest betrayed the struggle that rent him.

The poet had been unable to tear himself away from the sight of Sonya's house. That whole afternoon and evening he had been furtively watching her windows through the dusty panes of the tea-shop on the opposite corner. None of the shabby patrons about him looked as lost and forlorn as he. His eyes smouldering in a tragic head seemed to have no relation to his pitiful shred of a body. Drinking one glass of tea after another he had hung on every glimpse of Sonya. "Only to fill my eyes with her for the last time," he mumbled wretchedly.

With a wrench at his heart he had seen Manning arrive and thereafter his heightened imagination wove love scenes out of every passing shadow on Sonya's blind. Lipkin had been his own inquisitor, flailing himself on the rack of his hopeless love. He fumbled in anguish to touch the bottom of his sorrow—get hold of some reality even if it were only pain. But he only felt himself sinking, sinking lower and lower, far out of reach of human help.

It was utterly impossible for him to leave the sentry post of agony before Manning came out. And now, with a refinement of self-torture, he forced himself across the street to face the man who had beaten him, find out what manner of superior being this Manning was who could capture and tame the unconquerable Sonya.

"This is John Manning—yes?" a diffident voice stammered in the dark.

The philanthropist, startled out of his reverie, turned to a stooped and shabby form that he thought was that of a beggar. All in black, in a torn, wrinkled suit, Lipkin merged into the background of the night like a figure in a Rembrandt painting. His eyes, made lusterless by his sorrow, were bottomless pools in sockets as hollow as those of a skeleton. But forehead, cheekbones and lifted chin were high lights in the pallid mask of his face. Instantly Manning recognized the poet.

"Why, Mr. Lipkin of the *Ghetto News!*" And he put out a friendly hand in greeting.

"I wanted to ask you if you would favor us with an article on housing," ventured Lipkin at random, hardly aware of what he was saying.

"Certainly, any time," responded Manning enthusiastically. "You want to send someone to interview me?" But instead of waiting for an answer, Manning hurried on. "The best plan would be for my secretary to prepare the article for you. I have a wonderful girl coming to work for me to-morrow—Sonya Vrunsky. Do you know her?"

Lipkin winced as though he had been stabbed. He looked at Manning grimly and then shifted his glance. "I sent her to you that first time to write up the story of your settlement."

"Oh, yes, yes, I remember." Manning was abashed at his own absent-mindedness. "I'm taking her away from you, I fear. Do you mind very much?"

Lipkin did not answer for a moment. Resentment and stoicism chased each other in and out of his mind. The furrows on the forehead above the young face deepened. Then an inner light flashed up, etherealized the features.

"Sonya Vrunsky only passed through the dusty office of the *Ghetto News.* She is not a slave of jobs. She is not a person that lesser ones can hold down." There was a curious exaltation in the quiver of his voice. "She is a flame of destiny that will burn her way to the stars. You'll give her her next chance, Mr. Manning. And no one is more happy for her sake than I. But a flame she is that will burn on, ever higher and higher."

Not only was Manning amazed at the strange eulogy, but Lipkin himself was astounded at the words his own lips had framed. Why should he have said this, to Manning of all men? But it was true. And the almost mystic warning he had voiced seemed to give release to his soul.

Manning found no words with which to break the embarrassed silence that followed. Lipkin seemed to have forgotten the Anglo-Saxon's very existence and walked at his side in dreamy aloofness.

"After all," thought the poet, "the greatest thing that ever happened in my life is that Sonya's flaming wing had brushed against me as it passed, even though it had burned me and left me scarred. . . .

"Who am I? What am I that I should dare want to hinder the flight of a tameless bird like Sonya? What have I to offer her but futile dreams, a life of poverty, the wasted strivings of a tragic weakling?"

Suddenly he caught sight of his reflection in the mirror of a shop window. A wave of revulsion at his ragged appearance swept over him. In humiliation he surveyed himself. Everything about him down to the merest trifle of his costume bespoke of slovenliness and neglect. Buttons missing, collar frayed, his coat-sleeve torn at the seams.

The shadow of a passer-by recalled the poet to himself. He turned back to Manning. "My ideas fly away with me," he made an attempt to smile in humble apology.

Manning was roused from his own thoughts puzzling over the strange character beside him. He was disturbed by the age-old sadness of the poet's eyes. They were the eyes of a lonely man, restless and ineffective in the pursuit of illusion.

"The article you suggested interests me vitally," Manning said, in an attempt to resume the conversation. But Lipkin had ceased to hear.

Sunk in his introspection, he gave Manning a vague salute of farewell and flitted back into the dark.

"He answered nothing concerning the article," murmured Manning to himself, in blank wonder. "Those Jewish intellectuals—those chaotic dreamers are a mystery to me."

13

The Temple of Serenity

At the turn of the corner, Sonya passed and looked up at the Manning Settlement House to which she had been coming for the last fortnight.

"Two weeks," she mused. "Why, I feel as if I were born there. It's more part of me than the block in which I was raised."

In her gushing exuberance, her wild idealization of Manning, the settlement at which she had railed now seemed the most splendid achievement in the world.

"It shines like a light over all other houses." Her eyes drank in the bright red and green geraniums that decorated every window. "It's not just a house. It's a living beating heart of love. Every brick, every inch of plaster of that building is quivering—shot through and through with Manning's presence."

A few minutes ahead of time, Sonya walked up and down the block. The tenements, dingy bee-hives swarming with humanity, seemed lifted up from their black life of hurry and worry by the sheltering arms of the father-and-mother-like settlement.

"Our East Side which we're going to save together!" Manning's inspired words throbbed through her as she crossed the street; they made her feel mystically maternal. Her breath quickened, her cheeks flushed as she entered the temple of her new faith. The janitor, the elevator man, the drab book-keeper and office clerks—about them all hovered the golden glamor of Manning's personality.

"To think how I once hated settlements," her own fickleness struck back at her with sudden force. She remembered the shudder of revulsion that settlements had once aroused in her. Her brain knew, though her heart denied it, that this philanthropy was no different from others she had known. But her incorrigible gift of illusion had made it the very shrine of romance.

"Where else can a poor girl like me meet her millionaire if not in the settlement?" Sonya rationalized her inconsistency. "How did

Rose Pastor catch on to Graham Stokes? How did Mary Antin get her chance to climb higher up? How did Sonya Levien, a plain stenographer, rise to be one of the biggest editors?"

She grew more and more self-righteous in defense of her changing moods of mind. Her happiness was double-edged. In her zeal for the new gods she felt the wound that had been left in tearing away from the old.

"The thing that I hated in settlements was the stupid ignorance of the people who run them. But here, there are no rich, fat women to poison the air with their impudent uplift. Here, there's only John Manning's divine understanding and everybody takes the cue from him."

In her passion for self-justification, Sonya tore the last veil of deception from her eyes. "Why, there would be no fake settlements if they were only openly what they should be; marriage centers—clearing houses for ambitious youth, where live East Side girls like me can catch on to men higher up."

Sonya's flares of self-assertion had been the despair of her overworked, care-crushed mother. Her father, a dreamy-eyed religious fanatic, looked upon the untamed wilfulness of his changeling daughter as a penance for all his sins.

Born in the blackest poverty of a Delancey Street basement, yet the drab environment had no power over her. Even as a child her imperious craving for what she wanted dominated not only her family, but the tenement house, the whole block where she lived.

Her mother had tied her hair with torn shoestrings. The day before school opened she shocked her parents with her audacious demand. "When I begin school, I got to have a red silk hair ribbon like the American children."

"What?" shrilled her mother. "Why don't you ask me better for an automobile or a million dollars? *Gevalt!* Hair ribbons yet!"

Sony stamped her feet in a burst of rebellion. "I got to have a hair ribbon. I ain't no immigrant. I ain't going to stand for shoestrings on my hair."

Her clamor shook the basement. She ran out into the street with it and kept it up till all the neighbors had gathered. The cries did not cease till a strange passer-by, moved by the extraordinary vehemence of the child's will, stepped into the corner dry goods store and returned with the miraculous gift of a whole yard of red silk hair ribbon.

"Now, I hope the devil will be choked in you for a time," her mother wagged her head in secret disapproval of such pagan luxury. But the very next day she returned from school, her nose in the air. With childish arrogance she kicked the loose shoes off her feet to the other end of the room.

"I ain't going to wear charity shoes no longer," she burst out. "All the children laughed from me."

Scandalized, the mother gazed at this witch-child.

"Should I starve us all—take the money away from the eating to buy you new shoes?"

"Shoes that fit me I got to have," came in a cool, grown-up voice. "It wouldn't kill nobody not to eat for a day, so I could have what I need."

Desire with Sonya had always been a mere prologue to attainment. Throughout her childhood and youth her impulses had been creative, always carrying her forward to seemingly unattainable goals. She had left family and friends behind her in her driving need to possess the chimera just beyond.

Now, her enthusiasm for Manning and all that belonged to him was the culmination of her erratic ambitions. With the ardor of an adolescent convert Sonya had made of Manning the ideal of what she aspired to be.

Two weeks at the settlement.

And Sonya, the unadaptable, believed that she had adapted herself to a new race, a new culture, a new religion!

As she opened the door of her office she smiled her greeting to one from this new world who had in two weeks become her patron saint. It was Mona Lisa hung over Manning's desk. Sonya glorified the fifteenth century enigma as the mother, the eternal ancestress of Manning and his kind. In her inscrutable eyes Sonya felt the patrician race—the generations of self-control from which Manning sprung. This was a fascination she felt which would forever hold her serenity.

Searchingly, prayerfully, Sonya's eyes dwelt on every feature of La Gioconda, as though she would wrest from her the secret of her charm. "How much more alluring to men is what she keeps hidden about herself—her mystery of restraint, than our Russian madness to tell everything—to strip our souls naked in the untamed wildness of our desire!"

Turning from the picture Sonya touched with sensuous enjoyment the things on Manning's desk. Her hands passed slowly, clingingly over every object—held by a magnetism that she could not resist. "Everything about him breathes serenity," she thought. The dark amber of the oak-wood desk, the rich brown leather of his chair, every detail of his aristocratic setting exhaled the essence of fineness—selectiveness. "I feel the quality of his things flowing through my fingers like a voiceless song, like rich color quivering in the dark."

It came over her suddenly, the aesthetic value of silence as her eyes lingered lovingly upon his things. The ink well was set in a leather pad. All his desk equipment was sheathed in leather. Even the paper-knife had a leather handle to maintain the perfection of silence.

Till she met Manning all the people she had ever known had been steeped in noise. Silence was like a color to which they had been blind. Now she perceived that silence was eloquent and colorful, a refinement possible only to superior people.

Sonya looked back in anger at Lipkin's assertion that the Anglo-Saxons were emotionally an inferior race. It was not true. This silence was the poetry, the very pulse of emotion.

As the hour of Manning's arrival drew near, a tumultuous fever stormed through her. In desperate resistance she made her whole body rigid and sat down stiffly at her desk. In imitation of her new patron saint, she folded her hands and assumed a cryptic, impersonal smile.

A Salome of the tenements striving to be Mona Lisa!

So Manning found her as he entered. One swift glance. And he saw that she was more disturbing than she had ever been in the restraint that the office routine had imposed on them both.

"Is the mail heavy this morning?" he asked with controlled banality, casting another stolen side-glance at the girl.

Sonya shook her head stiffly because she could not trust herself either to speak or look at him.

He found her inarticulate greeting a little odd, but did not stop to analyze it. Sitting down at his desk, he fingered the pile of letters, drawing out sheets here and there without method, casting them aside unread. He consulted his desk calendar and was irritated at the list of appointments that suddenly seemed tiresome to him. For the first time in months he actually did not know how to begin the day. The routine bored and distressed him.

"Am I threatened with a nervous breakdown?" he asked himself, fatuously.

There were a dozen tasks waiting for him that morning, but instinctively he chose the one that would bring him into immediate contact with the girl. He picked up a memorandum book jotted with notes for his yearly report.

"Are you in shape for a long spell of dictation this morning?" he asked with a queer softness in his voice.

She picked up her note-book and spread it out in business-like fashion. Her head bent lower in her perverse determination not to look at him. "I'm ready, Mr. Manning," came in a low withdrawn voice.

Her coolness chilled him. And yet he moved closer as if for warmth.

"This will never do," he told himself and got up swiftly to pace in the sunshine that was streaming through the window. It pained him vaguely that Sonya did not follow him with her eyes. She was bent over the desk, her pencil poised above the paper. There was no excuse to delay his dictation and abruptly it came to him that it would be stimulating to stand close beside her and watch her while she worked. He moved to her very elbow and began:

"We have tried to build a strong foundation for the right kind of womanhood, manhood and citizenship. The past year has seen many errors—often expense of fruitless energy, but we feel we are learning slowly and each month we grow in understanding of our problems and closer to our community. Surely the fact that we are reaching nearly eighteen hundred people a week is the outward symbol of the inner worth."

He paused and came back to a tangle of statistics in which he lost himself.

"What is the matter with me? My mind is not working to-day," he thought in a panic.

A moment of embarrassing silence fell between them.

Manning ceased to make the effort to pick up the lost thread of thought. He no longer resisted the growing joy in which he had been revelling for the last few minutes. The sunlight on the black satin of her hair. The radiant life of her young flesh that bloomed through the thin waist. Stammering, he tried to check the intoxicating lure of her beauty.

"Will—please—Miss Vrunsky—read back your notes a page or two."

Sonya began in a collected voice.

"We have tried to build a strong foundation—" Her eyes ran wildly over the crazy notes of which she could make nothing further. Almost from the beginning she had lost the meaning of the words in the soothing music of his voice. Yet her hand had moved on mechanically recording nothingness.

She looked up for the first time, her lips trembling, her eyes seeking forgiveness like a frightened child.

"My head is not here to-day," she blurted confusedly.

"You poor child!" Both his hands were about her shoulders in an instant.

"Poor child! You're not well. You shouldn't be working to-day!"

He felt Sonya's body quiver under his palms. Swept by a sudden tide of emotion he longed to take her to his breast and cover her with kisses. But he drew back in terror. What was he thinking about? What excuse had he for supposing this girl might be in love with him? What a horrible breach of etiquette between employer and employee! He wanted to apologize but a feeling that apologies would only make it worse, bewildered and silenced him. He stared wildly at the girl for a moment and then strode out of the room.

Sonya sat numbly, her eyes fastened on the door, expecting him to reappear any moment. Certain at last that he was not coming back, she pushed note-book and papers violently out of her way. Her eyes turned beseechingly to Mona Lisa, but the picture seemed to grow cold and withdraw itself from her, under her very gaze. She half rose in a mood of desperation to get her hat and rush to her room—where she could be alone—anywhere away from this unfeeling, inhuman serenity. But the effort seemed beyond her strength.

She sagged back into the chair and crumpled up on the desk, her head on her outstretched arm.

Her whole body shook under a tornado of weeping. The tears ran out in a stream on the glass-covered desk. Her shoulder blades sticking up sharply rose and fell in spasms of sobbing. She looked very small, very pathetic—like a beaten child.

14

Love in Chaos

"Yet three more hours till he comes!" The little mahogany clock on John Manning's desk seemed to Sonya's tired gaze to have dead weights on its slender, silver dials. "If I could only smother my aching senses—lie still in my emptiness till he comes!"

The familiar surroundings of the office, the desk on which his arms had rested, the pen his hand had touched, the very chair on which she sat struck back at her as if she were still an intruder, a stranger in his world. Even the cool eyes of the framed Mona Lisa, above his desk, seemed taunting, mocking her.

"How sure she is of herself! How she laughs at this burning waste of my body and soul! But how can I get hold of myself? How can I make myself cold in the heart and clear in the head, when I feel myself dying for a smile—the breath of a voice?"

Sonya was now in revolt against the non-committal, expressionless face. Following Manning's departure, she had become incensed at the aggravating repose of her erstwhile patron saint.

But in spite of her turbulent mood, Mona Lisa's serenity rose over her, dominated her. She marvelled anew at the placid calm of the woman with the white hands. Surely this superior being had never loved, had never known passion. She recalled what Manning had told her of La Gioconda. It was the mystery of the face that so drew people. Was she saint or devil? Not even the artist who painted her knew.

A boy brought a telegram addressed to Miss Vrunsky. "It's from him," shot through her like a bolt. "*Oi weh!* He ain't coming!" Terrified, she tore open the envelope and read: "Regret, shall be detained a few days longer. Please cancel all appointments till you receive further word." And then his name.

It grew black before her eyes. The life in her suddenly stopped as though a current of electricity had been turned off. Mechanically she signed the yellow slip, then gripped the arm of a chair to steady herself, as the blue-capped messenger went his whistling way.

"I wish I had never met him," she sobbed. "For the little bit of joy how have I suffered and must yet go on suffering!"

She sank back a crumpled heap. "I hate his philanthropy that makes no room for me. What right has he with business at Washington while me he leaves dying for a little of crumb of love?"

Another messenger entered. This time, it was a ragged schoolboy, holding out in front of him a dirty envelope. Automatically, she took it from him.

It was a letter from Honest Abe. "The time of your note is up already and not yet are you married to your millionaire," he wrote. "So you must sign me up my second note, or I'll take you to Court."

It was for a thousand dollars that Abe was now binding her, but she saw the figures without realizing what they meant. Nor did she appreciate the sordidness of the pact that was getting her deeper and deeper in the pawnbroker's clutches. Blindly, she put her name at the bottom of the note and gave it back to the boy.

Through the whole transaction, her thoughts had not left Manning. Her love mounted to crazy hate of him and his things.

Sonya felt like throwing the ink well at the smiling fifteenth century siren on the wall. "I hate her!" Her voice rose in her throat, harsh with nervous tension. It jangled in the silence of the office, startling her. "He and his Mona Lisa are of one kind.

"Always at arm's length. Always cased in ice. So you can never touch them—never get near them. I never know what goes on in Manning's head. But everybody can tell what's going on inside of me. I'm naked—helpless—naked and helpless as a child just born. The blood rushes to my face and betrays me every time I look at him."

A wave of self-pity weakened her almost to the point of tears.

"My life lies in his hands. He can make of me what he wants—a black witch or a white angel. God will hold him responsible for my soul. For I have no soul without him."

A message came from the Oklahoma Senator to ask if Manning would be ready for the appointment at three. In lifeless tones she answered that he was still away. Then suddenly she remembered there was a board meeting at four and telephoned the secretary to call off the appointment.

"I never want to see him again," she told herself with finality. "I hate love. All the blackest hells I'll suffer—only never to be in love. . . .

"What's love but bondage? I want to be free—free from everybody—above all free from such a lifeless, bloodless piece of ice like him. . . .

"He is my chains—my prison. I hate the sight of him as I hate the sight of chains and prisons."

A plan for flight, a desire to cut loose from Manning seized her. She would leave the East Side—New York itself—travel to the other end of the earth, till the name and the memory of Manning were blotted out of her soul. But the next moment she knew that to sever herself from this man would be like plunging into the darkness of death.

"God help me! Will I never get hold of myself? How can I tear him out from the beat of my heart—the breath of my breath—the life of my life?"

Love and hate, the ache to cling to love and the urge of her free spirits to tear loose from this dependence on love drove her hither and thither within the cage where passion had entrapped her.

"I can't help it. I'm in him. My body is in his body. My soul in his soul. He—he alone can free me from myself."

The chairman of the housing committee called to remind her that the lease for the model tenements was to be executed by Mr. Manning. The president of the Women's Trade Union League came to ask Manning to address the mass meeting of strikers at Carnegie Hall. Other people needed him—important people—but she—she, in her terrible longing for him, needed him more than the whole world.

Sonya took from her bosom a letter of fatherly advice she had received from Manning the day before. The closing paragraph seemed to leap from the paper like the poisoned thrust of a dagger. "Identify yourself with your work. Work is the only thing real. The only thing that counts. The only thing that lasts."

What hollow mockery his whole code of sweet and reasonable

sanity! How cold and calm and collected he was! How deadly sane! As if he had never been young—never been alive.

Sonya tore his letter into a thousand bits. "If I could only tear his reason to shreds as I tear this! If I could only hurl him into chaos. Drown him in unreality. Strangle him with his own self-control! If only his soul were tortured with his impotence, his nothingness as I am tortured. Then maybe he too would become human."

A fear bred of exhaustion flung its black wings over her. Manning did not love her, never could be made to love her.

"That I should let myself go to pieces for a man that don't give a hang for me! Where's my brains? My self-respect?"

In defiance of her weariness Sonya rose to her feet. "I shall yet be master of myself. I shall yet be colder in the heart and clearer in the head than the American-born, *all-rightniks* of the educated world."

Resolutely, she covered the typewriter, straightened the papers and closed his desk. As she started to get her hat and coat she heard a murmur of women's voices in the outer office. The next moment the handle of the door was turned. Another one of those rich patronesses to talk over "How to Save the East Side." But when the door opened a thin desiccated face of sand and ashes peered in. It was Gittel Stein looking more than ever a victim of joyless toil, of virtue-enforced goodness, thought Sonya with a touch of contempt. The sight of Gittel irritated her at this moment even more than any charity worker could have done.

"You got to come with me to Lipkin," Gittel snapped acidly.

"I don't have to go where I don't want to. I got enough 'friendly visiting' down here."

A current of antagonism ran between them, the culmination of months in which they had barely tolerated each other. To Gittel, Sonya's talked-of success with Manning had become a bitter grievance, her ruthlessness with Lipkin a crime that she could never forgive. Yet, pocketing her pride and her animosity, she had come to plead for Lipkin's sake.

"You simply got to come," she insisted. "The paper has been going to pieces for weeks. He seemed unable to concentrate or do anything, but the last few days, he has sunk into a silence that terrifies me. He don't eat, he don't sleep, he don't see anyone. He just lies back, with the look of a dying man in his eyes."

"Well, what do you want me to do?"

"Go see him, talk to him."

"What good will that do?"

"You know he loves you, the sight of you will bring him back to life."

Sonya felt a twinge of remorse. It seemed to her unbearably pathetic that this woman who was so much in love with Lipkin had come pleading to her who had nothing to give him. But she masked her sympathy with cold reason.

"All I have for him is pity. And a man that rouses pity don't deserve even pity. A man who lets himself be crushed by anything or anybody is not a man worth saving."

"You're more heartless than stone," cried Gittel, enraged.

"The only thing to do with crazy love-sick fools is to let them have such a full dose of their misery and wretchedness that they learn to be sensible, and fall themselves out of love."

Sonya paused abruptly and gazed into space, as though she had forgotten for the moment Gittel's existence.

"I really believe that love is only a sickness like smallpox or typhoid," she said as though thinking aloud. "You can do nothing for a love-sick fool till the fever of illusion has burned itself out of his heart and brain. Any man or woman who lets himself believe that happiness lies in one particular pair of eyes, in the sound of one particular voice, in the thrill on one particular touch, such a person is stark mad."

"Then you don't believe there is such a thing as love?" Gittel stared at her aghast.

"If I had the law in my hand"—Sonya clenched her fist with feverish gesture as though she were fighting with herself—"I'd confine love-sick fools the same as lunatics and dangerous criminals, for you never can tell what harm love-sick madmen can do to themselves or the people they love if let loose."

Gittel looked blankly at the hysterical girl. She was searching for angry words with which to lash her for her selfishness, but Sonya turned in swift compassion, disarming her. "You love Lipkin yourself, don't you? Why don't you go to him?"

"I love Lipkin?" A rush of blood covered her face and neck.

"Yes, you do. You're foolish enough to worship him and think him too high a poet for you. But if you only had a little brains to study out how to play the game of love, you could have had him as easy as I snap my fingers." She paused and shrugged her shoulders. "Not that any man alive is worth the heart's blood you've got to pour out before you get him to crawl at your feet."

Gittel looked at Sonya with virtuous condemnation. "You know nothing about love. And the way you talk shows it."

"But I get the men to go crazy for me. Do you?" she jibed.

"I'm no schemer or plotter like you. When I love I *really love.* I love in silence."

Sonya gazed in pity at the starved, virtue-enforced virgin who condemned her.

"Failure is my religion," announced Gittel with apostolic fervor. "I accept failure in love and in life. The deeper, the finer you are the more you realize the vulgarity, the sordidness of success."

Sonya laughed mockingly.

"If I failed I'd have the honesty to look my failure straight in the face. I'd not let it crush me into such a pulp of resignation as you. I'm an American—not a crazy Russian. I want the vulgar sordidness of success." She flung out her arms in an abandon of desire. "Ach! Success—success! Everything else hides in the shade for it!"

"Wait only till you get a little older. What else is there in life but failure if you're deep enough?"

"What else? Why, there's life itself. The naked battle of it. The sense of humor that makes you laugh at the whole blind farce of it."

The champion of defeat made her last plea. "Are you coming? Yes or no?"

"You go to Lipkin yourself. Don't be a resigned saint. Go, get the man you love, if you really love him."

"I can't force myself into a man's heart as you do."

The direct charge startled Sonya. "I? . . ."

"Yes, everyone knows you got Manning by force. You knocked him senseless with your love-making." All the bitterness in Gittel's soul burst out unrestrained. "Just as in old times the cavemen used their clubs to beat the women into submission, so you vamped poor Manning with your crazy flattery."

"I made love to Manning?" came from Sonya in indignation and resentment.

"Didn't you, yourself, tell me how it happened? You stop a man in the middle of the street, and begin to call him 'Benefactor of humanity,' 'Savior of your soul,' so he had to invite you to lunch." Gittel's voice rose harshly. "Then you storm a Fifth Avenue store and get another strange man to dress you up from head to foot like a Delilah; then you vamp a landlord; hypnotize a helpless Honest Abe; turn the whole world upside down to get the setting for your man. And if you did catch on to him," she flung over her shoulder as she swept out of the room, "it's only because you're a heartless Salome and you don't care if you get your man dead or alive, as long as you get him."

"Have I got him after all?" thought Sonya as the door closed behind Gittel. She tightened her fists, resolutely trying to pull herself together.

"The coward! The make-believe! The milk-and-water philanthropist! Don't I know it? He ran away to Washington like a thief in the night—only because he's scared of me—scared of the breath of love."

Now that there was no one in the room before whom Sonya had to keep up a front, her whole body sagged into a chair as if her very bones doubled and broke with despair.

"What Gittel says, the world will say. In their eyes I'm a schemer and a plotter. Hollins is the only one that understands me. He knows that I only do what I *must* do. I only want to live. And no one can live without love. But he—Manning—what's all his cold manners—his higher-up education—his whole busy-about-nothing philanthropy—but a scheming and a plotting to live without love?"

With a determined tread Sonya walked through the hall to the resident's quarters, passed his room without any slowing of her footsteps. But when she turned the latch of her own door, her hands were a-tremble. She was weak and faint again. She knew that her battle with herself had only just begun.

A while before she thought she had gotten hold of herself. And now she was again at the point where she had begun—flung back into chaos and tumultuous darkness. She was not Sonya Vrunsky. She was a driven thing, lost in space, tossing and whirling in a void of pain.

She did not go down for dinner. The thought of listening to the

workers' chatter of their futile routine was unbearable. She was
faint for food and yet she could not eat. She threw herself on her
couch too weary to remove her clothes.

The endless night ahead terrified her. What was sleep to her
now but an ache, a weariness and an exhaustion! Her need of him,
this man who had been a stranger to her but a short time ago—and
the shame of her need of him, pressed upon her like madness—
drowned out reason—annihilated the strength of her will.

With an impulse toward self-torture she recreated the night of
tumultuous unrest before Manning's visit to her room—the night
of passion and roses. Her sleeplessness then had been sweet—buoyed
up by hope and glamor and illusion. Tonight there was nothing
but chaos and the ashes of emotion.

Terrible questions assailed her, hurled against her brain like
bullets, leaving throbbing wounds that ached and ached. Was her
love for Manning merely a delirium of the senses? Was that light
from his eyes that beckoned to her so irresistibly, his low voice that
thrilled in her such music, was it but the Lorelei luring her to
destruction? What was that driving madness to make herself beautiful for him, the fever that drove her to Hollins, the landlord,
Honest Abe—was it only the drunkenness of desire? Did other
women who loved go through the blood and fire of such disillusion?
Or did she suffer so merely because she loved a high-souled saint—a
John the Baptist—a man without blood in his veins?

How long she lay there, tossing her questions into space, she
knew not. Suddenly a familiar footstep in the corridor struck across
her confusion bringing her up in an instant to life and sanity. A
sharp joy leaped into her heart. She bounded to her feet wondering
if it was but another trick of her tired brain. Then came the light
tap at the door.

"I found the last moment I had to come back," a beloved voice
stammered apologetically. "About the leases—"

"The leases," she repeated vaguely as one waking from a dream.

A sudden faintness came over her as she met Manning's gaze.
All the bitterness that she had cherished against him, all the harsh
words she had lusted to throw in his face, melted in the flaming
passion the sight of him brought back. But like one dying of thirst,

yet unable to drink because his throat is seared by the long drought, she gazed at him dumbly.

"And also I did not want to miss seeing the Senator," Manning's voice droned on with startling unreality.

Baffled by Sonya's curious silence, the man felt the necessity of giving some plausible explanation for his precipitate return. How could he begin to tell her the real reason for his inconsistency?

He had gone to Washington on a pretext. He had tried to escape from the insistent, repeated demands she unconsciously made upon him. Her indomitable will, the torrential passion of her had worn him out—till he felt he must run or surrender. He needed time—a few days longer to marshal his forces—gain possession of himself. And so he sent the telegram only to realize the moment after that Washington was intolerable to him, the people he met in the streets—his associates, the city itself and its distance from her.

He had come back to her. He saw again the flash of her kindling face, felt again the rush of happiness that always wafted from her. He had so much to say to her and here he found himself stupidly talking to her about the reconstruction plans propounded by the Senator from Oklahoma. Almost without volition his voice ran on details infinitesimal—details about the remote affairs at Washington. In disgust and self-abasement he tried to change the subject, but instead found himself taking out a blue print of the model tenements. As he explained to her the architects' plans, he cursed the thing within him that held him from being himself—from saying the things he wanted to say.

A light came into her eyes—poignant—appealing—as though she were asking him for something. His heart yearned for her. He longed to put out his hand to her and ask her why she was so sad—so oppressed—but all his ancestral fear of women rose up in him, paralyzed him, and held him back as in gyves.

"There will be a model kindergarten on the roof and a public dining room in the basement," he went on—details, infinitesimal details.

His low, monotonous voice ran through her like fire. "Why is he talking to me about model tenements? What do I care about reconstruction plans?" she longed to cry out to him. "Here, I'm burning alive at his feet and he don't see it—he don't know it!"

Manning's voice broke off suddenly. Sonya was so pale—so disturbingly quiet. It frightened him. He looked up startled. Her face had taken on a swift ashen pallor. But as he gazed, a vivid flame leaped into her cheeks. Bungler that he was, he hadn't realized the strain, the responsibility of the work she had been under in his absence. There would be time enough to talk things over to-morrow. He must not keep her standing longer. Sleep and rest were what she needed. Before he knew it he heard himself saying good night in cold, lifeless tones. He closed the door softly and left her standing there—alone—without having said a word of what he had come to say.

She listened to his retreating footsteps, heard the jangle of his key ring as he fitted the key into the lock. The door opened and closed.

Now he puts his stick in the corner. Now he is taking off his tan overcoat, removing his hat. Then she lost track of his movements for a moment, but through a whirl of tenuous feelings, she reached toward him, burned through the walls, the space, the physical barriers that separated them.

Slowly she began to undress. As she slipped a thin nightgown over her head, she paused and smiled at herself. Had he gone methodically to bed, or did he stand now and think of her as she thought of him? After the long trip he must be tired. She remembered now there were little lines around his eyes that showed fatigue and sleeplessness.

She wondered how she had kept from putting out her hand, smoothing out his tired lines. Maybe it wasn't too late. She would go to him and ask him if there was anything she could do for his comfort. She had seemed so cold—so wrapped up in her own thought she had forgotten to ask him a single word about himself. Maybe he was sick and in need of her and that's why he had come back so unexpectedly—stoically making the leases the excuse.

How selfish he must think her! Yes—she was selfish to the whole world—but not to him. She would give her last drop of blood just to be the footstool on which he stepped.

His tired eyes—the tired lines—she could not get them out of her thoughts. They were calling to her like a hungry child to its mother.

She wondered if there were tired lines on her face too. She picked up the mirror nearly to drop it at the reflection that stared at her—blood-shot eyes—swollen lips—cheeks aflame as if the blood had run riot, twisting, distorting her features.

She flung the offending mirror on the couch. This minute she would go to him—put an end to all the intrusions—the unrealities that stood between them.

A thought, big, daring, wonderful, slipped into her mind. It wavered and dimmed and then flamed to sudden beauty.

"Why not? Why shouldn't he know? Why may not I tell him all—now—this very minute?

"As I am in all my weakness, my helplessness, my terrible need, I'll go to him. A moment's release—to lie in his arms, to rest my heart against his heart if only this once."

She stood where she was, riveted, her hand on the door-knob, drawn, driven. But the very pressure of her desire paralyzed her.

"Fool—Esau, that you are, clamoring for a mess of pottage! You are only a man-mad woman!

"Sonya Vrunsky! Get hold of yourself!" She swayed back and forth like a leaf in a hurricane.

Slowly her reason returned. "Lipkin, and dozens of others—I could have them all—any man of my own kind. But it's Manning—Manning only I want."

She staggered across the room to her couch and sat pondering. Her hot face seemed to burn the cold fingers that pressed against it. "The beauty, the culture of the ages is in him. To have him is to possess all—the deepest, the finest of all America. He is my bridge to civilization."

"Pfui! Civilization?" she flung at herself. "The people higher up—with all their book learning—I hate them and their cursed civilization!

"Will I set him on fire with my nakedness or drive him from me in disgust? Who knows? Men of my own kind—they would understand. But he and his kind, what do they know of life—of love!

"Ach! What's his civilization that I'm hungering for? Nothing but walls and barriers that hold back heart from heart. If he were flesh and blood, would he have stuffed my ears with model tenements—reconstruction plans?

"He and his educated kind—his whole heartless world of gentlemen—the best of them have less feeling than Sopkin, the butcher. How they can trample and murder in their cold politeness the helpless people who look up to them for their very lives!

"Bah! What release would there be for me to give myself to this thing that calls itself a man? Even in his arms—even in the closest embrace, there would rise up the barrier of his wholeness, his invulnerableness, his very gentleman-ness, the things that prove his poverty—his inferiority."

"Paler passions—paler needs; paler capacity—paler fire!

"Unless he stood stripped, broken, helpless as I, he could never fathom my need for him."

She put on a heavy bathrobe and slippers, and opening the window she stepped out on the fire-escape. For a long time she sat very still, feeling the darkness around her entering her being; resigning herself to her own inadequacy.

"I am not ready for fulfillment," she told herself with chastened humility. "Something in me shuts me out from the light of my own soul. Then how dare I sit in judgment on him? How do I know what locks him in from himself? Inside of me are vineyards of plenty and I keep stretching out my hands begging crumbs! Not he, but something unfinished, unripe in my own soul, keeps me from self-realization. There are seeds buried in the darkness of me that will never blossom—echoes, longings, suppressed desires of past generations clamoring for expression in me that will never find voice."

Her resignation calmed and stilled the tumult within her. "In the morning I'll give up my job here," she decided. "I'll just tell him it always was a lie to me—the very mission of the settlements. And the make-believedness of it all still chokes in my throat. I have to get away to save my soul."

*   *   *

John Manning left Sonya feeling that the problem of their relationship was growing more confused than ever. He felt vaguely that it had been a mistake to seek her out in her room at so late an hour. What he had to tell her could just as well have waited for the following morning. It would be wiser in the future not to go to her room—their conferences could just as well be held in his office, but the exigencies of this one occasion almost warranted it. She would understand certainly how anxious he had been to know of the things that had taken place in his absence.

He realized there would have to be many adjustments in their relationship—adjustments in which he must make clear to Sonya that the personal equation must not be allowed to obstruct the progress of their common work. The work and the work only must remain the issue.

Still only when he came face to face with Sonya in her room did he feel the subtle poignance of her charm—the primitive fascination of the oriental—he called it—the intensity of spirit of the oppressed races. The idea of having the girl associated with him in his work seemed logical and soothing. From the very beginning he had felt she would be tremendously helpful to him. She was one of the people to whom he had consecrated his life, and what was more, she could interpret those other strangers to him. And again he told himself that the work and the work only was the issue between them.

Her eyes seemed to follow him about as he prepared for bed. What was that questioning look? It pierced through the very roots of his being. All the loneliness of the immigrant—the hungry, the homeless—cried out to him out of those eyes. Sonya's eyes could not be shaken off. Silent—resistless—they stirred the inmost silences within him. Why was Sonya so sad—so disturbingly quiet? The wild, tempestuous Sonya he knew a little. But the disturbingly quiet Sonya? What was she striving to say to him? A great tenderness flowed out of his heart to her. Unconsciously, his hands reached out in the darkness. A mysterious, resistless force swayed him—drew him to her in her voiceless need. How he longed to take her up in his arms and heal her of the sorrow that paled her face and saddened her eyes! "But the work and the work only is the one absorbing passion of my life," he told himself with finality.

He went to bed at last as the first streaks of dawn were breaking over the tenement roofs. So tired was he that he fell asleep almost instantly to dream that he was John the Baptist loving with a self-destruction the white-fleshed loveliness of Salome, who lured and drew him with the dazzling color of her voluptuous dancing.

He awoke in a dripping perspiration from the battle that waged within him.

After tossing restlessly on his couch for what seemed to him an eternity, he arose, stretched out his exhausted limbs and after a cold shower started for an early morning walk through the streets of the Ghetto—"to get the cobwebs out of my mind" he told himself.

An hour later he returned. Calmly, steadfastly, he took the settlement house steps, setting each foot down with a confidence that said, "I am master of my destiny."

He was curiously unaware of the armor of sophistry with which he had tried to shut out the lure of the girl. He did not know that during his whole stay at Washington and through the chaos of the night interview, love had been hammering and boring through all his ancestral inhibitions.

But in the dim hallway, when he came face to face with Sonya, before he knew it he had her in his arms, showering kisses upon her lips. "Let's fly away," he whispered. In the contagion of her unfettered spirit he caught the very rhythm of her dialect. "Away from walls and work and settlements—darling—let's fly together."

15

Greenwold—"God's Own Eden"

"Give only a look! What's this?" The office boy nudged the janitor, pointing to Manning, arm in arm with Sonya.

"Where are they going so on fire?" gasped Hannah Hayyeh, leaning out through the window.

"It burns the earth under their feet," responded her favorite confidante. "Such a happiness! The sun shines out from their eyes."

"That little witch! Catching herself on to such a millionaire!"

"What luck! All her worries for bread are over!"

Manning did not see the staring faces, the amused smiles. He did not hear the whispered comments of the block gossips. He only hurried the faster. Now gazing ahead. Now turning and smiling to Sonya as he pressed her arm with savage tightness to his side—devouring her with man's hunger of long repression.

Gone was the mask of cool aloofness—the air of restraint that Manning always maintained when in public. Social barriers, genteel inhibitions were swept away in the hurricane of his emotion. He gazed at the girl beside him frankly, passionately—as helpless, as unconscious of his overwhelming absorption as any adolescent in his first love.

Sonya was a fluid flame that merged into the rapt ardor of his mood. But her keen ears heard every envious whisper. Her glowing eyes noted every jealous glance that escaped the love-intoxicated man.

She did not ask where he was taking her. Even after they had reached Grand Central Station not a word marred the ecstasy of silence between them. Nor did Manning himself know where they were going until he heard himself asking the ticket agent for two tickets to Greenwold.

"Where's that place?" Sonya whispered, raising possessive eyes to the amorous captive.

"My people's estate." And he released the hand that held his arm only to venture a bolder caress. His avid fingers touched her neck, moved behind her shoulder to rest for a moment around her waist.

Swift exhilaration seized her. A large feeling that the world was good and she the happiest of mortals. Without a word they settled themselves on the train. For some time they could neither speak nor look at one another so thick was the spell over them.

Into the haze of her dumb rapture, his hand came and enveloped hers. A thrill of sensuous delight shivered through her from head to feet. She could no more have drawn her hand away from his than severed it from her own body. Her skin clung to his wherever it touched as a filing clings to a magnet. Their fingers interlaced in a gentle pressure. Every slightest stirring was a new caress.

"Ach! Air! Open wide the window!" thought Sonya. And so intense was the clairvoyance between them that he felt her wish as though she had spoken.

Leaning in front of her to open the window, he tried to let go her hand only to find himself clasping it tighter. He threw up the sash with his left hand, then slipped back into his seat, brushing her hair with his lips, resisting desperately the impulse to clasp her in his arms.

Like the wine of their youth was the fragrant wind of the open country that blew into their faces. The film of pale green that beckoned to them from fields and meadows was like the budding delight quivering in their hearts.

"Philanthropist! Savior of humanity!" Sonya twitted roguishly. "You called a meeting of the housing committee and where are you now?"

"They'll get along without us," he laughed back into her eyes.

"But Mr. Preacher! Didn't you teach me that we must only identify ourselves with our work? Didn't you hammer it into me that work is the *only thing real*—the only thing that counts—the only thing that lasts?"

He threw his head up in brazen denial of all he had ever taught and raised her hand in a flash to his lips. "Love is the only thing real. The only thing that counts." And he kissed the fingers hotly before he released them.

They got off the train and tramped down a green road to a gate built like an archway of a Gothic castle.

"You run-away gentleman! Letting a whole settlement go to the dogs to make love to a nobody from nowhere. Where are you taking me—crazy philanthropist?"

"Why, there's no farther to go." Manning slipped a hand around her waist and drew her closer to him. "This is my home—Greenwold."

"Such a cold name! Is that what you call this beautiful place?"

"It's formal and English," he agreed. "But let's go in. There's no one there but an old caretaker."

"A house—now—for us?" Sonya gently swung her body free from his caress. She stopped in front of the iron grill, an enigmatic expression on her face. To enter his house too easily would be symbolic of surrender rather than conquest. Manning caught the look and moved nearer to her. His elbows slightly crooked and his nervous hands held in front of his thighs twitched as if he were about to seize and clasp her to him. From his stooped height his head was bent toward hers. Gone was the frosty aloofness in his eyes that maddened her in their early friendship. Now his eyes were blue and soft like the waters on the Sound that could be glimpsed on this May morning between vistas of trees.

"Let me take you to the sunken garden. Don't you like these grounds?" he cried enthusiastically, moving toward a flower bed.

Sonya shook her head. "I can't stand anything green with fences around it. It makes me feel I'm only in a city park." She threw a glance of distaste at the rigid landscape gardens—the gravel path with a box hedge and clipped lawns on either side. "These trees look like little dogs on a chain and the grass is as stiff as a lady in a corset. Ach! Take me where nature's got a chance to be natural. I got to have high mountains and open spaces—the whole sea pouring out its wild waves on us."

Soon they were out of the garden on a miniature cape thrust into the Sound, planted with Maine pine trees. The brown pine needles lay thickly, a fragrant carpet on which they sank side by side.

"It's like an island here," she whispered. Her knee had brushed against his and unconsciously she let a few minutes pass before she withdrew from the delightful contact.

"The whole estate is an island. You would scarcely notice it coming from the station, but it's separated from the mainland by a narrow salt-water creek, veiled by marsh grass."

The words he had used to so many visitors fell from him mechanically, but within his heart sang the joy watching the fluttering pulse in her young neck, the fine down on her cheek made visible by the sunshine.

"Don't call this Greenwold," said Sonya, feasting her eyes on the green and blue of land and seascape, the white of the drifting clouds. "Call it God's own Eden, where Adam and Eve made heaven together."

They turned to each other, deliciously aware that they were alone for the first time that day. The vast open of earth and sky, the sensuous quiet seemed to settle upon them like a mantle, enfolding them in a palpitating silence.

Through a blur of hot desire they looked at one another. The very magnetism that drew them so irresistibly quivered like a physical veil between them.

Manning fought an overwhelming madness to thrust civilization aside, tear the garments that hid her beauty from him, put out his hands over her naked breasts and crush her to him till she surrendered. But he was terrified at his own relapse to the primitive. And he appealed dumbly to all the traditions that had been bred into him to gain control of himself and save him from the fury of his desire. The sublimation that the momentary restraint gave to his love made her all the more ravishing. He was steeped in a divine lyricism—swung between the fear to profane beauty by possessing it and the God-like knowledge that only through their oneness could beauty be complete.

It seemed to him that on the East Side he had never perceived her irresistible attraction. In a theoretical way he had accepted her as a type of the people that drew him. Now, the woman beside him was a flame of life—a vivid exotic—a miraculous priests of romance who had brought release for the ice of his New England heart.

A swooning calm possessed Sonya as she returned his gaze. She was intensely conscious that at last she had pierced through the shell that had separated her from this man as by an impalpable wall. All those days of wasting suspense, the sleepless nights of consuming desire—the emotions that had burned her dry—that threatened to destroy her—were but a storing up of the spirit that had created the fulness of this moment.

She knew that now Manning was as much in love with her as she had ever been with him. This was victory—a vindication of her conquering power that made the suns and spheres of heaven and earth sing back her triumph to her. She *had* plucked the moonbeams out of the moon. She *had* drawn the sun-rays out of the sun. She *had* dried up oceans—levelled mountains—gathered all the forces of creation in the burning passion of this man.

Like dry grass thirsty for water after a long drought their hearts ached for contact. Swept up in the tidal wave of his emotion, he seized her in a bold embrace, his kisses quick and countless. Flesh and spirit yielded to his arms in breathless happiness. She was all love that wrapped itself about him, entered his very veins a subtle, ethereal essence. Without reserve, without shame they surrendered themselves to the maddening, keen pleasure of their togetherness. So complete was the mutuality of their giving it was as if their spirit had found expression at last through the flesh merging their hearts into one consuming flame of love.

* * *

They opened their eyes and saw how forest and meadow palpitated with the Miracle. Every bush had a million pulses. Every blade of grass was a thread of fire. Manning felt that they had come out of a union of ages, made finer, more beautiful, more spiritual by the fusion of their love.

"Lovely woman! How did it happen?" he asked her, marvelling.

She smiled at him tenderly, charmed by the innocent futility of his question.

"It's because we come from opposite ends of civilization that we fuse so perfectly," he persisted.

"High-brow and low-brow to marry themselves this way," she mocked gently.

"I have run away from my caste and you have risen out of yours. Destiny ordained that we gravitate toward each other."

The woman shook her head. "Bunk—all bunk. What's reason

and all the educated thoughts from your head compared to what we feel in our hearts?"

"What do you mean?" He touched his cheek to her breast. "Are we not the mingling of the races? The oriental mystery and the Anglo-Saxon clarity that will pioneer a new race of men?"

Sonya moved closer to surrender herself to the joy of his caress. "Why drag in high words from sociology books in happiness so perfect as ours?" Her lips pressed to his lips. "I can't think. I only feel that we are for each other as the sun is for the earth. Races and classes and creeds, the religion of your people and my people melt like mist in our togetherness."

She paused and gazed into space through and beyond him. "We are the sphinx—the eternal riddle of life—man and woman in love."

16

The Days After

Sonya walked like a joyous pagan up the red-carpeted aisle of the church of Manning's fathers. So enraptured with romance, so drunk with the wine of her love was she, that her wedding seemed no mere ceremony or religious rite, but a triumphant entry into happiness—a union that would last forever after. Revelling in the rich, blending colors that streamed through the stained glass windows, in the sensuous tones of the throbbing organ, she cared little whether the man who officiated was rabbi or priest. Her only god was love. She confided her destiny into Manning's hands. What ever he wished, she wanted her life to be.

A month's honeymoon at Greenwold. A month of glamorous absorption in one another. Sonya asked for nothing but to pour herself out to him. And the more she gave, the more bottomless became her urge to give more. She sought to plumb deeper and deeper into the personal, through an ever-closer fusion of the flesh to touch the spirit of the man she loved. But as the first veil of illusion fell between them, she began to see that she had more to give than he needed—than he wanted.

The honeymoon was over, but she felt that a deeper under-standing, a completer mating, awaited them in the city where their work was. Thereafter, the call of New York became more insistent.

"When I am choked in by houses, the open country calls to me," she confided to Manning, "and I see before my eyes the sea and sky and hills. But I'm really only myself in the crowded city among the tenements."

"But, darling, we'll go straight to the town house."

"Let's go this evening," she cried impulsively.

With an indulgent nod, he put his arms about her: "Whatever you say, darling."

He immediately proceeded with the packing, preferring to do it alone in his usual systematic way. But she followed him like a faithful dog. There was a tight, inarticulate feeling in her heart that gnawed her.

She held the fulness of her happiness, but wondered suddenly why she did not glow with it. Touching the collar of his coat in possession of him, brushing his neck with the tips of her fingers, she tried instinctively to rouse him to the language of love. He looked up with a smile of response, but it was more than a smile she craved. She wanted that, at her touch, his arms should open to her and enfold her. He did not move, however, from his kneeling position over the suitcase. Nervously, she turned to the window and began to drum on the pane.

"Don't, dear!" he reproved for the first time in their season of mating.

She burned to exclaim: "What don't? Why don't? You're impatient with me."

But the glamorous haze of her love still enveloped her, silencing her angry words. She wanted to throw herself on his shoulder and weep; at the same time, she feared to let him see any cloud of discontent on their honeymoon. So she quietly slipped away to her room and there gave vent to hysterical tears, the reason of which she did not understand.

On the train, Sonya wondered why the ache in her heart was so keen. What had happened? Why did she feel so dumb? She stole a glance at Manning, who was placidly reading an article in the Atlantic Monthly. Was this man with the tired married look the lover who had hung over her with such ardor on the way up? There was a numbing silence between them, and they had not begun to say things to one another. And he could sit there placidly reading an article in the Atlantic Monthly!

She wondered vaguely: "Does this always happen?"

She had thought that their great moment of love would only be a prelude to increasing interchange of more love. She still had things to say, but the gift of a thousand tongues that had possessed her before they went to Greenwold seemed to have gone out of her.

Dimly afraid, she drew closer to him and snuggled her warm shoulder under his arm. He was so tall that she fitted in perfectly, as though in reality she were only part of him. More and more dependent on his love, she could not help but cling to him. And yet his body was tightly drawn away from her. Embarrassed at his wife's over-demonstrativeness in a public train, Manning ignored her and concentrated on his magazine.

"And he doesn't even need to say things, or he wouldn't be reading so calmly," she thought. "How could such flames of feeling as we have known pass through him and leave him with the same educated coldness, the same hard reasonableness of the higher-ups?" The Atlantic Monthly had become an offense to her. "How can he read those lifeless words of the high-brows?"

Disheartened at his lack of response, she settled back in her corner. Instantly, he felt her withdrawal. He looked up. The frosty blue eyes softened with an affectionate gleam and he put his hands over hers with a calm possessiveness that offended, even though it seemed to reassure her.

"So we're going to our real home!" he beamed at her. "Five generations of brides have come to the room in my town house which will be ours."

"There we'll have another honeymoon," she flashed back eagerly. "There we'll say things to each other."

Her glance lingered on him with ardent questioning. Would the town house bring the deeper flood of love? Surely the warmth of all those five generations of brides would storm through him when he held her there!

Sonya was radiant again as she looked up at him. The thought that she was to be mistress of his town house filled her with keen anticipation. Remembering that night of black rebellion, when she had been full of hate for the heartless rich as she watched his social set walk up the carpeted steps in all their splendor, she thought to herself: "I am one of them now." And the next moment she questioned: "Am I one of them? Has our love made us alike? Just because I am his wife, have I become his kind? Will his people accept me—and will I accept them?"

Her introspection melted into an idealized vision of the Madison Avenue mansion. It would be a palace of shimmering beauty. The colors and textures she had craved all her life would permeate the place, culminating in the tender warmth of their room together. But when the great mahogany doors were thrown open to her by the erect, expressionless butler, it was not the house of dreams she had pictured.

It was so different from what she had expected.

The frigid dignity of the butler as he took their wraps sent a chill to her very bones. Clinging like a frightened child to Manning's arm, she followed him in a daze.

But at every turn, she felt herself sinking into an unknown world. Her every step was silenced in thick, rich carpets. Her every glance was entangled by mirrors, paintings and colored tapestries.

"Maybe the house is beautiful for those who know the cost of these rich things, this deadly durability of the furniture," thought Sonya. "But it hasn't the warm, soft coziness that makes the feeling of home."

Her thoughts went on:

"Solid, cold, impersonal—that's what these things are! Maybe to the educated, the cold, impersonal things are beautiful; but for me nothing is beautiful but what's intensely personal. Here I feel no person—only the heaviness of weighing-down possessions."

"Well, how do you like the house, dear?" asked Manning, as with familiar tread he led Sonya through the huge rooms of the lower floor.

"Oi, it's so big, so cold—like a museum, not a home!"

"You'll get used to it, my dear," he assured her.

They entered the somber, majestic dining room. An enormous candelabrum hung over the table, and the massive furniture with its old carvings lent an antiquated air to the place. Sonya walked uncertainly about the room, trying to familiarize herself with the huge sideboard loaded with old silver, and the china-closet crowded with antiques. Stranger to herself in this strange world, she found her bewildered hands tracing the outlines of animals carved deeply in the backs and arms of ancient chairs. Her fingers seemed caught in the mouths of these fantastic beasts.

The butler and an obsequious serving man pulled out the heavy chairs for them to sit down. "Do the rich need a man to waste his time to help them sit down?" she thought, with a look of scorn at the menials. She was not used to the accepted inequality of servants. But she took her seat with an attempt at gaiety.

"I'm so starved I could eat up the shells of the oysters and all!"

she cried, trying instinctively to break through the atmosphere of solemn dignity.

She reached for the largest fork and hungrily lifted an oyster to her lips. The mask-faced butler silently, but significantly, placed the correct fork in front of her. The blood rushed to her cheeks. She glanced at Manning, then down at her plate, shamed and confused. Her first impulse was to throw the correct fork after the butler, who had retreated behind his screen in the pantry. But she only bit her lip and forced back her tears.

Manning, pained at her embarrassment, tried to smooth the situation. "Have you thought, dear, of the friends you'll invite to our reception?" he asked, trying to resume the natural thread of conversation.

"My friends I can count on the fingers of one hand," was her impatient reply.

The butler removed one course after another from Sonya's place, untasted; but Manning did not seem to notice and talked right on.

"Ach! Why do you need receptions yet?" She flung out her arms in a gesture of irritation.

"Why, my dear," he murmured tactfully, "my relatives and friends want to meet you."

She looked up at him hopelessly baffled. She had never thought of Manning in relation to any human being but herself. And now the mention of his relatives and friends intensified her growing discomfort in his house.

"Take me to our room," she asked, the moment they rose from table.

Upstairs she found the same oppressive bigness, the stifling tapestries and smell of old, old things. But the bedroom with its quaint-patterned paper, its soft dotted Swiss curtains, seemed more homelike. Sonya hoped her husband would stay there with her for the rest of the evening, so as to shut out the depressing gloom of the house.

"I wish we'd better had one little poorest flat, one little room, with nothing in it but our love. I hate things."

She drew him down to her on the settee and laid her head on his shoulder.

"How much do you love me?" she asked pathetically. "More than you ever did? More every day?"

"Of course, of course! You know that I do, dear," he said, extricating himself from her clinging arms. "I must get down to Hopkins, my secretary. He is waiting for me to answer some letters which came this afternoon. I will dictate the replies and then come back."

His eyes narrowed on his wife for a moment. His look of cold scrutiny stabbed through Sonya, disrobed her of her human charm. In that one critical flash, she felt herself stark naked.

"Have I no shame?" she asked herself. "Am I only an East Side savage—a clinging female dragging him down from his higher life? . . .

"That's why he's running from me, because I can't hide my terrible hunger for him. . . .

"Why did he shame me so with his look? In those first days at Greenwold, there was no shame between us. Did he shame me because I feel for him so much more than he can feel for me? If he loved me as much as I love him, then there'd be no shame."

Sonya let him go without a murmur. But loneliness gathered over her, like the clutch of a cold hand on her throat. She thought on:

"The love in me can't ever stop, but if I don't do something my greedy love will burn out the romance between us. To hold him, I've got to get interested in his things—his relations, his friends, even those dead articles from his Atlantic Monthly."

She leaped to her feet: "Above all, I must get a new dress for his reception. I've got to see Hollins, then."

Mechanically, she began to unpack. The lulling reverie mirrored in her face was broken in upon by a maid, who appeared as if by magic.

"Madam," she said with faint reproof, "may I do it for you?"

The word, "madam," made Sonya wince irritably. She, plain from the East Side, to be called "madam." It jarred on her nerves like a falsehood. She was accustomed to live among nobodies, but everyone there hoped at least to become a somebody. This maid's servile deference was the language of admitted inferiority. She hated to have this obsequious menial touch her things. But against her will, she found herself yielding to the maid.

Standing back, she watched her clothes being laid out in the bureau drawer and hung in the wardrobe. All at once, she noticed the maid sniffing slyly at a cotton nightgown she had thrown into her bag the day she started for Greenwold. In quick resentment, Sonya chased the maid from the room. Not yet enslaved by the need of servants, like the habitual mistress, she felt free to do without her.

She made up her mind to tell Manning that she couldn't bear to have servants dogging her steps, but when he came back all complaints and disillusionments quickly vanished within the circle of his arms.

The next morning, Manning showed her the different wings of the house and dwelt at length on the ancestral portraits that dominated every room.

"This is my great-aunt Susan." He pointed out an austere, angular woman in crinoline and starched collar. "She was noted among the Mannings for her piety and self-control. She was so devout that when a relative came from China with a bale of silk for her, she refused the gift because she learned that it had been carried on a vessel that had sailed on Sunday."

"Was the silk she wore then only grown on week days? Did God prevent the silkworms from working on Sunday?" Sonya asked, amused.

He laughed and passed on to another painting.

"This is the second lieutenant-governor of Connecticut, my great-great-grandfather," he said proudly. "He helped to found Yale University and built the largest church in his town."

"Did he also burn witches?" she asked mischievously, as she looked at the grim, trap-like mouth and the shaggy eyebrows over gimlet eyes.

The ancestors seemed to follow her even when she took a stroll that afternoon. They repressed the free stride of her usual walk. They held in her swinging arms. She saw some East Side folks and in a burst of emotion wanted to rush over to them. Strangers that they were, she felt she knew them because they were her own people. But the scowling glances of the Manning ancestors inhibited her.

"Between trying to act I'm a lady for the servants and holding myself up to the ancestors, God from the world! where am I?" she sighed, bewildered.

17

The East Side Shakes Hands with Society

As Sonya looked about the luxurious reception room of Hollins' shop, all in delicate tones of mauve, infinitely more beautiful, more selective, than Manning's aristocratic house on Madison Avenue, she thought:

"How naturally Jaky Solomon made himself over and settled himself for a born higher-up! Why can't I be sensible with my good luck? Why can't I take Manning's house as a frame for me and make over my new world? Millions of girls are wishing themselves in my place, the wife of Manning the millionaire. Why am I still so lost in the air, a wild crazy from Hester Street?"

So magnetic was Hollins' personality that Sonya knew he had entered the room before he spoke to her. He came forward with a friendly: "How do you do, Mrs. Manning?" She felt now the composed manner of the professional artist, not the warm, responsive Jew she had found at their first meeting.

"I come to you again for something beautiful," she began, "and you must put your mind on the special thing for me more than ever before."

"More than ever before—" At the last phrase, Hollins' heavy lids lifted and dropped with a quick, penetrating glance.

"Always you can depend on me, Mrs. Manning. It's not hard to create beauty for the beautiful." His words were warm, but Sonya felt a tone of formal withdrawal, a polite aloofness.

"Ach, I got on me a reception! Manning's relatives and friends are coming to look me over."

He nodded in swift understanding: "I know the kind of gown for you."

As they compared fabrics and matched colors, Sonya tried to

bring him back to the old friendly footing. But he seemed abstracted, his mind busy with other thoughts.

"I suppose his head is full to-day with orders from his millionaires," she reflected. "I can't talk to him about real things as I used to before."

But at the next appointment for a fitting, he was not there at all. Only Miss Bernice and another assistant, who served her with expert but impersonal precision.

"Where's Mr. Hollins?" she demanded impetuously.

"Oh, Mr. Hollins only comes to the final fitting!" murmured Miss Bernice.

"But I have to see him," she ordered.

"Certainly, madam."

A few moments later, Hollins sauntered in. "Weren't you pleased with the fitting, Mrs. Manning?" he asked, with polite solicitude.

Hollins' professional business manner was unbearable to Sonya. "He knows he understands me. Then why is he making himself for a stranger?" she thought.

"The fitting is perfect!"—and at her impatient glance Miss Bernice and her assistant withdrew.

When they were alone, she faced Hollins with her usual directness:

"Don't you care nothing how I'm getting on in my new life?"

"You look so happy and radiant!" And he bowed gallantly.

"Ach! Stop your polite manners with me. You got politeness enough with your rich customers and I in my rich house."

"You'll never need politeness, Sonya, because you're so alive, so filled to the brim with yourself. Manners are only for tired people to hide their tiredness."

"Do they really make you so tired, your customers from the Four Hundred?" she asked naïvely, as though searching herself.

She moved her chair closer to his: "Tell me only! You're dealing every day with the higher-ups. Do you think I'll ever get used to Manning's social set?"

"Oh, Sonya!" he said. "You can handle yourself with any of them. But you'll be terribly bored."

She felt he had reached instantly to the truth about her, and went on in a groping, puzzled way:

"Tell me a little more about the higher-ups. Do they feel less because they think more? Does using the head hold in the heart? How do they educate themselves out of those burning feelings such as you and I feel?"

"Go on, Sonya—I like to hear you talk. Go on!" His voice was caressing, drawing her out, and she plunged deeper and deeper into the thoughts that bothered her:

"Do you think educated people ever really fall in love? I mean, does it ever shake them to the roots of their being? Does it tear through their body and consume their brain?"

"What a question!" He laughed aloud, to conceal his surprise at her unconscious self-revelation.

"What a fool I am, the way I tell out everything in me the minute I open my mouth to speak!" she reproached herself, chilled by his evasive laugh. "Does he draw himself away from me because I am another man's wife? And I thought he was like my own, he understood me so!"

The ensuing days were filled with details for the coming reception. When the invitations were ready to be sent, Manning turned to his wife:

"Have you ready the list of our friends?"

"Our friends?" she teased whimsically. "This is your reception. Your society friends can't be my friends—only, you insist I got to meet them."

Manning frowned: "Why, your friends and mine will be the same, dear. Why do you insist on imagining differences between yours and mine?"

"I'm not imagining, my dear, higher-up husband," Sonya laughed playfully. "I've lived. I know. If you came from where I come, you would see plain as day the solid difference between those on top and those on the bottom. . . . It's easy to stoop down when you're on top. Just like on a ship the first class passengers on top are free to walk into steerage. But will they let steerage passengers walk free upstairs?"

Manning waved her smile aside. He would not let her intrude the differences of their background into the harmony of their home. He rose and placed a tender hand on his wife's shoulder. "This is *our* reception, my dear—our opportunity to show the world that all social chasms can be bridged with human love and democratic understanding."

"Democratic understanding?" Sonya's brow puckered doubtfully. "Don't talk over my head in your educated language. Tell me in plain words how can there be democratic understanding between those who are free to walk into steerage and the steerage people who are not allowed to give one step up to the upper deck?"

Evading his wife's concrete question, he went on explaining in his usual, abstract way: "Why do you constantly emphasize differences which you and I both know to be false? I am giving up my life to prove my belief in the brotherhood of man," he continued with hurt pride. "The elimination of all artificial class barriers is my religion. And you harp constantly on class differences, as if you wanted me to lose faith in my work."

And so Manning had his way.

Sonya addressed the exquisite, engraved, formal invitations to her Ghetto friends, wondering as she wrote each name how many would muster the courage and secure the clothes to mingle with high society.

Elated with the feel of her perfect gown, Sonya was now eager to play the hostess on a grand scale. She could hardly control her primitive instinct of hospitality and wait till the butler formally announced each guest. She longed to open the door herself and draw all in with a warm, glad hand. It was even more than the racial passion of hospitality that shone in her eyes and throbbed in her open arms of welcome. It was a delirious feeling of triumph that she, Sonya, only a year ago a Hester Street nobody, had in one leap made herself the mistress of the Manning house.

She saw herself one of the million girl readers of society columns, who had suddenly been made mistress of the shining palace of pleasure she had only dreamed about. She felt like the poor girl who could only worship from a distance the hero on the stage, transformed by the magic of marriage into the heroine by his side.

The very Four Hundred that she had once watched with such jealous envy from the outside of Manning's house, she was about to receive from the inside as its conquering mistress. From this dizzy height of hostess in a millionaire home, she could afford to be generous, even to the born rich—even to the educated higher-ups.

The very débutante whose gorgeous evening gown had once made Sonya feel so poor, now came up with her mother.

"Sonya, my cousins, Alice Vandewater and her daughter Louise," said Manning. Sonya was triumphantly conscious of the look of pride in her husband's eyes as with one swift glance he compared her to the débutante cousin. He turned to receive new guests and Sonya, flushed by her husband's approving gleam, flung out her arms to mother and daughter: "Ach! So we're relations!" she cried with Jewish fervor.

But her hands dropped quickly to her side at the reserve which met her.

"I have been looking forward to meeting you," said the dowager. "Nowadays, one meets one's relations after marriage, not before."

"So interesting and modern, don't you think?" added the débutante with a doubtful smile.

She measured the hostess. "Astonishingly well-dressed," she had to concede; but the next moment, her envy found consolation: "Her gesticulating hands show her origin."

"You are really quite wonderful, Sonya," the dowager went on. "You've rescued John from confirmed bachelorhood after all our girls had found him invulnerable." She turned to her daughter: "Don't you think so, Louise?"

"Oh, I don't know, mamma! It is hardly fair to compare Sonya's opportunity to learn the wiles of the art with ours. Unluckily, we've been so carefully shielded!"

Hurt at the veiled thrust, Sonya struck out blindly: "The only art to win a man is brains enough to understand him and his work."

"Yes, that's quite true." Mrs. Vandewater's brows lifted and dropped. As she moved away, she whispered to her daughter: "It's John's so-called work that's responsible."

All the welcoming gladness went out of Sonya's eyes, as though a hidden current of electricity inside of her had been suddenly switched off. But she had no chance to indulge in her feeling, for new guests came crowding around her, morbidly curious to see how the Ghetto prodigy would conduct herself as Mrs. John Manning.

A woman in wistaria net approached and extended lukewarm fingers, while her eyes bored appraisingly: "It must have been charming at Greenwold this spring." She paused and smiled, as if wondering what to say to this plebeian. "John's box is next to mine at the opera. I hope we shall often see you there this winter."

"Opera? What are they playing—something good?" Sonya stammered words, scarcely knowing what she was saying.

"They're opening with Aïda. I know John adores it. Of course, you'll miss your Tchaikowsky, as played by your delightful little community orchestra. But the brass march ought to amuse you. Such a lively touch."

As the woman passed on, Sonya sought her husband. "I never know what they mean when they talk," she whispered, slipping her hand into his. "I never know what goes on in their heads. I never know what to answer them."

"Just be natural, dear, that's all." He pressed his wife's hand, then dropped it in quick embarrassment as he noticed that her ardent gesture had been observed by those near them.

He looked up with an expression of relief as the figure of Helen Moore approached them. He introduced her to Sonya and his face relaxed somewhat, as he saw the older woman greet his wife with genuine friendliness.

"I've looked forward with such pleasure to meeting you," she said, enfolding the bewildered Sonya with her warm, steady look. "And now that we have met, I think I shall begin by calling you Sonya, if I may. My name is Helen. Please call me by it, so that we shall start as friends. Some day soon we shall have a real talk."

These words and this voice Sonya felt were from the heart. The sincerity of the woman's kindly eyes came as a relief from the critical atmosphere surrounding her.

"One real person in a sea of make-believes," thought Sonya.

The influx of guests with their formal patter of words went steadily on. She felt their vivisecting eyes all about her. She no longer seemed the hostess. She was an outsider in her own house. She was lost among Manning's people like a stranger in a strange land.

Then, through the circle of cold, alien faces she espied Gittel Stein. The old maid of the Ghetto had dressed herself up in her best for the occasion. But the nap of her heavy, velvet waist was rubbed away in spots. Her skirts flapped awkwardly around her thin ankles and she was so flustered that her hat, with its hard array of cock's feathers, had swung to one side.

Gittel Stein had never been Sonya's real friend in Ghetto days, but now she was the first of her people to appear. Sonya was so terribly lonely that Gittel's face with its care-worn, homely features brought to her the warm feel of home. She rushed forward with open arms of welcome to greet her friend. At the same time, Sonya was painfully aware that the hostile strangers that watched her saw in Gittel's uncouth appearance as her friend, more ample and obvious proof of the crude and inferior social order into which John Manning had married.

"*Nu*, your four-flushing landed you your millionaire!" Gittel nudged. "But how do you stand it living up to the fake manners of society?"

Before Sonya could answer, the butler with appraising eyes announced her former landlady, Mrs. Peltz.

Wholly unabashed by glittering wealth, Mrs. Peltz strutted in, decked in the gaudiest finery of Essex Street. She wagged her head with proud self-consciousness that society in all its glory was not arrayed as she.

"I came to wish you good luck on your happiness," cried Mrs. Peltz, embracing Sonya. "The minute I heard from your after-wedding party, I knew I'd be the first by your table of friends."

She encircled Sonya's waist and drew down her head to kiss her again: "Ach! I soak in pleasure from your new riches like I was your own mother."

Mrs. Peltz released Sonya from her maternal embrace and smilingly threw back her shoulders stooped by long years at the washtub.

"*Nu*," she whispered raspingly in Sonya's ear. "I can also look with other people alike when I shine myself out in holiday things."

She thrust out a thick thumb at society. "They don't have to know that what I'm wearing is the lend from all the neighbors on the block." Then she proceeded to enumerate: "This silk waist, Mrs. Finkelstein from the fish market lent me. And the diamond earrings is from the butcher's wife. Mrs. Smirsky from the second-hand store let me wear this hat for to-day. But don't it all fit me together like I was a lady born? They all said I shined up the block with my clothes. Everybody turned out from the windows to give a look on me."

As other guests came to meet Sonya, Mrs. Peltz took hold of Gittel's arm and dragged her round the room. Sonya saw Mrs. Peltz pawing the draperies. She bent down to test the quality of the carpet, then pushed her fist into the upholstered arm-chair to feel its downy softness. Then Sonya heard Mrs. Peltz's penetrating whispers as she priced the furniture.

"God from the world!" came from Mrs. Peltz loud enough for others to hear. "The price of this one carpet would be enough to feed the whole block for a year. Only a little from that silver on her side-board would free me from the worries for rent for the rest of my days. If she'd have a heart, she'd divide with us a little of her good luck."

Sonya was keenly aware of the unfriendly backs turned upon her gaudily-attired and loud-voice Ghetto friends. But a greater embarrassment was yet to come. Again the butler appeared in the doorway. She felt the unspoken sneer directed at her.

"Miss Sophie Sokolski," he chopped out.

Sonya looked in astonishment at a full-bosomed, round-hipped girl, unknown to her, but who recalled the buxom saleswoman of Division Street.

With both hands outstretched, the new-comer rushed over to her.

"You don't remember me yet?" she cried, giving her hostess a resounding kiss. "I am a third cousin of your great-aunt." Seeing that Sonya made little response, she fingered nervously the coral beads on her neck. "Don't you remember we were in a shop together by shirt waists? But I've worked myself up to be a hair-dresser now."

Sonya noted a glance from her husband and became aware that he thought she was neglecting his people. She turned nervously to say something agreeable to Mrs. Vandewater, but was interrupted by a pluck at her sleeve. The voice of Sophie Sokolski hissed in her ear:

"Now, with all your riches, you ought to have a hairdresser to yourself. Honest to God, I'd like to live here! And I'd do your hair for nothing."

Mrs. Vandewater stood listening with evident amusement on her face. Again Sonya's eyes sought her husband, and he turned toward her. Her head dropped on his shoulder and her hand felt for his.

"I don't know where I am in this buzz of make-believe," she complained helplessly. "It freezes me, the cold looks of their fishy eyes."

"You'll like them when you know them better. Why, dear, you've been too occupied to eat anything, that's what's the matter. Let me send your salad and a cup of tea," he said, gently setting her aside.

The small, red-lidded eyes of Mrs. Peltz widened at the gallantry with which Manning spoke to his wife.

"*Nu!*" She shook Sonya with boisterous warmth. "Wouldn't your dead mother jump out from her grave if she could only give a look on your happiness!"

Sonya offered her salad to Mrs. Peltz and Manning told the butler to bring another plate, then turned away to speak to some one.

Mrs. Peltz picked up the queer small fork and looked about wildly. Then in desperation, she stabbed a large lettuce leaf and raised it dangling to her lips. After a desperate effort with this inadequate instrument, she grabbed the leaf with her fingers and stuffed it into her mouth.

Sonya, seeing her friend's predicament, nervously and none too successfully tried to roll a lettuce leaf on a fork as a demonstration. But Mrs. Peltz refused to profit by example. Instead, she glanced about and, seeing curious eyes upon her, stuck the lettuce from her hand on to the fork, then laid it down in despair.

Sonya stood bravely by through the salad course, but when Mrs. Peltz began pouring out her tea in a saucer in the regular East Side fashion, Sonya's nerves began to snap inside of her. Leaving Mrs. Peltz in the care of Gittel, she slipped out unobserved up to the dressing room, to cool her hot face and get hold of her taut nerves.

Manning, moving from group to group, greeting one, laughing with another, suddenly become conscious of the isolation of Gittel and Mrs. Peltz. Bowing hastily to the lady with whom he was talking, he came quickly forward to rescue the hapless couple.

Gittel smirkingly extended her hand: "Did you believe that the East Side would come as far uptown?"

"It's no harder for you to come up than it has been for me to come down. The pleasant part is that we meet."

Gittel's sensitive pride heard only the words, "come down." She could bear no more. "What do you mean?" she flared.

"I mean there's no coming up or going down. We all belong to the people. I see no differences."

Mrs. Peltz, who sat placidly sipping tea from a saucer, caught the phrase, "no differences." She put down her tea and faced Manning.

"*Nu*," she said. "Even downtown we got differences. Let me and the landlord's wife go to the butcher store for meat. For who will the butcher pick out the fattest piece of meat? For me, who bargains herself for every penny, or the landlord's wife what pays him over any price he asks?"

At Mrs. Peltz's loud-voiced proclamation of the concrete facts of class distinction there was a sudden silence. Ears eagerly waited for Manning's defense of his theories.

Thus cornered, the host struggled for an answer: "The values of life are not to be measured by material things. Democracy is of the spirit."

Mrs. Peltz looked critically at Manning's slender form and thin, aristocratic features. Then she shot forth, emphasizing her words with her gesticulating palms: "With all the money to buy yourself the fat of the land, you got this idea to live by the spirit! No wonder you got no meat on your bones."

An outburst of spontaneous laughter released the tension of silence. In the buzz of conversation that recommenced, Manning found opportunity to slip out and go in search of Sonya.

As Sonya powdered her hot face before the mirror, she swallowed rising sobs. She thought that none in the whole assembly of people below felt as lonely as she. "Mrs. Peltz is having the time of her life pricing rich things. Gittel has at least the sensation of envy. What have I? Where do I belong among them?"

But controlling her feelings of loneliness and futility, she walked slowly downstairs. To make her re-entrance as inconspicuous as possible, she started to go through an alcove into the drawing-room.

As she stole quietly over the soft rug and raised her hand toward the curtain, she heard a voice:

"The East Side in full regalia . . . in the Manning drawing-room . . . what a picture!"

"And the way she follows John about . . . He won't endure it three months . . . No man can stand being made love to in public . . ."

There was a malicious laugh. Sonya could almost see the shrug of Mrs. Vandewater's fat shoulders as she added: "That kind of love-making, even in private, is not done by our men—after three months . . ."

Sonya found herself listening without at first realizing that she was eavesdropping. Her mind told her that she ought to go, but a painful curiosity held her rooted to the spot. "Whom will I hurt if I hear what those society cats are thinking of me?" she told herself, and stayed on.

Another voice started:

"John's melodramatic vaudeville of social equality . . ."

Sonya moved closer to the curtain. Right or wrong, she must hear everything.

"Indeed! One could consider it as the latest amusement. You remember the Newport monkey dinner that was given to a pet monkey? I would be better able to find it amusing if it were not that I'm fond of Manning . . . Giving a dinner for a pet monkey is one thing and marrying one is quite another thing . . ."

"Do you think she could be bought off, if John came to his senses? . . ."

"Even if his father were alive, he could not offer to step in and buy off the girl. Why, John, you know, is over thirty, and obstinate . . ."

"Men will be like that . . . But most men get caught as the result of careless play. John did this in deadly seriousness."

A moment's pause. A rustling of silk, as of some one approaching. And the same voice assumed a different tone:

"Do you not think, Helen, that this misalliance will at least cure John of his radical theories of giving himself to the poor along with his money?"

"Cure him? Why, it's his ultimate achievement of living the ideals he professes."

"But Helen, be sensible. You realize that girl is impossible."

"John has something besides his background," Helen Moore defended. "Impossible for others—yes. But for him, she's his ideal of the people. She is so alive, so vital. And so in love with him!"

"I am glad, dear Helen, that you can call it such pretty names," Mrs. Vandewater answered. "Personally, she may be what she calls—in love, but"—with an insinuating drip in her voice—"in old-fashioned parlance, I should call it by a different name."

"They say," broke in another voice, "Russian Jewesses are always fascinating to men. The reason, my dear, is because they have neither breeding, culture nor tradition ... With all to gain and nothing to lose ... They are mere creatures of sex ... And much as we may dislike to admit it, men uptown and downtown are the same ..."

A pause, as some one seemed to move away. And then the same voice went on in a lower tone:

"Helen Moore makes me tired, the way she's always sugar-coating the facts of life ... You and I know ... Why do our débutantes go to theaters and cafés? To imitate, my dear ... Let us recognize, my dear, that our smartest clothes are but imitations of the creations of the demi-monde. ... We may imitate their clothes, my dear, but—"

"But the East Side girl hasn't the clothes," broke in the innocent voice of the débutante.

"She needs none, my dear ... She gets the man she wants ... without them." There was a laugh at the ambiguous phrase.

Sonya could hear no more. Quickly but silently, she made her way back upstairs.

"Let the whole reception go hang! I'll not go down again. Culture! Breeding! I saw them naked, too!"

Walking wildly up and down the room, she suddenly stopped. She heard Manning's step. In another moment, he had entered. He looked at her. What killing coldness came to her from his blue eyes! She had never seen such an expression of anger and insulted annoyance on his face before. When he spoke, the chilling frost of his voice cut into her flesh like sharp knives.

"Your guests are still here, Sonya," he said, as though carefully choosing words that she would understand. "Surely, even on the East Side you realize some form of hospitality—some duty to others, beyond our own selfish emotion!"

The cold harshness of his words was like the spark struck from flint that set fire to the smouldering feelings she had suppressed all afternoon.

"Form!" she shrieked, flinging out her arms like a maddened savage. "Is it form to force me to go down and tell your people I love them when I hate them? Hate them like poison!"

He looked at her with alien eyes.

"Possibly, you do not realize that you agreed to give this reception with me. I have done my best to be courteous to your friends. Surely, even you must realize it has been difficult. It is only fair, I think, to insist that you make yourself as presentable as possible. Make the best ending to a most unfortunate afternoon."

"I simply can't do it. I hate them all."

"Your likes and dislikes are scarcely of importance," he said with icy decision. "You are my wife, and as such the hostess of this house. I insist that you go down at once."

Quite suddenly, all of Sonya's emotion left her. She was spent—exhausted—extinguished! Extinguished by an attitude and its language, which was not only alien but antagonistic to her. Her lover, her husband, had suddenly become one with the people below. She could not endure it. She would suffer anything, tear out of her heart all her likes and dislikes, make herself the slave of his least wish—only to have him hers again.

"I will go," she said with downcast eyes. "I will do anything you want," came in a low, beaten voice.

Manning's features instantly relaxed. He came to her and kissed her on the forehead, much, she felt, as he would have patted a dog he had just punished. "Bathe your face," he said, "and powder. I will go down and explain that you will soon join me."

After he had gone, Sonya looked at herself in the mirror, hardly able to realize that the face staring back at her was hers. She felt crushed, beaten by something vague and intangible. A terrible loneliness cried in the dumbness of her heart.

Her husband had kissed her of his own volition. But in that kiss she recognized for the first time a silent admission of her incapacity to meet him fully in his own world.

She went slowly downstairs, feeling for each stair as if it symbol-

ized a step in the unfamiliar road of her husband's world, which
she must travel.

Back in the drawing room, she stood quite quietly by her
husband's side. But the light was not in her eyes and her shoulders
had a tired droop, as she went through the dead form of conven-
tional hospitality.

She shook hands automatically with the departing guests, heard
herself echoing her husband's farewells. She wondered, as Mrs.
Manning, would she always have to be the puppet of a form, the
echo of a language that had no meaning for her? "To please my
husband, will I always have to make myself for a parrot of words
and a monkey of manners, like those born in high society?"

And then it came over her suddenly: "What would Hollins say,
if he could look into my face and see into my heart? Would he
despise me, or pity me?"

When the last caller had gone, Sonya looked up at Manning
dumbly, waiting for him to speak. Something in the look of her
eyes, in the droop of her shoulders, brought him to her with a
quick, enveloping embrace. She had obeyed him. She was his—
doubly his! Because he felt how much she had to learn from him.

At the touch of his arms around her, the icy hostility of her mind
took fire in her blood. She was a flame of wild longing for him. At
the same time, her brain kept boring in to her helpless heart. "Do I
love him because he has beaten me? Do I love him because I hate
him so? Why do I feel this terrible sense of defeat?"

Sonya's thoughts raced on, as she smoothed tenderly the head
on her shoulder: "I'm no longer angry at the catty talk of those
society snakes. It was only the poison of jealousy burning them up.
They were only eating out their own gall because I got him and they
didn't. But have I got him? Which has him most—his kind or I?"

She wanted to shut out the persistent reasoning of her brain in
the drugging opiate of an immediate possession, in the reassuring
supremacy of their passionate oneness. Instinctively, she pressed
her body against his and closed her eyes in a gesture of hungry
desire.

Manning put her gently from him with almost paternal patience.

"I am sure you are glad now, that you came down like a sensible
girl," he said, with affectionate tolerance. "You will find very soon,

my dear, that you can adjust yourself to the form of the society in which you have to live."

At his reiterated reference to the word "form," her tenderness turned to swift antagonism.

"I could never choke myself into the form of your society friends," she said, with a coldness equal to his when he had insisted that she obey his form. "Can Mrs. Peltz make herself over for a Mrs. Vandewater, or Gittel Stein for a Helen Moore? No more can I make myself over on another person's pattern. I'm different. I got to be what's inside of me. I got to think the thoughts from my own head. I got to act from the feelings in my own heart. If I tried to make myself for a monkey, I'd go crazy in a day."

Unable to comprehend the unreasonable torrent of her changing mood, he said very gently: "I met your people on their grounds, as one of them. And you must also learn to meet mine as one of them."

"God from the world! How he fools himself!" thought Sonya, staring at him too stunned to speak.

"Maybe, for a while, my dear," he hesitated, fumbling for words, "it might be better for a while, if you saw principally only my friends, and that we do not mix our circles. It is not that your friends are inferior to mine. You and I are one in the sight of God. And so are our friends. But I—unfortunately, I have a family tradition, which to some extent I have to live up to. That makes it necessary that you, as my wife, should be able to meet my friends in their way."

"You say that my friends and your friends should better not meet. Well, at least my friends, with all their East Side manners, don't insult people. And what's more, the sight of God, in your eyes, is only your family tradition, whatever that is—"

He stretched an appeasing hand to hers and tried to reason with her, but she moved her hand away.

They looked at each other with strange eyes.

18

The Crumbling Temple

Sonya and Manning, tricked into matrimony, were the oriental and the Anglo-Saxon trying to find a common language. The over-emotional Ghetto struggling for its breath in the thin air of puritan restraint. An East Side savage forced suddenly into the strait-jacket of American civilization. Sonya was like the dynamite bomb and Manning the walls of tradition constantly menaced by threatening explosions.

And so, for the first time in the history of the Manning family, its placid routine had been upset by a temperamental bride. Manning was gentleness and forbearance itself to all of Sonya's erratic moods. Her very unreasonableness drew her to him the more. He found his wife more elusive, more incomprehensible, more unattainable, after marriage than before.

Whenever the maze of misunderstanding between them became hopelessly tangled, Manning took refuge in compassion and toler-ance for her ignorance and lack of tradition. When she had shamed him and his guests at the reception, he had thought:

"Poor child! How can I expect her to comport herself like an American, like"—he hesitated even in his thought—"like a lady?"

But there were times when the atmosphere became so overcharged with Sonya's emotionalism that Manning decided that the sooner they got back to their work at the settlement, the better.

"Shall I get your office ready for you?" he asked at supper one evening. "Next Monday we might start on our program for the winter."

For answer, Sonya jumped up and hugged him. Her cheek seemed to cling to his and her breath was hot on his neck.

"There, there!" he said gently, setting her aside. "With a great work before you, you'll not be so restless."

Glowing with zeal for their mission of regeneration, they rode downtown together in the subway. As Sonya looked at the jostling strap-hangers, a warm feeling rushed into her heart. With the joy of an exile just released from a long bondage among strangers, she gazed at her own people. Out in the old familiar Ghetto streets, every face was a lamp of light after the grey fog of smothering respectability on Madison Avenue. The raucous noises of hucksters, screaming newsboys and brawling children were like a burst of music after the muffled voices of servants, with their "Yes, madam," and "No, madam."

She felt like going over to the passers-by and crying out: "I'm here again! I'm home again!" as though she had been away for ages from her own.

At sight of the settlement, the beacon-light of the neighborhood, Sonya darted ahead of Manning. With shining eyes, she leaped up the steps two at a time. The romance that had once shimmered about the walls of the place throbbed for her again. It was the same, yet not quite the same—more sober, more everyday. "Is it because I'm married?" she asked herself whimsically.

In the office, she saw that her desk and its fittings were the same as Manning's. She looked up at him gratefully for his significant gift that made her feel they were co-workers. She sat back in her chair and turned to her husband with a formal mock-manner, as though she were his old secretary again:

"What's the business to-day, Mr. Manning?"

"Model tenements for model couples," he smiled.

At this gleam of response, she bounded from her desk and settled herself on the arm of his chair.

"I can't hold myself in any longer," she cried. "I'm so on fire to do something—something real."

She drew him to the window and pointed to the swarming masses below.

"Ah, my beautiful philanthropist, look—look only on them all! I am they, and all these people are me. I feel what they feel. I want what they want. All they want is a little bit of love, a little bit of beauty. Dearest, all we've got to think out is how to change your millions into love and beauty."

"Don't be so over-emotional, dear," he admonished, feeling none the less warmed in the radiance of her ardor. "To accomplish anything, you have to work on the plane of reason."

"*Oi, weh*, school teacher! How can I reason? I'm in love with the people."

"Be in love, dear. Idealize the people all you can. We need ideals. We need love. But we have to start with common sense."

"*Nu*, I can't be so cold in the heart and clear in the head, like you Americans! But tell me anyway, what are your common sense ideas?"

He was delighted with her open state of mind and at once launched forth on his hobby:

"This settlement is not founded on blind impulse and mere good intentions. I have had social experts make for me a scientific survey of the needs of the neighborhood, and one by one we meet those needs on the plane of reason."

The words "social experts," "scientific survey," "plane of reason," were to her educated phrases that were like icy winds over her enthusiasm. But she controlled her longing to refute his platitudes and listened with outward passivity.

"In this settlement you'll find every phase of social service. Take a stroll through the building. Study our activities and concentrate on those where you can fit in best."

"Fine!" She grasped his hand, glad to escape from this homily. "I don't look yet like a dignified Mrs. Manning. So I can get around unobserved, and tell you what I see."

As she stepped out into the passageway, the institutional character of the building suddenly depressed her. "Till now, the settlement was the office, with Manning together," she thought. "How cold it looks without him by my side!" Why, it was almost as chilling as a school building, or an old ladies' home that she had once seen!

Across the hall, a door was held ajar by a knot of late-comers, who were waiting for the teacher to finish her demonstration before taking their seats. Screened by these girls, Sonya looked in. On the blackboard was the subject of the lesson: "Milkless, butterless, eggless cake."

The teacher held up a dark, soggy loaf and expounded enthusiastically:

"Class, this cake will feed a family of six, and all it costs is nine and an half cents! That makes a dessert for a cent and a half per person."

A pale, anemic girl got up: "Teacher, without milk, without butter, without eggs, what strength is there in the cake?"

"Whom should we fool with such a cake—our own stomachs?" commented another girl timidly.

"You can't afford plum pudding. Wouldn't you rather have a cheap dessert than none at all?" returned the teacher crushingly.

"Yes," thought Sonya, as she stepped away from the door, "better no dessert than to train them to be thankful for cheapness and doing without. I'll change all this. No more milkless, butterless, eggless cakes for the poor when I take hold of this work. I'll teach those teachers something. The poor also got a palate in their mouth!"

She wanted to flee to Manning at once, to point out to him the waste of such faked, futile home economy; but on her way, she glimpsed through a half-open door a better-dressed group of women. "Evidently social workers," she thought, noting the stiff-tailored, graceless severity of their clothes, the school-teacher tightness about their lips, the self-conscious look of virtue in their eyes.

"What is there so terrible about professional goodness that makes them look so hard, so ugly?" Sonya asked herself. "Even Hollins' art couldn't warm their coldness and make them beautiful."

Again concealing herself, this time behind a pillar, she listened. By the very voice, she knew that this lecturer was the rigid woman in a white starched collar who directed the "friendly visiting."

"For the sake of the worthy poor, we must guard against impostors—"

The words "worthy poor" made Sonya shudder. She wanted passionately to interrupt, to demand what this uplifter meant by "worthy," but she restrained herself.

"We want to be kind," went on the lecturer; "but for the good of the truly deserving, we must guard against fraud, ladies. Only yesterday afternoon, I walked into a widow's flat and I found her cooking *chicken!* Where the woman got the money for it, I'm sure I can't tell. But there she was, accepting the regular rations for our pensioners—cornmeal, rice, macaroni—and secretly cooking chicken! In another place, where I came in unexpectedly, I found butter and eggs for breakfast. The woman said she had nothing in the house, but when I looked at the pantry shelf, there I saw a frying-pan full of half-fried eggs, where she had shoved it as soon as I entered."

By this time Sonya did not care whether she was seen or not. She turned a violent back to the lecturer and dashed out of the room, slamming the door in such a fury that the seats shook.

"So it's a crime to eat chicken if you get charity," Sonya's thoughts surged hotly. "The taste for butter and eggs should be punished with a sentence in black prison! Worthy poor—those who are content with cornmeal!"

Her resentment leaped beyond control. She could not articulate it. She could not go to Manning in such a rage. So she paced the hallway up and down, to get hold of herself.

All at once, the gymnasium door was burst open by an excited group of girls, and rebellious voices shrilled:

"The impudence of that old maid!"

"This settlement is no orphan asylum to hold us like dogs on a chain!"

"A girl got a right to do what she hell pleases with her own face!"

"Does she want to make us over for left-behind old maids like herself?"

Sonya's mood of excitement was swept up in the tumult of emotion about her. She seized the arm of one of the rebels:

"What's the matter? Tell me."

The girl pointed to the end of the hall.

"Look only, that cat, Rosie, carrying off all the boys! And that Miss Smith done it all."

"How? What? How did she get all the boys?" asked Sonya, fascinated by a Carmen-type factory girl surrounded by a circle of adoring youths. Her rouged cheeks and highly tinted, full lips were flaming like roses. Her robust young body was vibrant in a tight-fitting princess dress that was the last word in Grand Street fashion.

"That snooping Miss Smith made such a fuss over her painted cheeks, she put her out," cried one girl.

"So right away all the fellers got stuck on her like flies on a pot of honey," put in another. "And without the boys, Miss Smith can keep her dancing to herself."

The girls dispersed to the washroom and Sonya turned toward

the gymnasium. The director was ahead of her on a tour of inspection. A glance at the room and he gasped:

"Miss Smith? What's this? Where's your attendance? Why no dancing?"

Tremblingly, with averted gaze, Miss Smith stuttered: "I had to discipline—a girl came with painted cheeks, and—and the boys ran after her."

A hiss of sarcastic derision came from the director:

"Discipline! Is this discipline, an empty dance hall? What will you say to Mr. Manning when he comes around?"

He beat a tattoo with his hand on a table:

"This room has to be filled with boys and girls. Find an attendance—make an attendance—if you want to keep your job."

Now Sonya was all on fire to see how Miss Smith was going to meet the director's challenge.

For a moment, the dancing instructor cowered against the wall like a beaten dog. Then she flashed out of the gymnasium, passed Sonya without seeing her, and charged into the washroom.

"Girls, have you made up your minds to be good?" she smiled ingratiatingly. "You don't want to take an example from Rosie. See how she was turned out."

"Yes—and all the fellers after her," tittered a girl.

"How quick the fellers got stuck on Rose the minute you said her cheeks was redder as ours!" taunted another.

Emboldened by Miss Smith's silence, a girl took out her rouge box from her stocking and began applying color to her face.

"Where should we get our red cheeks—from the fresh air and sunshine in the shop? We got to take our redness from a box."

Loud guffaws and jeers echoed the taunts of the girls. Seeing the last shred of her authority vanishing, Miss Smith began to simper coaxingly:

"Now, girls, stop all that fooling. I am going to give special prizes for the best dancing. A box of nutted candies and two silk handkerchiefs."

She encircled the waist of the ringleader: "Now, dearie, go after the boys and tell them. And, to give every one a fair chance for the prizes, Rosie can come back, too."

Sonya's former rage melted into compassion for Miss Smith's

bitter way of earning her bread. "Her lot is even more galling than that of a Division Street puller-in." she thought. "In Division Street they're plain out for a living—no doing good to nobody. Here she must even lie to herself. Even when she's got to pull the boys and girls by the hair to get her attendance, she still tries to do them good."

Sonya thought on:

"So these are Manning's social experts! So this is their plane of reason—'reason' forced down the throats of the people! Hireling telling lies to hireling! All of them lying to him! But they can't lie to the people."

Before her marriage, she had willfully blinded herself to what was going on in the settlement. It had been enough for her just to be Manning's secretary, thrilling and intoxicating herself with his delusions. She had told herself that his personality must humanize the most inhuman activities of philanthropy. Now she was seeing his settlement, as she had refused to let herself see it before her marriage.

A mood of complete dejection weighed her down. Slowly, in a chastened spirit, she entered the office. She found Manning, with beaming face, immersed in charts and statistics.

"Come!" he cried, beckoning. "Come here, dear! These are the expansion plans for extending the work of the settlement. Do you see that mounting red line? That shows the tremendous increase of attendance in all our departments. The director is asking for funds for more cooking classes, more friendly visiting, a large dance hall."

Suddenly aware that he was doing all the talking, he turned to her:

"And what have you seen?"

Her whole being shut tight, choked with dumbness, her tired voice trailed the words:

"I've seen so much, I can't tell you."

Manning's face lit up. So sure was he of the stimulating good in all his activities, of the inspiring social achievements of his settlement, that Sonya's mere statement she had seen it all spelled unconditional approval. Overwhelmed by the greatness of his work, Sonya would at last find an outlet and there would be peace again in their home.

"Because of what this day has meant in both our lives," he said tenderly, "I'll make available the funds for the whole programme of expansion."

A wild instinct urged Sonya to cry out to him: "Stop it all! Burn up your settlement! It's only waste and worse than waste!" But Hollins' sardonic words flashed through her mind: "Playing with poverty is more exciting than knocking golf balls."

Here was a rich man who might be spending his money on self-indulgence—automobiles, race-horses and champagne. Should she stop his generous hand to the people? What better had she to offer him?

Stunned by the tragic impasse, Sonya slumped into her chair. Her head sank on to her breast and into her darkened eyes came the age-old look that is sometimes seen in the youth of the poor.

"Oi-i-i, weh-h!" The cry broke from her.

All tender solicitude, he put his arms about her.

"Oh, but you *are* tired!" he exclaimed. "You mustn't do so much in one day. For the sake of the great work ahead, you mustn't let your enthusiasm consume you so."

19

Only Paying Up

A bolt of reality was awaiting Sonya the next morning. It was a letter from Honest Abe. The crabbed characters of his uncouth handwriting jumped up at her from the page: "If you don't prompt bring me to-day the thousand dollars that's coming to me, then I'll have to collect to-morrow from your millionaire husband."

The blood seemed to run out of her hands and feet, leaving them as cold as ice. She crumpled the letter and thrust it into her pocket. Guiltily, she turned to Manning to see if he had noted her shock, but he was now absorbed in the director's yearly report and smiling with pleasure over a statistical digest of the attendance in the various clubs and classes.

Unobserved, she put on her hat and coat, slipped out of the building and hurried to Honest Abe. She was ashamed to find, as she approached the pawnshop, that she feared to be seen. She, Sonya, ashamed and afraid! Like some mean criminal with stolen goods, she slunk into the shop. At sight of her, Honest Abe scuttled from behind his counter like the pouncing spider that he was.

"*Nu*, have you got my thousand?" he croaked hoarsely. He showed by his evil sneer of triumph that he knew she did not have the money—that she was in his power.

Sonya took out from her handbag three hundred dollars, her pin money allowance for the month. "That's all I got. I'll pay you out every cent if you'll only wait."

Craftily, he spirited the three hundred dollars into his cash-box. "Why should I wait?" A mocking grin cracked the yellow parchment of his face. "A bargain is a bargain. My dollars helped you hook your millionaire and I should yet wait for my little per cent?"

"If you don't wait," came from the desperate Sonya, "you'll lose everything."

"I lose?"

Honest Abe grinned. The spark that a courageous, triumphant

Sonya had once lighted in him had now wholly vanished. Weakness and helplessness roused the fiend in him. His eyes gloated in the knowledge of his power over his victim. It was as if he felt her soft throat in his bony grasp.

"Yes, you'll lose. If my man gets to know about this deal I'm lost and done for. Then how could I pay you?"

A sardonic smirk twisted the pawnbroker's features. He turned to his safe and drew out the note she had signed, tapped her signature with his hairy finger, "Here I got the signed name from John Manning, the philanthropist, what loves the hand of the poor in his pockets, what loves to see his Jesus Christ face shining in the front page of all the papers—"

"His signed name?" broke in Sonya, white with terror.

"His signed name by the law."

"You old bluffer! I signed this before I married him. Even by law you could only collect on a wife's signature after marriage."

"You are smart. Yes. By legal law I got nothing."

He paused and fixed his gimlet eyes on her, tapping his forehead with his crooked finger. "But I got something to collect on him cheaper and better as courts and lawyers. I got the newspapers and reporters. They work free."

Choked dumb with fright she glared at him. Her mouth opened but no words came from her quivering lips.

"It would be a kindness to God to show the poor how to milk your millionaire for some real money. Only, I got yet too much heart for my business. I feel I went with you in partners to rope in this cow what gives the golden cream and I like your smart little head. I like to hold you for my partner for more business. And since you got no seven hundred dollars you owe me, then sign me this note for only fifteen hundred dollars."

Sonya's eyes darted here and there, like the eyes of an animal in a trap. The appalling danger of signing this new note, of being swept under by a tide of debt with which she could never cope unless she appealed to Manning, stung her into frenzied action. She pulled off her engagement ring, a great solitaire set in platinum, and thrust it at the pawnbroker.

"Take this, my engagement ring, only let me free."

He seized it greedily, screwed a lens into the horrible socket of his right eye and appraised the glittering diamond. In an instant, Honest Abe knew it was worth more than a thousand dollars.

"*Nu*," he parried craftily. "I'll think it over. Let the diamond stay by me." And he slipped it noiselessly into his cash-box.

Sonya's head hung in stricken anguish. She stared blindly at the empty place on her finger. It seemed to have left her hand naked, and suddenly a realization of disaster came to her.

"My engagement ring! I can't! What will John say?" she muttered. Then she sprang at Abe and seized his claw-like hand.

"Give me back the ring," she ordered fiercely.

"*Shah!*" he hissed, leering over her like a foul octopus. "It's mine. It's only paying up what you owe me."

He took out a paper from under the counter and showed it to her: "*Nu*, I'll tear up the thousand dollar note and so we'll be even."

Frenzied, she cried: "No, no! I got to have the ring, or I'll call a policeman." And she struggled against him toward the cash-box.

"Run to the policeman," he jibed. "Take your case to the police court, so in all the papers your millionaire will read about you."

She paused, stunned.

"I got to have the ring back at any price," she gasped.

He looked at her from under his grinning mask of triumph. "Sign the fifteen hundred dollar note, then," he commanded.

Sonya signed.

Honest Abel blotted the note with meticulous care. After he placed it in the safe beyond the girl's reach, he rubbed his hands and shrugged his shoulders. "*Nu*, I got the law of the newspapers and I got yet also now, the law of the courts."

20

The Chasm

For some days Sonya had ceased to go down to the settlement. She had eluded Manning, withholding the impetuous warmth of the old days. Her evasions baffled and roused him. He missed the over-demonstrativeness, the ever-gushing torrent of emotion, that had once embarrassed him. He wanted the old Sonya back. But he tolerantly made excuses for her present mood, not at all perceiving that it was anything but the superficial perversity of a young wife.

He took himself to task and reviewed his daily life with Sonya. Had he been considerate in money matters, in making allowances for her crudity in dealing with guests and servants? Had he been tender in serving her, in maintaining the atmosphere of their romance? He found himself blameless in every detail. He had been as thoughtful of her comfort as any model husband could be.

And yet, why sudden aloofness? She seemed almost deliberately to turn her eyes away from him at table. Several times, she had risen much earlier than he, and in the library, evenings, before retiring, she pored over books, barely noticing his presence. Why, she seemed almost to shun him!

His work suffered. His daily programme became an irksome routine. He could not concentrate as he was accustomed to do. A little frown haunted the placid forehead and his blue eyes were shadowed with restlessness.

On an impulse that was strange to him, he left the settlement early one evening and went home to have a talk with his wife. Astonished not to find her in the library, he sought her upstairs in their room. She was already in bed.

"Are you asleep, dear?" he murmured, bending over her.

A tender feeling rushed over him. How like a little child she looked, tucked there under the covers! Her slender body was half turned over, her face down and the thick hair spread loosely like a shimmer of black satin over the white pillow. A picture of fragile grace she was, as she lay there. Even the round hip, upthrust, seemed frail and childlike to the paternal pity welling in his heart. How he longed to take her in his arms and pour his strength into her!

A network of little lines crinkled the high cheek bones, and the blue eyes softened into a warm smile as he watched her, waiting for her to wake up. But she did not stir. He took up a book—Kant's "Critique of Pure Reason," it happened to be. His efforts to concentrate were in vain. The printed page was blotted out by Sonya's face, enigmatic as it had been for him during the past few days. Looking up, he was startled by a vivid flash of imagination which revealed her naked body through the covers. Her breasts... her hips... her slender flanks... the whiteness of her flesh glowing in contrast to her crown of black hair.

The puritan in him stiffened in alarm. What madness had come over him, what carnal indelicacy possessed him? he questioned, bewildered. But the next moment, he convinced himself that he was sleepy and prepared for bed.

He lay down beside her. Slowly, his arm reached out and hovered over her. A fine hesitancy deterred him from waking her, sublimating his desire. Gently at last his hand closed over her breast. He trembled violently, fighting back the impulse to sweep her up and crush her to him.

Close as he was to her, feeling under his palm the rise and fall of her bosom, he did not suspect that Sonya was awake, as she had been awake when he entered.

She had crept into bed early, hoping for sleep, but knowing only too well that her heart and brain were too racked for sleep. Her worries goaded her more cruelly at night than in the daytime. That afternoon, Honest Abe had stabbed at her again with another blackmailing letter. She had sat shivering in the chilly house, aching to escape—but where? At the settlement the very air was poisoned with the busy-busyness of philanthropists and their hired band of social workers.

As she brooded through sleepless hours, the fear that Manning would find her out and fail to understand became an obsession. How could she make him understand—he whose mind was so clear and straight—that her very crookedness in her evil pact with Honest Abe was at bottom only a consuming love for him? How could she make him, who was so sane, so logical, see the burning madness of her passion, which had destroyed every trace of prudence and self-preservation that she had once had like other people?

And yet she had to tell him about her degrading deal with Honest Abe. She had to tell him, too, that the settlement had become a hideous mockery that she could no longer endure. Her own lies gathered around her, coiling about her throat until they were strangling her.

She was in no mood for caresses now. She wanted to face him and tell him all—know where she stood with him. His hand on her breast, his body edging closer, became an invasion of her soul when it was wrestling with such cruel problems.

Pretending to wake up suddenly, she shook him off with a brusque movement and turned farther away from him to the edge of the bed.

Startled and hurt, he tried to withdraw far over to his side, but his hot desire only drove him closer to her. Again his hand fumbled on her shoulder and slipped into the valley of her breast.

"Don't, don't! I'm so tired! she said sharply, stinging him with the ice of her indifference.

He lay a long while wondering what had happened to the ardent passion of his priestess of romance, who had been so eager to give all to him at Greenwold! A wounded pride that he thought unworthy of him stabbed him to the core. A sensitiveness that forbade him to force himself upon his wife made him seek to control his desire, to calm himself, to try to sleep.

But sleep was impossible to him. And sleep was impossible to Sonya. They lay a long, long time listening with sharpened nerves to each other's breathing. The scent of her young body intoxicated his brain, permeated his senses irresistibly.

Throb by throb, all Manning's attempts at self-control ebbed. The fear of being repulsed again by her made him suffer agonies, but his hand involuntarily reached for her under the covers. To his amazement, instead of a tense, unresponsive body, he found a yielding softness to his touch.

Sonya's mood had imperceptibly changed. Sheer propinquity had softened her resistance. A desperate hope had come to her. Now, if ever, when he desired her so keenly, was the time to confide to him the tortures and humiliations she had suffered from the sordid pact with Honest Abe. Now was the time to open up her soul to her husband and tell him how she had been driven by day and night to win him—how the wild urge to please had seemed to justify lies and self-abasement and all manners of subterfuge. She ached to confess all—everything—only to assure herself how deeply he understood and forgave. A moment of yielding closeness. A moment of love. Then, after such a moment, would be the ideal time to unburden her heart to him.

She turned frankly toward him, laying her cheek against his. In his pleased sense of victory, he abandoned all subtlety. He pressed his hard lips to her lips, and violently strained her to him.

His instant of thrilling triumph was tinged swiftly with shame. He felt vaguely that he should say something to her. But there was nothing at the moment in his puritan heart but an apology for his lust, and silence seemed more delicate. Turning away from her he lay on his back, staring baffled into the dark. What was this sharp sense of guilt that so quickly blotted out his passion? Slowly a wave of physical languor crept up his body, engulfed his brain, and he fell asleep.

Shame and disillusion charged through Sonya. The disaster to her thwarted love was reflected in her wounded, quivering body. Her flesh was raw and hurt by the insult of his incapacity for love. Real love, real tenderness, the imaginative subtlety that makes togetherness beautiful, were not in him.

She had been too enamored, too illusioned, in the first weeks of their honeymoon, to demand anything but the opportunity to give. The coldness, the shallowness, of his emotional nature had seemed to her at first an alluring reserve that impelled her to seek him more and more. Till now, she had felt that behind the rich, still curtain of his puritan austerity was waiting for her a great revelation—a flame of a soul higher and finer than hers. At last the curtain was down. There was no revelation, no flame—only the pale flicker of a burnt-out star, only the winter coldness of a sterile race.

She had expected suns to burst forth at the consummation of their togetherness, and all it had led to was a dark, impenetrable void that none of her ardor could pierce. She knew now that there had never been any real togetherness between them. There had never been on his part any spiritual reaching out to her, any personal seeking that gives life and substance to a love. For all the fire and passion that had rushed out of her heart to him, there had always been a chasm between them. She had been too blind to see till now the furious animosity of temperaments that clashed as theirs clashed. But as she watched him sleeping there beside her with his calm saint-like face, she knew that just as fire and water cannot fuse, neither could her Russian Jewish soul fuse with the stolid, the unimaginative, the invulnerable thickness of this New England puritan.

With her, passion marched naked: with him always veiled—shame always when the veil was drawn.

All night long, she tossed about, choking with outrage—burning up with hate of the man sleeping so serenely. Anger mounted sullenly in her as the hurt of her roused and unsatisfied desire tore through her body like a torturing fury. By morning she had reached a pitch of smouldering wrath, ready to flare out at the slightest provocation against her treacherous saint.

She could no longer endure lying there beside him, her wrought-up nerves racked with sleeplessness. Before dawn, she rose and dressed hurriedly to escape from their stifling bedroom. Through empty, forbidding rooms she paced and finally fled to the yard for a sight of the sky, a breath of air. When she turned into the house again, he was at the breakfast table, waiting formally for her to appear.

Innocent of any suspicion of misunderstanding, he beamed with pale dignity.

"Good morning, dear. Are you coming with me to the settlement to-day?"

Sonya looked at him coldly, wondering how a man in whose arms she had lain, a man she had loved and lived with, could be so obtuse. Did he not realize how he had hurt her last night? Could he not feel the blow he had dealt to their love?

"I am through with your settlement," she flung with finality.

"What do you mean?" He straightened up severely and stared at her. "Have you lost interest in the work?"

"Settlement business ain't work. It's only a make-believe, a fake. Your settlement is a lie, like all settlements are lies."

"Why—Sonya!" He leaned across the table, rendered almost speechless by her heresy, the offense against his whole theory of life.

"Last night I wanted to tell you things about myself, only you fell asleep so quick." She paused to see whether he understood the cause of her bitterness, but he remained untouched—self-centered in his righteous amazement. "Settlements!" she challenged, bringing her fist down on the table. "It's fit for jokes in comic papers, the whole show-off of uplift work. And you make printed reports from it and read your own lies for the gospel truth. I thought your settlement would be different. But your own report that you're so proud of is a comic paper in itself."

"Sonya—is it you or I who have gone mad?" came through tight lips. "What is there so comic about my report?"

"Friendly visits! Five hundred and fifty of them—five hundred and fifty insults added to the injuries of the poor! The large attendance at your social room! Do you know how your hired workers 'pull in' the boys and girls by hook or crook? I can tell you—I know!"

He stared, baffled. "You? Good God! You were so eager to join me!"

"Yes, but it was a lie," she hurled at him. "Only one of my lies, because I was in love with you, fool that I was!"

"Lies?" he gasped. "What? When?"

Sonya clutched at her bosom, fighting for breath, forcing back tears. Even in her fury she wondered how she had ever been capable of so much passion for this man.

"I don't know how it began, one lie after another. But it was all because I was so crazy for you. I can't tell you a thing that you'd understand. Each one is worse than the next. But—yes—I will tell you this: I got you by lies. I got to pay Honest Abe, the pawnbroker, fifteen hundred dollars. He—he tortures me with his blackmail. He—"

Manning made a quick movement toward her. "And you had this burden on your mind all this time?" came in a tender voice, as he put his arm around her. "Why didn't you tell me, dear? You know, darling, I never wish you to lack for anything again. You know what I have is yours."

Sonya drew herself away from him, violently, unable to speak.

"Poor child!" Manning grew more tender. "You are nervously overwrought. The only thing I cannot understand is why you have not told me before. Was it for some of your family that you are in debt? Tell me, dear."

"Family? Nonsense! I've done nothing for my family!" She flung the words at him with an up-raised hand. "I'm no charity saint like you. I've done nothing for anybody. I lied—lied—lied! For me—me—myself! God! How I lied! How I tore and twisted everything in me—only to get you!"

"So much you loved me," he said fatuously, "that you would suffer all this to get me!" Then with sudden harsh suspicion: "Or was it my money you wanted?"

"Money? You fool! I wanted *you!*"

"Wanted me? You got me."

"What have I got? A house like a prison. Servants like jailers. Have I got a lover? No! I got a husband. I'm starving. I'm dying under your very eyes. And you don't see it. You don't know it. I want love—love. I cannot live without love!"

Something deep down in him answered the cry of her youth. He made an instinctive movement toward her. He wanted to seize her in his arms, crush her to him, make her utterly his. But the pride of generations of Mannings held him back as the torrent of her insulting reproaches burst forth.

"I lied to get *you.* But what did you get me for? To make me over? To make me part of your social experiment—part of your Christian reform? . . .

"I am a liar. But you are a cheat. You go around preaching democracy and the brotherhood of man. But you don't want my people. You never loved me for me, myself. You only love dead traditions. Your only religion is your family pride."

Exalted by her anger, Sonya was as on a mountain-top, judging, weighing and seeing utter loss.

"What have I lied to get? A cold fish. A high-brow. An educated hypocrite. A man who talks high words about the soul and hasn't spirit enough to get even my body!

"If we had children, how would I know that they'd be flesh and blood, or something like you? The lowest from my people that you sneer at, has more life in his body, more fire in his soul than you, with all your higher education."

His tradition, his background, all that he stood for in a formal world of convention bade him scorn her. But her words bore down upon him with a resistless force, held him listening against his will with an intentness with which he had never listened to her before. He felt suddenly near to life as if Sonya were tearing away veils between him and reality. Perhaps at this moment he was more truly in love with Sonya, more held by the untamed passion of her spirit than ever before. She ceased to be merely a beautiful body, but became for him woman—the sphinx—the eternal mystery. The girl whom he thought so simple suddenly loomed over him—an unknown personality.

"Last night, how I wanted you to love me! How I needed love! But not love as you know it. I wanted to be you and you to be me. I wanted from you life and you gave me death. Your kisses and embraces last night were not love."

"What was it then?"

"It was the murder of love. The kind of love a man goes to a street-woman for. I don't sell my love. I give it."

"You're insane, Sonya," he said coldly.

"You've lost complete control of yourself. We will end this discussion, here and now, and continue it only when you know what you are saying and can talk reasonably. I assure you, I do not hold you responsible for anything you have said now."

"You can't shut me up. I know what I am saying. I'm not yet crazy. You must listen. You shall listen. I lied because the world cheated me of my youth. It burned in me for beauty and here I was trapped by poverty in a prison of ugliness—dirt—soul-wasting want. What chance had I to tear myself out from the black life of poverty but to marry myself rich? If I waited till I could save up enough from my wages for one Hollins dress, I'd be old and wrinkled and baldheaded and toothless as Rockefeller. I couldn't wait. I'm young. I wanted things now—now—now! I wanted life. I wanted love. I wanted beauty while I was still young enough to live and to love and enjoy the beautiful. Why shouldn't I lie for what my youth cried?"

She came close to him and snapped her fingers in his face in a gesture of utter contempt. "Do you hear? Do you understand, my high-brow husband? I owe a pawnbroker fifteen hundred dollars to get you."

Angry at the shame her confession roused in her, she suddenly pulled from her bosom the letter demanding fifteen hundred dollars, the amount of the note she had signed to Honest Abe. She flung it at him and demanded, "Read this."

With a dazed frown, he took the letter and read it twice before he grasped its significance. Then his face grew harsh as he turned to her.

"You owe this pawnbroker fifteen hundred dollars—*my name* involved! What does it mean?"

His grimness hardened her.

"I needed money. I needed to have my room beautiful when you came to see me. Honest Abe only lent me a hundred, but he made me sign to give him five hundred after—after—"

"After what?" he cried.

"After I married you. But I was ashamed to ask you for money right away, so he made me sign a bigger note."

Manning looked again at the letter.

"I see," he said, cold and frowning. "You borrowed on your prospects. Is that in the note?"

"Yes."

"It must be paid instantly. My name in the hands of *that Jew!*"

His scorn scorched and crushed her, as he almost leaped out of the dining room to the study where the safe was. He returned in a few minutes.

"You must come immediately with me to the Jew's place."

"I won't. I won't take orders."

"Very well," he cut and froze her with his icy tone. "I'll go alone. Your Jew won't refuse cash."

He paused and penetrated her with the steely coldness of his cold blue eyes. "Now," he panted, for the first time betraying emotion, "now I see why you dared not look me in the face."

"Then you don't understand nothing?" she pleaded.

"There seems nothing to understand except that I'm through with you."

"What do you mean?" came from pallid lips. "You want we should divorce?"

Colder than ever, the puritan glowered at her.

"Divorce!" he said with frigid contempt. "There has never been a divorce in the Manning family. I am married to you. We stay under one roof. But we are through."

"Why, why?" she shrieked wildly, snatching at his hand.

But he folded his arms and sat in stolid silence, a bleak smile on his lips. So this was his priestess of romance—the woman of the people that was to bring him new life, for his work—a schemer, an adventuress! He felt his blood congeal to ice as he stared at her.

"Hit me, hurt me, yell at me, but don't sit there condemning me, you dead lump of self-righteousness!"

Like granite he sat, a grim judge who had already passed judgment.

"You faking saint—bloodless higher-up! You *allrightnik!* You never lied in your life! You never did wrong! You never budged from the straight footsteps of your ancestors, because you're as dead in your stony goodness as those in their graves!"

A withering pity, an insulting toleration, showed in his face as he got up without a word and left the room. She heard him slam the front door and hurry down the brownstone steps.

Stunned—outraged—Sonya stumbled blindly to her room. On the way, she met the butler. His pug-nosed face, stiff with silly dignity, thrust silent condemnation at her. She could have struck him, the repulsive blockhead! But she made her way up the stairs. On the first landing, an insolent titter sounded and an assembly of inquisitive maids scattered, throwing backward glances of veiled criticism. Never before in the history of the Manning household had a quarrel been heard, and wherever she turned she could feel them gloating greedily over the scandal.

The corridor leading up to her room was lined with the portraits of Manning ancestors. They seemed to step out of their frames and follow her, grimly reproving. She did not know which she hated more—the veiled contempt of the pussy-footed inferiors, the servants; or the trap-like mouths, the gimlet eyes, of the arrogant higher-ups, his ancestors.

"I, Sonya Vrunsky—I a Manning!" she cried at her rebellious

face in the mirror. "I, married to that empty, stupid higher-up, that self-righteous cold fish that calls himself a man? Never would I let the ashes of such a bloodless name smother me."

She snatched a pillow and hurled it at the painted features of the pious great-aunt who had refused to wear silk that had come in a Sunday boat.

"I, a living, breathing human, tied up for life to a cold mummy like him? I stay with a man I hate and despise, under one roof? No—not all the marriage rites in the world, not all the dead pride of Manning's virtuous ancestry that never knew divorce, can keep me in this prison a moment longer!"

And without stopping to pack or to take any of her belongings, she seized her hat and coat and rushed out.

21

"For the Truth They Burn You"

Darkness! Helplessness! Sonya felt herself losing consciousness of everything except the terrible sensation of sinking—sinking—lower and lower into an unknown, unutterable sea of darkness.

Slowly, like a drowning man rising to the surface again, she felt breath by breath her consciousness returning. She opened her eyes. She looked about her. Where was she? What had happened to her? How did she get here? Thread by thread she tried to piece together her straggling thoughts.

She had had a fight with Manning that morning. She had left his home after that. She taken the bus and ridden till it stopped. Then walked till she was too tired to walk any further. Evening was coming on, but she was too tired to walk back and find a place to sleep for the night.

She felt like something dying that cannot bear the sight or sound of life.

Her body was—spent. But her mind could not stop thinking. Her mind went on and on. Physical exhaustion only sharpened the throbbing nerves of thought and feeling.

She saw with burning clearness every detail of her life with Manning. With an agonizing reality she relived her love-making, her marriage, the slow piling up of disillusion upon disillusion until the final crash when all that had once been love had turned to hate.

Her mind kept going round and round in the narrow circle of her past. Like a tantalizing tune that cannot be shaken off, it cried in her, "Waste—waste—emptiness and waste!"

"Ach! Only to stop thought! Only to deaden feeling!" She struggled vainly with herself. "Is there no bottom to futility?"

But like a piece of machinery that has been wound up, so her mind kept going on and on, without her volition.

A picture of herself as she had been in Mrs. Peltz's dirty, little hall-room! She saw herself a living thing caught in the trap of poverty, ugliness and dirt. Her youth cried in her: "Escape! Escape! Push—push—up—up—up where the higher-ups live! Up where the worry for bread and rent does not exist! Up where there's life and love and beauty!"

Then Manning, the prince of higher-ups, came. He would be her savior. With him she would realize all that her heart desired. Then everything in her centered on one thing—one thing only—to catch on to him—to marry him!

Well, she had achieved what she had set out to achieve. She had made herself Mrs. Manning. And what had she gotten out of her conquest? Nothing—nothing. How unreal, how less than nothing were the million emotions she had experienced in her mad infatuation! She felt like a lunatic who had gone up in a balloon to grasp the colors of the rainbow, suddenly awakening with a crash back to earth. The only thing real in her unreal experience was the gnawing sense of nothingness.

Hours passed, but still Sonya sat no more moving than to sink lower her head. The far-off clatter of a milkwagon, the rumbling of a car roused her slightly. It was night no longer. With the coming of morning her introspection merged into the immediate practical question of what to do now.

Her dreams had fallen but she was still left. She had to go on with what there was left of her. Resolutely, she rose to her feet and went back to the subway.

The trains were crowded with people bound for work. In the faces of all about her Sonya recognized the hounded look of those driven by the struggle for a living.

Her heart tightened with fear. "Ach! I wanted to run away from the worry for bread and here I am back again to where I started.

"Who can help me get a job?" she asked herself, remembering that she had less than fifty dollars in her purse.

A quick thought of Hollins flashed through her mind. She was not Manning's wife any longer, so she could go to Hollins. He would understand her. To him she would go for advice. She realized with surprise how the months of absorption in Manning had blotted out the thought of Hollins. With new clarity, she felt now that Hollins was infinitely the superior man, "an artist with a born understanding for crazy people like me," she thought. The man who had dressed her so divinely for the love of beauty, who had valued her for the very things that Manning hated, he would help her now in her great need.

A new light leaped into her eyes as she murmured, "To Hollins I will go immediately."

With buoyant step and beaming face she got out of the subway and almost ran in the direction of Hollins' workshop. She had not gone very far when she stopped herself with a sudden bitter realization that this was quite a different crisis from her first need of Hollins.

"Then I was all inspiration and fire. I didn't ask him for anything—only clothes. But now I'm a beggarin. He'd either have to take money out of his pocket, or give me a job. And I can't stand that—not from him."

In an instant, she was dashed down from the heights and driven forth, a bruised and broken Hagar wandering in a wilderness toward an unknown goal.

"*Oi weh!*" She clutched at her bosom. "I want so much to go to Hollins. I'm dying for a little understanding. Only I can't—I can't go to him—because—because—"

To her own amazement, she burst out weeping in the middle of the street.

"Anywhere else I'll go—to Gittel, Lipkin, anybody, anywhere, to get help. But not from him."

A torn and tragic figure, Sonya rushed up the steps of the *Ghetto News,* half an hour later. She who had always been so fastidious, so super-sensitive about the details of her dress, looked now a dishevelled, crumpled thing. Her face was stained, her eyes ringed, black and hollow with sleeplessness. Wisps of her hair stuck to her forehead and the coat she had thrown on in a hurry was buttoned all awry.

"Gittel, '*that Jew,*' he said to me—'*your Jew!*' With all his high words of brotherhood, it came out, his hidden hate of the Jew."

"Who? What? For God's sake, talk connected!" Gittel peered bewildered through thick-lensed glasses. "You jump in like a crazy from a lunatic asylum."

"Me he holds for the same thing like the crook, the bloodsucker, Honest Abe!"

"God from the world! Who are you talking about?"

"Manning, the cold fish, the *allrightnik!* I left him."

Gittel's dull eyes flamed up with cruel satisfaction.

"*Nu?* Was I right your saint would find you out?"

Immersed in her tragedy, Sonya did not see the triumphant gleam in Gittel's eyes, so she rushed right on.

"He didn't find out anything. I *told* him everything myself, but it was like talking to a stone wall. What hurt me the most was the quickness with which he rushed to clear his name. *His name,* that's all he cares about!"

Gittel's quick mind pieced together the broken bits of information that Sonya threw at her hysterically. For the first time since she had known the girl, she felt justified in her condemnation of Sonya as a vampire, a love pirate, who would some day meet her deserts. Her own mediocrity seemed vindicated by Sonya's downfall. She, Gittel had never climbed, so she had never fallen.

"Tell me all. How did it happen?" urged Gittel, feigning sympathy only to hear more of the other's heartbreak. And as Sonya went on laying bare her wounded pride, the bitter pangs of her disillusion, the spinster found balm for her own inferiority that had never dared wrest from the years one live experience, one mad moment of surrender to her ache for love.

"The Anglo-Saxon coldness, it's centuries of solid ice that all the suns of the sky can't melt. Nobody can tell what that frozen iciness is, except those that got to live with it. Think of the bloodless inhumanity of it, when we hate each other like poison, when our eyes stab each other like daggers, he wants me to stay with him yet under one roof, for the sake of his puritan pride that there was never a divorce in his family!"

Gittel drank in every word, making honey out of Sonya's bitterness.

"*Nu,* so what are you going to do?" asked the older woman with smooth sympathy, envious even of the pangs and hurts of this broken romance.

"This office feels like warm heaven to me now," cried Sonya, her face beaming again with recuperative youth. She ran her hands over the broken plaster on the wall, seized a handful of papers loaded with dust, picked up a grimy chair. "*Oi weh! Gottuniu!* Give me dirt, rags, confusion, only never to live again with pussy-footed servants and dustless rooms. I've come back to my own people, to my real work. Where's Lipkin?"

Gittel's smouldering jealousy flared into swift anger.

"Your own people!" she taunted. "Who are your own people, after you married yourself to a Christian?"

"Well—" stammered Sonya. "But my work—"

"And what's your 'work' but to vamp men?" flared Gittel. "Didn't you kill Lipkin—make mush of your Anglo-Saxon saint? They all said his settlement began to go to pieces the minute you got hold of him."

With a gesture of scorn, she spat on the floor;

"*Pfui!* What are you after—*more* limelight? The papers got tired featuring the poor slum girl who married a millionaire. So you're putting on another setting for your stage!"

"You false thing! And I thought you my friend."

Sonya leaped to her feet, ready to rush out of the place, when she saw Lipkin in the doorway.

"You here, Sonya?" He paled in amazement at the sight of her.

"I want to see you in your office." She followed him to the dingy room and closed the door, so that Gittel should not hear her.

So stunned was Lipkin by the haggard, tear-stained Sonya that he stared dumbly, his hands twitching.

"I want my old column back. Can you fix it for me?" Sonya pleaded.

"Column—you again for that work?"

"I can do it a million times better now. You'll see. I left Manning like I stand, like I am, with empty hands, and I got to get a job at once."

Lipkin shrivelled with embarrassment. He looked at the woman he had once worshipped, fallen from her heights now, with a sordid request for a job. Pathos and terror fought in his breast at this specter of his old love that had come to put an end to his illusions. His instinctive horror of coping with reality caused him to hate the sudden responsibility thrust upon him.

"I am not the boss," he stuttered, shamed at his own inadequacy to meet the situation like a man. "The publisher's the boss. I got to ask him. The column was discontinued, you see."

"It's a matter of life and death for me to get something to do—at once. Ain't you the editor? Can't you make for me a new job?"

"*Ut*, now you take me by the neck to help you!" A harsh rasp came into his voice as he muttered in querulous protest. "Why did you sell yourself for that faker's millions, only to come back to me?"

Sonya's chest caved in with her sinking spirits. His failure to respond to her need bruised her at the moment—a treacherous betrayal of the love he once vowed to her. She could not defend herself; she could not speak. But she felt her heart one great sob.

"*Oi*, how you look now!" came from Lipkin, unable to hide his shock of revulsion at the change in her. Her broken spirit, her poverty, made him shrink from her now, as once she in her power had shrunk from him. "You're like a ghost from the grave. How could a Jewish paper take you on now? You killed yourself with the people after your Christian marriage."

For a long, long moment, Sonya looked him squarely in the face, straight into his eyes. Her lips parted as if to speak, but no words came to her. Buttoning up her coat, she turned, head high, and fled from the room.

She walked blindly through the streets of the East Side. Again the thought of Hollins came to her, and this time in a clearer flash of intuition. She realized with finality that she could not go to Hollins in the bankruptcy of her spirit. She could not go to him as a suppliant for help. Something deep down in her that she could not understand—she knew it was not pride—it was not anything she could name; but she could not show herself to Hollins while she was merely an uncreative failure.

"Never will I go to him less than an equal. But how can I make myself with Hollins alike? I got to do something, make something of myself. But how? What?"

She paused in front of a Grand Street shop window. With an abstracted gaze, she scanned the display of gaudy, cheap dresses. How horrible they looked! What a complete antithesis to the Hollins clothes to which she had so quickly and so naturally become accustomed! Her mind leaped to an obvious conclusion.

"Why can't I do something to make me with my love of clothes?

It will tear me to pieces if I don't work it out into something—this need for the beautiful. That's what Jaky Solomon had the sense to do."

The whole history of Jacques Hollins' romantic rise from his Division Street basement to his palace of fashion on Fifth Avenue surged in her memory like bubbling champagne. The eternal urge of her race to rise—to rise—to transmute failure, heartbreak and despair into a driving will to conquer—swept her up to the heights of hope again.

"I can't go to Paris, like Jaky Solomon did, but there's a school of design in New York. There's where I'll learn it all."

Without loss of time, she found the address in the telephone book and summoned a cab as if she still had John Manning's fortune behind her.

She darted up the steps of an imposing granite building entirely devoted to the various arts of design. In the office of the dress department she paused, then charged up to the desk marked "DIRECTOR."

"I want to make myself for a designer," she panted breathlessly. "How quickly can I learn it?"

A man with a thick neck and small eyes set close together, looked up and answered stolidly:

"Our course is two years, and the tuition fee is three hundred dollars a year. Payments must be made in advance."

"Three hundred dollars down! Two years!" She stared at him imploringly and fumbled at the few remaining bills in her purse. "Only forty dollars I got. Can't I pay you out later on?"

He frowned unsympathetically. "If we went in for that sort of arrangement, where would we land? Our rule is cash down. Otherwise, we'd go out of business in no time."

The man's callous indifference to her need stung her like a personal insult. Hollins had spoiled her for such sordid dickering.

"Is it only for business you teach how to make beautiful things?" she demanded.

A snicker shook the plump form of the director. "The Fifth Avenue shops are designing for love, aren't they? If you don't believe me, go to Jacques Hollins and find out how much he charges for a gown!"

Sonya's cheeks became bloodless. An engulfing faintness silenced her. The very mention of Hollins' name depressed her now. Even this thick-necked director knew enough to admit that Hollins was first in design. How long would she have to struggle before she came up to him?

"What's happened to me?" she asked herself in a grip of fear. "I—Sonya Vrunsky—turned down by a man! I used to be able to get anything I wanted when I only wanted it enough. All doors used to fling open for me the minute I knocked. And now they all turn me down." Her hands clenched in panic. "Is it because I no longer believe in myself? Did that frozen philanthropist kill the fire in me?"

Walking down the steps of the School of Design, her knees weakened. She leaned against a pillar for breath and remembered she had not eaten all day. At the first hotel, she dragged her self in, ill-looking and distraught, and asked for a room. She felt she must throw herself down somewhere and rest a moment before she could eat.

The clerk scrutinized her suspiciously.

"Where's your baggage?" he asked with an offensive leer.

"I have none, but I'll pay in advance." Sonya fingered nervously at her purse.

The bill that she thrust at the clerk seemed to embarrass him. He turned it over, clearing his throat and frowning.

"In the circumstances, I must ask for references," he said formally.

"Why references?" she flared. "Ain't my money good enough?"

"We have no more vacant rooms," he evaded, with dignified finality.

"Are you refusing me because I got no baggage, or because I got no escort?" Sonya asked in bitter revolt.

"Both," he answered. And he shrugged his shoulders and turned away.

"For the truth they burn you!" From some deep racial well of her being, strange words that she vaguely remembered flashed across her mind. "For the truth they burn you!" she repeated. "God from the world! For the first time in my life, I wanted to be honest with myself. For the first time I wanted to lift myself out of my lies. And that's why they're all down on me."

Outside in the street she found she was crying. The clerk's insulting manner had been like a blow from a bully. And she was powerless to defend herself now. She was helpless—shelterless.

Lipkin's and Gittel's bitter words burned through her again: "Why did you sell yourself for that faker's millions?" ... "You killed yourself with the people after your Christian marriage." ... "Your work? What's your work but to vamp men?"

Sheer exhaustion seemed to drag her to the ground and she leaned against a cold iron lamp-post for support.

A cry broke from her: "Why is it, when you learn already a little about life, then the chance to live is gone from you?"

Her very despair roused her for battle. "My chance to live gone from me? Are these pin-headed worms I met to-day my chance to live?

"Lipkin—Gittel—my once-called friends, what are they? Vultures ready to pounce on my bad luck, only because I had the brains to rise over them."

She started to walk on and then paused, lifting a tragic face to the sky.

"Where in this whole world can I turn to? Even the gods are against me, because I couldn't stand the mean luck to which I was born. Because I wanted to grab by force love, power, the place higher up, the gods got jealous of me."

Rebellion clenched her fists.

"I did what I did because I had to," she cried.

As Don Quixote once tilted at windmills, so Sonya Vrunsky flung out her arms in battle with the deaf and dumb air.

"I'll fight the whole world against me. I alone, without a roof over my head. I am I. Now that I've no one to hold on to, I have me, myself. In me is my strength. I alone will yet beat them all."

She walked on. A few blocks distant was a woman's hotel. Sonya knew it was the only place she could get immediate shelter. The room to which she was shown was narrow, cell-like, devoid of any touch of individuality. As she flung herself on the white-enameled bed and looked at the blank walls, she felt that the dark, dirty little rooms of Mrs. Peltz's Essex Street tenement were far more livable than this hard, institutional cleanliness deprived of one breath of human warmth.

But the complete sense of desolation did not take hold of Sonya until she got down to the dining room. The sea of segregated women buzzing at all the tables around, made her feel lost in a desert of nonentities, as in a swarm of neuter bees. There were all kinds of professional and business women and working-girls. But they had one thing in common—abnormal repression of femininity. Their faces were devitalized, ardor-less—the faces of women who have shut love out of their lives.

"Self-condemned nuns, without even the satisfaction of religion," thought Sonya. "It's a living sepulcher of old maids. Who but Anglo-Saxon women could so sterilize out of their hearts the hunger for men that makes life? This prison of females is more killing than a settlement!"

Back in her cell of a room, the fear of her uncertain future thickened about her like a stifling fog.

It came to her with a ghastly shock that she was like one who had been at a gay party, the center of light and color and song. Suddenly the lights had been switched off and she found herself in the dark, alone.

"I had in my two hands everything I once dreamed and longed for when I was in the Essex Street tenement by Mrs. Peltz. I had everything—husband, house, beautiful clothes. Why did I have to leave it all?"

She paused in her thought and then answered herself: "Because I really had nothing. Even my love for him was only a lie, because you can't love a man that drives you to be different from what you are. Never with him was I me, myself!

"From him I wanted beauty, and I lost even the little beauty that was in me, because I lived a lie with him. There is no beauty for me unless I can express myself, unless I can be in the open what I am."

She was determined to get out of the dehumanizing atmosphere of the woman's hotel. The very next day she would look for a job. With a humility that was strange to her, she conceded that she would have to begin at the bottom.

"Anything—anywhere—waitress, typewriter, saleswoman—any work I'll start with—only where there are living people, not uplifters and not old maids."

22

The Feel of the Beautiful

For several days, Sonya had been struggling to adapt herself to the soul-killing work of a waitress. When she applied for the job at the Herald Square buffet, the front eating-room had seemed so warm and inviting, so superior to most restaurants, that she felt herself lucky to be taken on immediately. But contact with the tough girls who worked with her, the fat, vulgar cook in his steaming kitchen, filled her with disgust.

Bringing in the food to the customers was not half so trying as removing the messy dishes. But the thing that most revolted her aesthetic sense was the sight of chewing mouths—of gluttonous faces bent over full plates—which she had to see from morning to night.

Remembering the detailed orders seemed an impossible task. Many a time when a diner asked for griddle cakes and she brought him ham and eggs, she would have been discharged if it had not been for the indulgent attitude of the men. At first, she was grateful for the smiles and apparent friendliness with which they excused her awkward mistakes. But she soon discovered the motive of the men's forbearance with her.

After one of her earliest errors, the customer looked up with a wink.

"That's all right, dearie," he said, grinning. He pushed forward a thick paw and rubbed her wrist exploringly with his finger.

Sonya turned away angrily. She served the next order to a quiet-looking older man, who glanced at her with fatherly interest. She was about to confide to this man the annoyance she had suffered from the last customer. But even as she bent over the table to place his food, he deliberately moved his leg against hers in a gross, lewd way. Her whole body quivered with revolt. Grinding her teeth together to gain self-control, she fled to the boss to tell him of the outrage.

"Some of those men should be kicked out," she cried. "They're low-down beasts."

The red-faced, thick-necked boss would have silenced her sharply, but he knew the value of a pretty waitress, so he smoothed appeasingly:

"Me insult my good customers—preach them out of my store when they come for big orders of steaks and chops! No, girlie!" He put a hairy, gorilla-like hand upon her shoulder. "It's up to the girl to look after herself."

She had to cope with a dozen vulgar attempts at flirtation in the first day or two. Men approached her in all sorts of ways. They tried to discover if she lived with her family, or alone. They asked her to ride in their machines. And the more crude ones invited her flatly to come to their apartments.

Sonya would have thrown up her job in a moment. But she felt that she must prove to herself her ability to stand on her own feet. She had left Manning and the ghetto had shut her out. So she must stick tight to whatever work presented itself. She must expiate her madness until she had found some way to learn the art of designing, the one work in which she could find her deepest self-expression.

But through the long days of grinding drudgery, the thought of Manning kept goading and nagging her. How had he taken her flight? Had he remained hard and hostile toward her? Or had he ceased to care whether she was dead or alive? Had he done nothing to trace her?

Remembering the sensational nine days' wonder that her marriage had been for the press, she scanned the papers daily to see if her disappearance had leaked out. Not a word, not a line about herself, did she find. Manning was mentioned only in a brief paragraph in the society column, which stated that he was taking a vacation from his arduous settlement work and that his physician urged a trip West.

In cutting loose from Manning, she had torn and wounded herself. Her whole body still ached at the thought of him. How was it possible, she wondered, that he had not even written a line to her? Then she remembered she had left no address with any one. She had cut herself off from the world—but the world of New York is not so large a place, after all. Hurrying from the restaurant to her

little furnished room one night, she ran into Gittel. Sonya tried to
dart past without speaking, but her old friend seized hold of her
arm.

"There's a letter for you I've been carrying around for days," she
said, and thrust into Sonya's hand a square envelope. "It came to the
Ghetto News and I didn't know where to send it."

The old maid was eager to gossip. Her dull eyes took in Sonya's
tired look and the shabby working clothes that seemed to Gittel the
final proof of the upstart's downfall.

"Where do you hold yourself? By what are you working? Where
do you live?" she questioned.

"Nowhere," snapped Sonya, shrinking from the other's imperti-
nent curiosity and making her escape as quickly as possible.

The sight of Manning's handwriting, the feel of his familiar
stationary, made poignant again emotions she had thought long
dead and buried. It was not so much regret over the sordid break
with Manning, but the thing that stung her unconsolably was that
so much ardor, so much passion, so much beauty of illusion had
turned to dust and ashes. Ach! yet less than dust and ashes!

She could not trust herself to read his letter in the street. She
needed privacy, for fear that she might break down. Once safely in
her room, she opened the heavy bond envelope. How characteris-
tic the letter was:

"Dear Sonya:

"I blame myself to a great extent for what happened between
us the other morning. In my astonishment at your confession,
I spoke hastily to you. I now offer an apology.

"If I can forgive your selfish egoism, the least you can do is
to remember that you are legally and publicly Mrs. Manning.

"Your rash flight laid us both open to disagreeable publicity,
but I have been able to silence the newspapers. Nothing has
appeared in print about our domestic troubles, and if you
will return at once, even my relatives and friends need never
know.

"I urge you to reflect seriously, if by any chance you plan to
make our separation permanent. The scandal of divorce is

almost unendurable to me, but in those circumstances I should be constrained to divorce you.

"Faithfully,

"John Manning."

The smugness, the stolid self-righteousness of this letter killed the last quiver of feeling that still lingered in Sonya's heart for Manning. " 'Your selfish egoism . . . If I can forgive . . . My relatives and friends,' " she repeated. "I—I—I—that's all he is, the unselfish saint!"

In a rage, she tore the letter into bits and burned them up. Now more than ever was stamped out of her the idea of remaining "legally and publicly Mrs. Manning," as she quoted bitterly.

Much as she hated the work of the restaurant, she was determined to stick it out at all costs until by strictest economy she had saved up enough to go to a school of design.

She started work next morning with a new rush of enthusiasm, but that very noon she was startled by a man who looked piercingly at her and then turned to his companion. She instinctively moved nearer to hear what was being said. The man's look had been so obviously not that of a masher.

"Did you notice that waitress?" he whispered. "Doesn't she look like Mrs. Manning?"

The other man nodded: "I could swear it was the same woman."

Black fear swept over her. She realized the danger of working in a public place like a restaurant, if she was not to be found out and tortured by reporters before she had had a chance to make of herself a person.

She must leave at once, but it was pay day and the money she had earned was vital to her. She would have to struggle through till nine o'clock.

The afternoon was slow agony. She suspected now that every diner might recognize her. Two men who entered when the luncheon rush was over cast a casual glance at her, and at once she trembled with fear of being again detected. Suspiciously, she lingered behind their chairs, but the subject of their conversation swept the thought of Manning out of her mind.

"That designer—worms should eat him! My gall bursts watching

him waste out my goods. What he used up for only the flounce was
enough already for a whole dress."

The speaker was a thin, nervous East Side Jew, plainly a business man, but with a touch of the artist about him. The soft
tailoring of his suit, the colorful quietness of his tie that blended so
tastefully with his shirt-front, marked him as more sensitive than
the cut-and-dried manufacturer.

"And the bunch of trimmings that sport orders me," he went on.
"It gets black for my eyes when I give a look on his samples. It's only
fancy for Delancey. He got no more head for style as a fish-peddler."

"A good designer is the hardest thing to get," answered the other
man. "Look only on the big money I pay mine, but he's worth it. He
knows how to save up an inch of goods and his samples is thought
out from his head, not stolen from another shop. That's again a
thing you got to watch out for, Mr. Ziskind."

"Yes, and with all his smartness, I found out what a liar that
crook is," said Ziskind. "I signed him up for the year because I
thought his first samples were so swell I was getting a bargain. And
what do you think came out yesterday? Why, he was only a sample
hand in a Fifth Avenue place. He stole those models and faked
them on me—the swindler!"

As soon as the other man had gone, Sonya edged up to Ziskind,
eyes wide, hands tense as she gripped the tray she was carrying.

"I see you're in the dress trade," she began. "Maybe you can tell
me if there is a school of designing where it doesn't cost too much."

"School of designing," he scoffed. "No real designer yet came
from a school."

"But how—where could a girl learn?"

A flame rushed into Sonya's face. She looked up to this chance
customer as one divinely ordained to save her.

"Mr. Ziskind," she pleaded. "I'm crazy to learn designing. Look
only on me. I know I got it in me. That's why I want to begin from
the bottom. Take me in your shop as machine hand, anything, only
so I could work myself up for a designer."

The very next day Sonya started with Ziskind as a sample hand.
But her whole mind and soul and body was absorbed in watching
the designer, the cutter, in studying sample after sample. Every
detail in the making of a dress was to her a sublime discovery.

After the shop closed, she sat up half the night reading fashion books, poring over designs. At lunch time, she hurried through a scant meal and greedily spent every moment in the department stores, pretending to be looking for clothes, but in reality studying how the more exquisite gowns were made.

One day, while sitting at her machine, watching the designer at work, Sonya became inflamed with an idea. The gown he was draping on the figure could be so much better with less trimming—a simpler, more sympathetic line. Afire with creativeness that for the first time knew what it wanted to achieve, she asked Ziskind for permission to stay in after the others had gone home.

"I got something in my head for a sample," she said.

For some weeks, Ziskind had had his eye on the eager, questing talent of the girl that the artist in him perceived. He had noticed the fineness that had distinguished her work on the samples. He was stirred by the inspired sureness of her look. Here was a hand that seemed born to do big things.

"I trust you even to cut into my goods," he consented, encouragingly.

All night long, she worked like a thing possessed. The gown she had dreamed and longed for had seemed simplicity itself, the easiest thing to do. But as she tried the tricotine on the figure, it fell into hard lines, and hardness in a woman's dress was an unpardonable sin to Sonya's eyes.

She brushed back her hair slowly.

"Ach," she mused, "what is it I want? I want that beautiful plainness that only the rich wear. A dress that looks simple enough for the poor only that it's different."

What she wanted was a costume, plain enough for everybody but distinctive enough to make it effective for any occasion. She wanted the wearer to have the joy of a dress that could be slipped on in a moment, and yet give the luxurious sense of a fitted gown. A supple, clinging thing in everyday serge, veiling yet revealing the lovely curves of a woman's body.

She looked at the other samples and realized that she must keep within the prevailing fashion, in order that her creation might be a commercial success. Braid was being indiscriminately used on dresses and suits that year, and of all adornments braid seemed to Sonya the most repellent, the most ineffective hard trimming that had ever been devised. She applied her mind to the problem and found that the worst atrocity of the prevailing mode was the excessive surface of the shining braid. She solved it by cutting the braid in half widths and inserting it edgewise between soft folds, running it along under surfaces, so that a bare thread of it appeared, lending richness to the shadowed parts of the dress.

She pinned up her model time and again, experimenting with every line over and over before she finally cut into the goods. It was almost dawn when the sample took shape under her flaming fingers.

She stood back speechless, her eyes half closing with rapture. She had once thought that love was the greatest joy that could ever fill the heart. But now she knew the released passion of creation. Now she felt that art was as great a god as love. It gave her the completest emotion she had ever known.

"*Ach!*" she breathed, touching the dress reverently. "It's Hollins' hands working in me."

Now that it was done she realized that her heart's blood had gone into the making of it. Suddenly she was very tired.

By the time she reached home, she was ready to collapse from fatigue. She did not stop to undress, but threw herself headlong on the bed. Instantly she fell asleep. The soundest, richest sleep was hers. A thrilling dream came to her in the last sensuous moment of transition between slumber and waking. Hollins had been seeking her, and she had been hiding from him in her emptiness. But now, with her new creation, she rushed to him and flung it at his feet and cried:

"That beautiful thing—that's me—myself! They all said I was a faker—a vamp. They said I was a Salome wanting the heads of men, but you know I was only seeking—seeking for the feel of the beautiful."

She woke from the dream exalted, believing it was a vision of her inmost being more real than reality. "But I'm not ready for Hollins yet," she told herself. "So long I've waited, I must make myself wait a little longer."

She was late in getting back to the shop. And then—wonder of wonders!—Ziskind and all his sales force were standing before her dress, as though it were a living thing. An ecstatic chorus greeted her:

"Such a Fifth Avenue look!"

"Such a Vanderbilt style!"

"Fit for a princess!"

"Made with golden hands!"

Greedily, Ziskind's fingers ran over the singing lines of the gown: "Ach, so plain! So nothing at all! How it dances, the beautifulness from this dress!"

Then he caught sight of Sonya and turned to her. "It's like designed in heaven," he chuckled. "*Oi*, where did you get the idea?"

Sonya's hand went up to her breast: "Here's where I got it—from my heart, my soul. The dress I wanted to wear for myself, I designed for all women."

That same morning, Ziskind raised Sonya's salary.

"You'll be my second designer," he said, "and so soon as my contract with my *schlimazil*—a black year on him!—is up, I'll sign with you for even higher wages. Only try your best by me and I'll look out for you."

Sonya did not need any urging to do her best. For the first time in her life, she was doing the work she loved, for the love of it.

Ziskind in his enthusiasm had named her creation the "Sonya Model." As long as it did not cost him anything extra, he was lavish in his appreciation of her work. His dream for years had been to get his dresses sold in the first class department stores. And this "Sonya Model" opened the doors of Wanamaker's, Macy's, Franklin Simon's, Hollander's, Gidding's, all the houses that had hitherto been inaccessible. Before the dress had been copied, he had received such large orders that in one season he cleared a small fortune.

Success made Ziskind more eager to establish a permanent hold on Sonya. The week before the contract with his other designer expired, he was anxious to see for how little he could sign her, and for how long.

"I ain't no cheap-skate," began Ziskind. "I want to give a worker what I feel comes to him. You got till now fifty dollars. How would you like a raise of ten, fifteen—no"—he flung out his arms dramatically—"I'll take my hand away from my heart and make it

for you twenty-five dollars more—seventy-five a week. Think only!
A little girl like you, a beginner from the machine, to give a jump to
seventy-five dollars a week! Ain't I good feller?"

Sonya smiled enigmatically. Her noncommittal manner chilled
Ziskind a little and he felt obliged to offer her some new flattery.

"It's more than high wages you get from staying by me," he said.
"If we work together, in a few seasons we can move over to Fifth
Avenue and beat Hollins yet."

"Hollins?" repeated Sonya, startled.

"Yes, I was talking to him only yesterday and he himself said that
our last two samples at Gidding's is equal to Paris models. Think
only, he invited himself to come up by us!" Ziskind winked. "Think
only, Hollins from Fifth Avenue wanting to rub sleeves with us!
That's a satisfaction to you more than money, ain't it?"

Sonya was choked by a swift rush of emotion, but she managed
to say:

"And do you want him to come?"

Ziskind shrugged his shoulders. "I don't want him around, looking
over my samples. But that man, he acts like he's the whole world.
Nobody couldn't say no to him. He just orders himself what he
wants to do with people. To-day—this morning yet, he's coming."

"Hollins—to a wholesale house—when he makes his own designs?" stammered Sonya.

"He says maybe he'll lend me money to open up a larger place,
but to tell you the truth I think he only got big eyes on my sudden
luck." Ziskind glanced at his watch. "*Ut!* any minute, he'll yet
come!"

Sonya was swept by a panic. If he was coming, she wanted to run
and hide, and yet she was eager to see him. She stood up nervously
and was about to flee to the workroom when Ziskind added in a
hoarse whisper:

"There he is, the Fifth Avenue king from Division Street. A
thunder should strike him for taking up my time."

Hollins entered, but the sudden sight of the girl stopped him at
the door. A swift pallor spread over his features. His eyes leaped
toward Sonya. But the shock of seeing her choked his speech. For a
long moment, he remained staring at her from the doorway, then

controlled himself and walked across the sample room with the fastidious elegance he had acquired in Paris.

Ziskind made the introductions a little grudgingly:

"Meet Mr. Hollins himself—Miss Vrunsky."

Her cheeks flushed crimson. Her knees shook. Like Hollins, she, too, was robbed of speech. "How did he find me?" she asked herself wildly. Intuitively, she knew that this meeting was no mere coincidence.

Sonya was right. Hollins had been one of the first to discover her break with Manning. A letter he had sent had remained unanswered and when he had tried several times to reach her on the telephone, the butler's evasions justified his suspicion. He had then tried to get her where-abouts from the *Ghetto News* and failed. He was glad that the inevitable had happened so quickly. Hurt a little because she had not come to him, he had understood and had set out to find her. When he had seen the "Sonya Model" at Gidding's, a sixth sense had told him that the creator was his Sonya.

"So this is the Sonya of the 'Sonya Model'!" Subtly conscious of the chaos of emotion in the girl's heart at his unexpected coming, Hollins tried to banter. "I thought I detected my influence in all those wonderful things you have been doing."

"What?" shouted Ziskind in alarm. "Was she also a sample hand and stole her ideas from you?"

"No, no!" laughed Hollins in broad amusement. "I did not mean that." He threw a quick glance at Sonya. "But we are friends. I once had the pleasure of designing for this lady herself."

Ziskind gasped. "You dressed her! Why, I picked her up from a waitress and learned her everything she knows."

Hollins turned his back on Ziskind. Not troubling to answer him, he said to Sonya:

"Why didn't you come straight to me?"

"I'll tell you after," she murmured.

Ziskind, seeing the look between them, threw up his hands and rushed out, tearing his hair.

"*Oi, oi!*" he cried. "I lost her already. Why did I let in my shop that crook, Hollins? A black year on them both!"

23

Understanding

Sonya and Hollins had been busy designing Jeritza's gowns for her new play. She finished draping the material, stuck in a pin here and there where his eye dictated, then glanced up, warmed by the look of approval shining to her from his artist's face.

In another moment she was all absorption in the costume she was shaping.

"How it flames with life on the figure! A poem in silk! Jeritza's breath throbs through every line of it!"

Her ecstatic lyricism, her unceasing joy of discovery in every stitch of her work, brought Hollins back to his colorful Ghetto days—days of poverty, but rich dreaming. He felt like a tired man who had come in touch with a rejuvenating sun of youth. The virgin ardor of creation, which had cooled with the mastery of his technique, glowed again in him through contact with her unfolding genius.

She turned to him the fiery wonder of her face.

"Which part did you do, and which did I? Where did I begin, and where did you end? It's as if one mind did the whole thing."

"One mind *did*," he smiled, his head on one side, taking in the complete effect of the gown. "Together we work as one mind." His hand groped for hers and he pressed it lingeringly.

Sonya's eyes became moist and dreamy. How different it was being with Hollins, where her work flowed like a song, from those chaotic days wasted with Manning's uplift schemes in his settlement! Then she had been a torn and twisted thing, reaching out to false gods. Then she had been a lie, and everything her hands touched turned into a lie. Even the work with Lipkin on the *Ghetto News* had been more or less of a make-believe. But now she was herself—a thing unbound—straightening out her limbs like a sapling in the sun. Now everything she did pulsed with reality.

"Tell me," she pressed with impersonal affection. "Is there anything in the world so real, so thrilling, as *real* work?"

He searched her penetratingly, the man in him hungry for the passion she lavished on mere gowns—jealous of the overflow of instinct, the maternal exuberance that rushed out of her to her work. Her dynamic womanhood called to him, compelling—resistless. How could he stand by without mastering her even in her poetic flights! He could not endure being left behind, and summoned all his magic charm to bring her back to him.

"Love!" breathed Hollins, triumphant conviction in his voice. "The thing that makes work so real for us is love."

He moved closer to her, eager for her reassuring arms about him. But Sonya's glance wandered far off into space. A shadow clouded her brow. "I'm almost afraid of that word, 'love,'" she shuddered. "I so mislived that word. Once I thought I loved Manning. God from the world! what lies and hypocrisies I practiced in the name of love!"

"You did not know love then, Sonya."

But nothing could stop her self-searching denunciation of her past.

"When I was so crazy for Manning," she went on in a burst of confidence, "when I lied and made believe I was everything I was not, even then I ached for the truth. I used to wake up in the night and ask myself: 'Can I speak to him only through veils of make-believe? Can't I show myself for what I am? Is there never to be any truth between a man and woman in love?'"

"It's on the ruins of our first blind romance, on the infatuations that break us, that we come to understand the meaning of real love."

His words quieted her torrent of self-condemnation and brought her back to him. She nodded in full agreement: "I guess you're right."

A pause fell between them—each with his own searchlight on his past. Then she pierced him with a quick, sharp glance. "And you, too, went through lies of love that were real to you once?"

He hesitated. "Well—that's what enables me to understand you," he parried.

But Sonya was not to be evaded. "*Oi, weh!* I'm a fool to be jealous, but I am—I can't help it."

Sonya's flare of jealousy was to Hollins rich, red wine. His hold on her returned. He felt her back on solid earth, close to him again.

"Tell me, since you knew that we were for each other from the beginning, why didn't you come to me the very day your madness with that fool philanthropist had burned itself out?"

"Ach! I was so miserable then, I didn't want to be happy any more. Besides, when I just ran away from one man, I wasn't going to hang myself on another man's neck."

"Foolish Sonya!" he chided tenderly. "In your need, you could think of me just like any other man?"

"If I could only tell you how I was aching to come—but—but—"

A rush of feeling choked her words for a moment, but she gazed at him with heart-to-heart directness.

"How dared I dream that you loved me, when you knew—knew about Honest Abe, about everything?"

"It's because I know everything about you that I love you so."

Beautiful memories shone from Hollins' eyes, as he leaned toward her.

"From that very first day when you burst into my office, you had me—had me for always, then and there. The savage wildness of your mood fired my heart. I felt you were a princess of the soul, for all your shabby rags. I loved the battered toque on your crazy hair—the broken shoes in which you rushed to me. I loved every little hole in your worn-out gloves."

Tenderly reminiscent, he touched each of her fingers to his lips.

"From that day, I have only waited and waited for you."

As she listened to his outpouring, she bowed her head before the splendor of such a rich gift of love. It rang like mighty music from some higher world.

"I have no beautiful words like you," she breathed. "But so much I love you!"

For weeks Hollins had been postponing his yearly trip to Paris, in the hope that she would go with him. Now he renewed his plea.

"Don't hold me off any longer, life of my life. Your marriage with Manning was never real love, that it should bind you so."

"Yes. We belong to each other." She slipped her hand into his. "And I'm going with you. Only, you know Manning's trip West means he's divorcing me, and I want to wait until I'm free and clear from all that."

No matter what the delay, the assurance that she was wholly his brought him back to the same serenity of their daily comradeship. With the enthusiasm of a boy, Hollins drew vivid pictures of their coming days together in Paris.

"Sonya, with your eyes I'll see Paris for the first time. Not the Paris I saw when I was struggling with the last breath in me to get on. Not the business Paris of my yearly trips for new twists in style. Now fresh things come up in me. We'll see what Poiret is doing, what Worth is bringing out this season. So many new ideas we'll get for decoration and costuming from the painters' exhibitions."

He talked animatedly, the long pent-up enthusiasms rushing out of him in staccato torrents. Sonya had made him again the impulsive East Side Jew he once was before he became a successful artist.

She listened rapt, gleaming-eyed, following him with little nods of ecstatic "Yes—yes!" And he suddenly became aware of how poignant was her understanding of his interests, and stopped. Just as a man shut in darkness feels delicious pain in a swift flood of light, so this joy of opening up his soul to the woman he loved struck through Hollins like some exquisite agony, intolerably sweet, that he could not bear.

Carried up on the tide of his mood, she broke in: "We'll forget the world—forget business. Nothing but ourselves and our high thoughts."

"And the silks and laces for Mrs. Van Orden's daughter's trousseau," added Hollins in a back-to-earth tone.

The name of Mrs. Van Orden made Sonya shudder. The huge, solid figure of the dowager rose like a wooden idol in their visionary Eden.

"To think that you make beautiful clothes for that fat thing, only because she has the money to pay for them!" she cried, flinging out her arms in temperamental revolt. "I'll never be content to work with you only for the rich. Beautiful things should be for those who long for beauty. There are millions on the East Side dying for a little loveliness, and they *never, never* have it."

"Sonya!" He seized her outflung arms and held them down to her side with gentle masculine firmness. "There aren't so many millions of the poor that desire beauty as passionately as you say. Nor are all the rich people wooden Mrs. Van Ordens. The feeling for beauty is a rare gift of the few, no matter where they were born. It belongs to no one class."

He enjoyed Sonya's incorrigible unreason, yet he liked to reason with her.

"What about Jeritza?" he went on. "Think of all the artist women who have earned the means to buy beauty for which they longed!"

"Buy beauty!" she stormed illogically. "That's what's so wrong. Beauty should be for those who love beauty, not only for those who can buy it."

"Well, my crazy Don Quixote," he said, with a lover's generous concession to every whim of his beloved. "You'll have freedom enough to try out your wild dreams in the air. When we come back from Paris, we'll open up on the side a little shop on Grand Street—see how it will work out—beauty for those that love it, beauty that is not for profit."

Tenderness and proud gratitude welled up to him out of her eyes.

"Ach, that's understanding! I never burned so for something in my life like I burn for this. In the midst of the ready-mades of Grand Street, a shop of the beautiful—that's to be my settlement!"

24

Revelation

As the day set for her marriage to Hollins drew near, a vague, unutterable sadness possessed Sonya. Hollins' love gave her every reason to be happy, but something deeper than herself sobbed and sorrowed within her.

"Why do I feel guilty when I'm happy?" she asked herself. "Is it because I'm a sentimental fool? Is it the craziness of Russian youth that feels a secret shame at happiness?

"I have found the man with whom I can be my own free self. With him I can work. With him I can play. Whether I speak or whether I'm silent, from his eyes flows understanding. Then what is the matter with me?"

She could not reason it out. She only felt the tug of something under the surface of living and loving. She ached to touch it and yet could not touch it near enough to know it. She saw herself moving toward an inevitable goal—not rejecting and not accepting. As one from a height she watched with puzzled wonder her bruised soul struggling to tear itself free from the past. But she could not rid herself of the past nor get hold of the present. A blinding fog rose between her and the Reality of things.

Her being was stabbed with a sense of invisible things. A thin distant voice seemed calling to her. Memories, dead, forgotten, haunted and brooded over her. A sorrow wept in her happiness and a beauty ached in her sorrow.

This new pensive mood lay like a haze over Sonya. It was in the wave of her hair, in the droop of her head, in the soft shine of her eyes. It was a new elusive beauty that Hollins felt in Sonya like the scent within the rose.

Sonya had been preparing supper in her rooms for Hollins. With a poignant look of longing he followed her about. But she seemed not to see the caressing love in his eyes.

A silence lay between them—they were veiled within themselves.

As the silence thickened, their self-consciousness increased. Something vital and impending throbbed through their self-consciousness. Something which they both knew must come and feared.

Sonya put the tea-kettle on and moved to the table near where Hollins was sitting. Suddenly he could bear her evasions no longer. He rose and snatched her in his arms.

The bell rang sharply.

Startled, they drew apart.

In the open doorway stood Manning. With a strange look he stood there. His lips tightened. His hollow eyes narrowed terrifyingly. His face that was always in repose quivered with the uncontrolled upwelling of a storm.

Sonya rubbed her hand across her eyes so as to bring herself back to earth. And yet she was not surprised. The past from which she had tried so hard to tear away was always present with her.

"I must see you alone," came the command, in a cold formal tone, barely hiding the outrage that shook him.

In a panic of bewilderment, Sonya stared from one to the other. Jumbled, blinding pictures of the past rushed before her as she stood there. Manning, the lover, tender, passionate, jealous, angry. But most wounding of all was the icy aloofness with which he was hurting her even now. Like a solid wall of ice he stood there, polite, aloof even in his wrath, defying the other man.

Hollins turned possessive eyes on Sonya. The veneer of the gentleman which he had acquired in the years on Fifth Avenue dropped from him. He was the primitive oriental guarding his woman.

"Will you go?" Sonya's lips scarcely formed the words. "I want to see him now."

In sullen silence Hollins dragged himself to his feet. The eyes of the two men clashed like swords. Hollins flashed back hatred for hatred.

Throughout the silent battle Manning remained fastidiously aloof. Like the grim judge whose will is law, he watched the other man put on his hat and coat and depart.

The door closed.

A moment of tense suffocating silence.

"So it was this man!" he hurled.

Wild with the hurt of her betrayal, Manning abandoned all restraint. Anger, hatred, injured pride were in his black look, his vindictive voice.

"So it was this man!" he repeated violently.

"Yes. A man—*a man!*"

Her words were like a whip-lash taunting a savage beast. This woman who had once begged on bended knees for his love scorning him! This woman who had been his, in the arms of another man! A crowding came in his throat.

All the bitterness of rejection he had suffered the past months burst. With an inarticulate cry he seized her in his arms, savage passion in his eyes.

"You—you—you're mine. Mine. You belong to me. You're part of me. Mine. I want you. I can't live without you. I dream of your lips—your eyes—your hair. I'm hungry for you. Oh, my beautiful maddening Jewess!"

Custom, tradition, every shred of convention, every vestige of civilization had left him. He was primitive man starved into madness for the woman. His hungry hands wound themselves in her hair, clutched at her neck, her bosom, fluttered ravenously over her whole body. His eyes bored into hers. His hot lips drew closer and closer—

Utterly lost in his passion, incoherent ravings of love poured from him as he smothered her with kisses, unseeing, unheeding her struggles against him.

"No—no," she cried, "let me—let me go."

With a violent twist of both arms she pushed him from her.

Dazed, struck into sudden awakening by her repulse, his burning gaze covered her from head to foot. Hair dishevelled, waist torn away, revealing the heaving bosom, the white throbbing neck, she stood there, superb, ravishing in her fury.

Sudden realization flashed through him. Like lightning, killing every nerve. His head dropped. His hands fell limply to his side.

Her scorn stripped him naked, exposed him to himself.

"So this is Manning, the Anglo-Saxon gentleman, the saint, the philanthropist—the savior of humanity."

Wonder was in her eyes and cold anger in her voice.

"You didn't want me when I was burning up for you," she

laughed harshly, remembering how she had lain beside him night after night, sleepless, nerves unstrung, hungering in vain for a kiss, for a breath of response, for a sign of his need of her. "Now I don't want you."

In the triumph of her sex which he had once so cruelly mortified she looked fully at him. This was her moment. She had it in her to bring this wreck back to life—to give him the warmth, the passion, the ardor that none of the women of his kind could give. There he stood perishing for her.

But her triumph over him died as it was born, for it was not the gentleman, not the arrogant Anglo-Saxon who stood before her. It was a human being—suffering—wounded—despised and rejected in his hour of need.

Suddenly she saw that she was the cross on which he bled. Hers was the mad passion that had roused in him this fiery famine for love. And now she denied him.

"I'm sorry," he said brokenly. "I didn't know, I didn't understand."

Her hands reached out to him. Anger, bitterness, were gone. Here was a child that needed comforting. And she was a woman. For the first time in all her life she was a woman. And in the knowledge of her womanhood she said with real tenderness:

"I'm sorry too."

Their eyes met with no shields, a clear look of absolute revelation flashing between them. For one instant they were to each other not gentleman and East Side girl—not man and woman, but human beings driven by bitter experience to one moment's realization of life.

Long after Manning had gone, Sonya still sat in the same chair. She made no move. She uttered no sound. Doubled fists thrust between her knees, she sat there, her head sunk on her breast.

"No man on earth can ever make me suffer as much as Manning. But only Hollins understands me as I am . . ."

"Whom do I *really* love? Manning or Hollins? Or do I love both? Or do I love neither? Is this the price I must pay because I want beauty? Always to be torn on the winds of doubt and uncertainty—never have rest—never find peace?"

As she lay awake that night she wondered if ever her spirit could so closely touch another human being as Manning's and hers had touched.

"He's not my own kind, but for that one moment he was closer to me than my own can ever be.

"So at bottom we're all alike, Anglo-Saxons or Jews, gentlemen or plain immigrant," her thoughts went on. "When we're hungry, we're hungry—even a gentleman when starved long enough can become a savage East Sider."

Till now, Manning had been to her a shadow, an echo of a human being—that had no life—no fire from within.

She had thought of him going through the years making speeches in educated language, using handed down words in high sounding phrases that were as empty, as meaningless as the scientific goodness of his settlement work.

Now he was real. He was human.

A newborn sense of humility came into her being.

She saw how men and women helplessly and unknowingly destroy themselves and each other in the blind uprising of brute passion which lies like a sleeping dog within the consciousness of the divine soul.

For a long time she lay crushed by the weight of this truth. Then the fog lifted. She saw beyond.

"Yes," she admitted wistfully. "We kill the divine in us. We kill the beauty in those we love. But the very killing makes immortal the contact.

"And now I'm pledged to Hollins," she told herself.

Going into a new experience, she knew, could bring her no forgetfulness of the past, nor the closeness of spiritual identification which she had found at the moment of parting with this man of a different race.

She knew now that Manning was an experience which had burned forever into the texture of her life. She had seen him when he was all dressed up for the world in the cultured manners of the Anglo-Saxon gentleman and she had seen him behind closed doors when he was a naked savage. But the essence of him as a whole was fineness—an unutterable gentleman-ness.

Always she would be finer because she had known his fineness.

Always she would be more human because she had touched the heart of his humanness.

"After all," she thought, "the way he loved me at the last was what I dreamed of him at first sight. He will be to me always Romance. The madness, the daring, the deathless adventure of youth."

Triumphant, she rose.

"It's only we who die, but the spark of love, the flash of beauty from eye to eye, the throb from heart to heart goes on and on forever."

ANZIA YEZIERSKA, author of the acclaimed *Bread Givers*, was born in a Jewish ghetto on the Russian-Polish border and emigrated to America as a young girl. Her writings detail the conflicts of the Jewish immigrants' struggle for identity in a new land, specifically the position of the immigrant woman. Although her works lost popularity in the 1930s when interest in the immigrant experience waned, she continued writing until her death in 1970.

GAY WILENTZ, associate professor of English at East Carolina University, is the author of *Binding Cultures: Black Women Writers in Africa and the Diaspora* and has also published in *College English, Twentieth Century Literature, African American Review, Research in African Literatures,* and *MELUS.* She is currently working on a book about the relationship of culture and health in ethnic women's writings.